THE HIGHLANDER
AND THE
GOVERNESS

Michelle Willingham

MILLS & BOON

First Published in Great Britain 2019
by Mills & Boon, an imprint of HarperCollins*Publishers*
1 London Bridge Street, London, SE1 9GF

© 2019 Michelle Willingham

ISBN: 978-0-263-26934-5

MIX
Paper from
responsible sources
FSC® C007454

This book is produced from independently certified FSC™ paper
to ensure responsible forest management.
For more information visit www.harpercollins.co.uk/green.

Printed and bound in Spain
by CPI, Barcelona

To Mom:
You have supported me, stood by me,
and you have always been there for me
whenever I needed you.
I love you more than any words can say.

Chapter One

❧

Scotland—1813

Everything will be all right.

Frances Goodson suppressed the tremor of nerves in her stomach, uncertain whether it was panic or luncheon that roiled within her now. But she stiffened her spine and reminded herself to find her courage. It didn't matter that she was alone or that her family had turned their backs on her. She had an offer of employment and a roof over her head. Surely it would be enough.

The agency had trained her to be an excellent governess, although this was her first position. She had never expected to choose this path, but when a lady became destitute, there was no choice but to resort to desperate measures. At least being a governess was somewhat respectable, even if it was not the life she had planned.

Frances prided herself on her education, and she felt confident that the Laird of Locharr would be quite pleased with her work. His daughter would become the toast of London after the young girl completed her lessons in etiquette—she was convinced of it.

She gripped her hands together before smoothing the grey bombazine dress she wore. Her blonde curls had been tamed and pressed inside a matching grey bonnet, and she looked all the world like a virtuous woman. No one in Scotland would know about her past. This was a new life for her, a new country, and a new beginning.

It was a pity that her new beginning involved torrential rain. It slapped against the windows of the coach in punishing sheets of water. Scotland was rather formidable, so it seemed. A heavy mist lingered in the air, obscuring her view. Even so, she would not let the terrible weather dampen her mood. She tried to imagine a blue sky with puffy white clouds, for surely it could not rain all the time.

The coach pulled to a stop in front of the laird's castle, and Frances craned her neck to look at the grey stone fortification. It looked like something out of a haunted fairy-tale. She counted seven towers nestled at even intervals around the castle, with arched windows and parapets. Best of all, it overlooked the sea, resting atop a cliffside. She'd never expected Lachlan MacKinloch to own a castle of this size. It was far larger than she'd imagined, and she was beginning to wonder exactly how wealthy the Laird of Locharr was.

Although her heart was pounding out of anxiety, another part of her was delighted to live in a castle—even if it was only for a year or two. How many young ladies could boast of such a thing? Not many, she'd wager.

Frances let her imagination take flight as she envisioned giving history lessons in a room with stone walls and perhaps a medieval suit of armour in the corner. Or, if the laird's daughter did not care for exciting stories of knights and battles, perhaps she could give the young lady botany lessons in the garden. She smiled at the thought, hoping his daughter would be a sweet girl, eager to learn.

That is, if he had a daughter.

A spear of uneasiness thrust into her stomach. She hadn't really considered the possibility of a boy. The agency had been vague about her pupil's age, saying only that the laird required an experienced governess who could train a student in manners and etiquette of the London *ton*. Surely, he meant a daughter. Frances was one-and-twenty herself, but she had been brought up as a well-bred young lady. Her mother had drilled her in all the lessons necessary for finding a good husband. She was completely confident in her ability and knowledge, even if she had been unable to use it for her own purpose.

Frances supposed it *was* possible that the laird had a young son who was not old enough to be sent off to school. She had no information about the child, but that didn't matter. She had prepared for anything, and the agency had given her a trunk filled with borrowed books for all ages.

The coachman opened the door and held out an umbrella for her. Frances took a deep breath, gathering command of her nerves. She straightened her posture and raised her chin, hoping that if she behaved in a confident manner, her courage would return. 'Thank you,' she told the coachman as she took the umbrella.

The gravel was soft beneath her feet, and she was careful not to step in any puddles. Behind her, the coachman followed with her bags. She didn't see a servants' entrance, but instead walked up the main stairs. It was possible that inquisitive eyes were watching her from the windows.

Frances knocked at the door and waited. It took some time before the door opened, and she saw an elderly footman with snowy hair and a white beard. 'Are ye lost, then, lass?'

She straightened and said, 'I am Miss Frances Goodson, the new governess. The Laird of Locharr sent for me. I have come to instruct his daughter.' Frances forced a smile on her face, clenching her shaking hands.

'The laird has no daughter,' the footman replied.

Oh, dear. Panic caught her in the stomach, and Frances blurted out, 'Then he must have a son in need of my tutelage?'

'The laird has no children. I'll bid ye a good day and be on your way, Miss.'

No children? Before she could make sense of that, the footman started to close the door. No— she could not let him throw her out. Not until she had answers. Frances stuck out her foot to hold the door open. From her pocket, she withdrew the letter she had received from the laird and held it out. 'Then please explain this to me, sir. I have travelled hundreds of miles to be here, and if there has been some mistake, I need to know what has happened.'

The footman took the letter, but before he could unfold it, a voice commanded, 'Let her inside, Alban.'

Frances didn't stop to wonder who had given the order, but she closed the umbrella and stepped across the threshold. Her gown was damp from the rain, and she tried to smooth it as she gathered her composure. Then she squared her shoulders as the laird approached.

Lachlan MacKinloch was the tallest man she'd ever seen. Judging by his broad shoulders and raw strength, he looked like an ancient warrior more accustomed to wearing chainmail than a kilt. His brown hair was unfashionably long and rested upon his shoulders. There was a faint tint of red to it, and his blue eyes stared at her as if he didn't quite know what to make of her. Across his cheek, she saw an angry jagged scar. It made him appear more of a monster than a man, but she forced herself not to look away. From his fierce scowl, he appeared to be accustomed to frightening others.

Frances didn't know what was going on or why this man had hired her. If he had no children, then the footman was right—there was no reason for her to be here. She couldn't, for the life of her, understand what had happened.

Her errant thoughts were distracted by his attire. He wore a blue-and-green-striped tartan coat over a white shirt, a blue waistcoat with brass buttons, and another blue and green kilt with a leather belt that slung across his right shoulder down to his left hip. A blue bonnet rested upon his head. His stockings were also tartan, bold and fitted to his muscular calves. There was no denying his Scottish heritage. In his demeanour, she sensed stubbornness and a man who always got his own way.

She remembered her manners and sank into a curtsy. 'I am Frances Goodson, the governess you sent for.'

He regarded her when she stood and commanded, 'We will have words in the drawing room.' Without waiting for her to agree, he walked away.

Frances stared at the laird, wondering exactly what sort of position she had accepted. A sudden wariness seized her, and she questioned whether his intentions were nefarious. But then, she was far away from London, and it was too late to leave now. Better to follow him and discover why he had hired her. Perhaps there was another child in need of her help.

With a quick glance behind her, she saw that the footman had slipped away, allowing them privacy. It wasn't at all proper to be alone with the laird, but perhaps Locharr didn't want the servants to eavesdrop about the reasons for her employment. Even so, she kept the door to the drawing room wide open in case she needed to call out for help.

It was a lovely room, exactly the sort she might have chosen herself. The curtains were a rich sapphire, and the white wallpaper had scrolls of matching blue. The furnishings were creamy white with rococo gold. Two of the windows in one corner were made of stained glass with blue birds and flowers. The laird stood in front of the window, staring outside at the downpour. For a long moment, he said nothing.

Frances wasn't certain if she was expected to sit or stand, but she couldn't resist the urge to sit upon one of the gilded chairs. She straightened her spine and cleared her throat. 'I am pleased to make your acquaintance, Locharr. But I must admit, I am rather…confused as to why you have employed me as a governess if you have no children.'

He stood at the window for a while, and she had the sense that he was choosing his words carefully. 'Show me the letter, Miss Goodson.'

She gave it to him, not really understanding why he wanted to see it. Unless someone else had sent it instead?

The laird's expression turned grim, and he crumpled the letter, tossing it into the hearth. 'I am sorry you made such a journey. My mother wrote the letter, not me. But you may stay for the night and be on your way in the morning.'

All the air seemed to leave her lungs. 'Why— why would she send the letter? I don't understand.'

The laird crossed the room and stood by

the window. 'I didna hire a governess. But my mother apparently believes I need help.'

Dear God. She had been hired to tutor a grown man. The very idea rattled her composure, making her question what to do now. She couldn't possibly be a governess to the laird, as wild and untamed as he seemed.

But then, the idea of going home was far worse. The thought of enduring another journey by coach for a second week, made her stomach twist. And worse, her mother would sigh and claim that Frances was, yet again, nothing but a disappointment and a failure.

No. These might not be the circumstances she had imagined, but she intended to make the best of them. She had the knowledge he needed, and there was a chance—only the barest thread of a chance—that she could stay here. But only if she handled the matter in the right way.

'I am so sorry if my arrival was a surprise to you,' she apologised. With hesitance, she added, 'Might I ask…what sort of help does your mother think you need?'

He didn't answer for a long moment but continued to stare out the window at the pounding rain. His silence stretched on between them, making her feel as if a departure in the morning was inevitable.

'Is your mother here, Locharr?' she ventured.

Perhaps the matron could help her decide what to do next.

'Nay. She's travelling. I dinna expect her to return for another month.'

'Oh.' Frances stood from the chair, wondering what to do now. Her position here was tenuous, and clearly, the laird did not want her. There was nothing else, save to beg for another chance. She went to stand beside him, hoping her pleas would help in some way. His physical presence intimidated her, and the scowl only accentuated the fierce scar on his face. His hair was ragged, as if he'd cut it himself. There was a feral quality to this man, and she wondered if he had shut himself away from the outside world.

'I realise that you do not want me here,' she murmured. 'You should know that this was to be my first position as a governess. I may have journeyed here under the wrong circumstances, but I really do wish to help. Would you consider granting me one day? And if I am of no use to you, I will return to London without argument.'

He turned to stare at her. 'I don't need a governess, Miss Goodson.'

Her heart was pounding with fear, but she forced herself to meet his blue eyes. 'No. But I desperately need this position. It's all I have left.'

There was an invisible battle of wills between them, but she kept her gaze fixed upon his. Let him throw her out if that was what he wanted. But she would not surrender this task without a fight of her own.

At last, he admitted, 'I am getting married in London in three months' time.'

It was all Frances could do to keep her expression neutral. 'My felicitations on your impending nuptials, then. Your bride will be fortunate to live in such a beautiful castle.'

'I've no' seen her in ten years,' he admitted. 'Our marriage was arranged by our fathers.' He crossed his arms, his mouth a tight slash of annoyance.

'Do you…not wish to wed her?' Frances ventured.

'I'll wed her,' he answered. 'It matters not to me. She can do as she pleases, once the vows are said.' There was a dark shadow to his words, and Frances wondered if he intended to abandon his bride. Her mind started to piece together his circumstances. If he was going to travel to London in three months for his wedding— and his mother had hired a governess to help him with his manners—then undoubtedly, Lady Locharr believed her son would frighten the bride. He was a beast in need of taming, and Frances understood all too well that society would ridicule anyone who did not inherently understand the rules.

Whether he wanted her help or not, he needed her. But like Scheherazade, she would have to earn her place, one day at a time. 'How long has it been since you've visited London?'

'Four years. I've no' left Scotland since my father was buried.' In his voice, there was a raw note of pain, and she studied him more closely.

'I am sorry for your loss,' she said quietly. 'Might I ask the name of your bride? If you don't mind revealing it, that is.'

He shrugged. 'Lady Regina, daughter of Ned Crewe, the Earl of Havershire.'

Oh, dear. Frances had met the lady once, and the tall beauty was proper and cool in her demeanour. Rather like a statue of ice. Scandal would never dare to touch a woman like her, and Lady Regina had turned down countless suitors—even a duke. Why then, had her father settled for a marriage to a Scottish laird? It made little sense.

The Laird of Locharr appeared to be slightly older than herself, but his rigid demeanour would terrify most of the London ton. As the son of a Scottish landowner, someone must have taught him manners, long ago. But perhaps he had forgotten his etiquette.

It was likely that his mother had enlisted her help, to ensure that Locharr would not be embarrassed by gossip.

Rain droplets pounded the window overlooking the garden, but while he continued to stare outside, she stared at him. Lachlan MacKinloch really was quite a handsome man, in spite of the scar. If he cut his hair and chose different clothing, he would indeed catch any woman's eye.

Frances was beginning to consider the prospect. Tutoring an unmarried man was scandalous, yes, but they were in Scotland, away from the rest of society. No one would know of her efforts to transform him.

Her heart softened at the thought of helping the laird win the heart of Lady Regina. If he allowed her to help him, he could become one of the most well-mannered gentlemen in London— a suitor Lady Regina would be proud of.

'Would you grant me one day to help you?' she asked. 'If my instruction is not of any use, I promise, I will leave.'

He expelled a heavy sigh. 'As I've said, I have no need for your instruction, Miss Goodson. My mother made a mistake.'

Frances's brain was spinning with frustration, but she forced herself to remain calm. 'Let us start with the evening meal. I will watch you eat.'

'I ken how to eat,' he retorted.

'I will need to speak with your cook to ensure that several courses are served. In London, you will be expected to attend supper parties where

Lady Regina is in attendance. There are subtle ways to ensure that she is enjoying herself.'

He eyed her as if she'd spoken a foreign language. 'Why would I care?'

Frances steeled herself against his annoyance. 'If your bride is happy, then you will enjoy a pleasant marriage. This arrangement might be a moment of joy in your life.' She offered him a bright smile, but the look in his blue eyes narrowed upon her. For a moment, she felt like a deer staring back at a wolf, half-afraid of being devoured.

'Alban will show you to a room where you can rest before supper tonight. Then you will depart in the morning.' He started to turn, but she felt the need to correct him.

'Locharr, you should acknowledge a lady with a nod before you depart. Or a bow if she is of a higher rank. Lady Regina will expect you to know this.'

His expression held a wicked gleam, but he gave a sweeping bow that almost felt like mockery. Frances bobbed a curtsy, but inwardly wondered how long he would allow her to stay.

Two hours later

Lachlan wanted to cheerfully murder his mother. *Why* would she hire a governess for him?

Did she think he was a baw-heided lad of six? He saw no reason to bring Miss Goodson all this way for naught. It irritated him that Catrina had interfered in their lives like this.

He had kept himself apart from the world for the past two years, since Tavin had died, and he preferred the isolation. His wounds from the fire had healed but not the guilt in his heart. For a time, he'd forgotten about the arrangement, until Lady Regina's mother had written to him, asking him to come to London. The countess had explained that the wedding could take place in May, if he had no objections.

The thought of marriage made him feel nothing at all. It was an arrangement, and he saw no need to court Lady Regina. He intended to arrive in London, arrange for the licence, and be done with the wedding. Why, then, had Catrina intervened? Did she think he would behave like a foppish gentleman, with his hair tied in a neat queue, bowing before his bride-to-be? Damned if he would embarrass himself in such a way.

The governess sat across from him in the dining room, braving a smile. He had to admit that she was bonny in her own way. Her hair was pulled into a tight topknot, though the blonde curls were escaping in soft tendrils around her face. She had green eyes with flecks of brown in them, and they reminded him of a river—beautiful with a hint of mystery. Her grey gown, however, was worn and colourless. It was too short for her, and he noticed several seams that revealed where she'd mended it. *It's all I have left,* she'd said about the position. And aye, it might be true that she needed the work.

Miss Goodson had chosen a chair near his, and beside her, she had brought a sheet of paper, along with an inkwell and a pen.

'Do you always bring a pen and paper to the dinner table?' he remarked. 'I didna think that was good etiquette.'

She brightened. 'You are correct, Locharr. Under normal circumstances, I would never do such a thing. However, I intend to take notes on what lessons you'll need. That way, I can be of use to you.'

'You're no' staying,' he pointed out. 'I am granting you a meal, but there's no need for notes. I ken how to use a fork.'

Miss Goodson set down her pen and took her napkin, folding it in her lap. 'Of course, you know that. But there is still a great deal to learn about etiquette in London. There are many unspoken rules.'

Lachlan eyed the door, wondering if it had been a mistake to allow Miss Goodson to join him at supper. He was accustomed to taking a tray alone in his room. It had been years since he'd had a formal meal, and he wasn't about to change his habits.

The governess appeared entirely too cheerful, as if she thought she could talk her way into becoming his tutor. There was a brightness about her, of a woman filled with joy and enthusiasm. Perhaps she thought it would change his mind about sending her away. Far from it. It made him want to push back, to behave like a wicked barbarian. And so he glared at her, letting her glimpse his bad mood.

'Is something the matter, Locharr?' Miss Goodson appeared concerned. 'You seem angry with me.'

Good. His plan was working.

'It doesna matter what I think of you. You'll be gone, soon enough.' He kept his tone deliberate, not bothering to be nice. It would be cruel to lead her on, to let her think she had a chance of staying—even if she did need the position to support herself.

Miss Goodson's expression dimmed, but she picked up her pen once more. They waited for Alban to bring in the food, but there was nothing yet. The clock ticked away a few more minutes, and finally, Lachlan called out, 'If you dinna bring the food out soon, Alban, you'll have to fetch shovels to bury us! For we'll both be dead of starvation!'

Miss Goodson's eyes widened at his shouting. Her pen scratched rapidly over the paper, but she did not correct him. Aye, he knew he wasn't supposed to bellow for his servants, but Alban might not hear the bell. The elderly man's hearing had worsened over the years.

His younger footman, Gavin, entered the room, carrying a tureen of soup. He plunked it down on the table and ladled out a healthy serving to Lachlan before he turned to Miss Goodson. She did not say anything, but Lachlan corrected the footman, 'You should be serving the lady first, Gavin.'

'I'm sorry, Locharr. Miss Goodson.' The footman gave a slight bow and took the tureen away.

Lachlan eyed the soup, waiting for her to eat first. The governess was staring at him. When it became clear that she was not going to taste the soup until he did, he picked up his spoon and took a small sip.

'Very good,' she said.

'I wasna going to pick up the bowl and drink it,' he told her.

There was a veiled smile playing at Miss Goodson's lips. 'No, of course not.' She wrote another note on the paper and then set her pen down. 'I can tell that you *have* had some instruction, Locharr. Your table manners are not bad at all. They only need some minor adjustments.'

'Which are not your concern,' he reminded her.

'It could be.' She smiled at him, and the encouragement in her eyes caught him unawares. For a moment, he watched her eat. Her hands were small and delicate, her motions graceful. There was a strand of curling blonde hair that had slipped free of her chignon, and it hung against her neck. Although she had done nothing untoward, there was something about a good girl that made him want to discover if there was more beneath the surface of propriety.

'Why did you seek work as a governess?' he asked. Miss Goodson was quite pretty, with the fresh face of innocence. Surely, she could easily find a husband. Why, then, had she travelled alone to Scotland?

'Poverty is an excellent motivation for employment,' she answered. Though she spoke with a lightness of mood, he believed there was far more to her story.

'You were a lady once, weren't you?' he predicted.

Her face flushed, but she did not answer his statement. Which meant it was likely true. If she had fallen upon difficult times, being a governess or a wife was her only option. It seemed that Miss Goodson was a woman of secrets, and Lachlan wondered what they were. He supposed he would never know. He reached for his goblet of wine and drained it.

She eyed him and bit her lower lip. Then she frowned and dipped her pen into the inkwell, writing furiously.

Aye, it wasn't right for a man to finish his wine in one gulp. Even so, he couldn't deny the urge to tease her. He reached for the decanter and poured himself another glass. There was a pained look in her river-green eyes, and she bit her lip, drawing his attention to its fullness. She was a bonny lass, indeed. Whether she knew it or not, Miss Goodson was a danger to herself. She might be posing as a governess, but this young lady was a walking temptation.

'Would you be wanting some wine?' he offered, holding out the decanter.

'No, thank you. I do not partake in spirits,' she answered. 'And next time, you should ask your butler to pour the wine. Or a footman.' She dipped her pen in the inkwell and wrote a few more sentences on the scrap of paper.

'If I waited for them, we'd have no food,' he pointed out. 'They're no' exactly making haste to get here.'

'Be that as it may, if you are a guest at a supper party, wait for the servants to pour the wine.'

A few minutes later, Alban brought out the next course. It was a mutton pie, and Lachlan cut into it with his fork, while steam rose from the pastry crust. Miss Goodson was still writing furiously, in between bites of her own meal. What could she be worked up about now? He'd done nothing wrong.

Finally, she set down her pen and took a sip of water from her glass. 'How long ago was this marriage arranged with Lady Regina?'

He stabbed the crust with his fork and brought up a bit of mutton and gravy. 'Our fathers went to school together and were good friends. They spoke of it for years, though 'twas only in jest. After my father died two years ago, Havershire wanted to fulfil Tavin's wish. We set the wedding date for this May.'

At that, she set down her fork. 'Without asking Lady Regina? And you haven't seen her in ten years?' Her expression was aghast.

'Nay. But she's an obedient lass.'

Miss Goodson took a bite of her mutton pie, but he could see her thoughts turning over the matter. 'Why would you agree to marry a woman you haven't seen in that long?'

Because it had been his father's greatest wish. Lachlan had wanted to give that gift to Tavin, even if he hadn't been able to save his life. A dark twist of guilt rose at the memory, prickled with grief. He didn't want to marry anyone, and he knew he was hardly a fit candidate for a husband. Lady Regina would be horrified by the sight of his scarred face. But if he fulfilled his father's last desire, at least it was one thing he could do for the man.

'As I said before, Lord Havershire and my father wanted to unite our families together.'

'Even so, why would you agree to wed her without meeting her first?' Miss Goodson enquired. 'You might not like her any more.'

'I like the twenty thousand pounds her father has promised.' Lady Regina's dowry was money he needed, because repairing a five-hundred-year-old castle was costly. The offer of marriage was a welcome means of absolving him from financial ruin, for he hadn't realised how deeply Tavin MacKinloch had fallen into debt. Lachlan had already cut back on as many expenses as possible, but he didn't want to dismiss any of his staff. They needed their wages, and he'd do whatever he had to if it meant protecting his clansmen.

'That *is* a great deal of money,' she agreed. 'But I don't understand why Lord Havershire would offer so much.' She set her fork down and pondered a moment. 'Lady Regina has plenty of suitors. She simply turns them all away.'

'Because she's promised to me,' he countered.

'She doesn't want to marry anyone,' Miss

Goodson predicted. 'I have met her on several occasions. They call her the Lady of Ice.'

Lachlan didn't concern himself with his fiancée's reluctance. There was no reason for her to raise objections to the marriage—particularly since he intended to let her live her life as she chose.

'Lady Regina values a gentleman with manners,' Miss Goodson warned. 'If you wish to marry her, you will need to make a good impression. I could help you with this.'

'I've no need of your help.'

But the young woman ignored him and held out her list. 'I've written down possible lessons for you. Dining, dancing, conversation, and so on.'

Dancing? Lachlan despised dancing, and he would never engage in such a pastime. 'I won't be dancing, Miss Goodson.' He loathed the very thought.

'Oh, but you must. At a ball, you will be required to dance with Lady Regina. Only once, of course, but it is necessary to making a good impression upon her.'

Lachlan would rather cut off his thumbs than dance in public. 'I willna make a fool of myself.'

'Of course not,' Miss Goodson answered. 'I will ensure that you are well prepared. And you may find that you enjoy dancing. It can be delightful.'

'You won't be here to give any lessons,' he reminded her. 'The coach will be here first thing in the morning.'

'But I just thought that—'

'You'll find another position,' he said. The last thing he wanted was a woman staring at him and making lists. 'I don't need you. I don't want you here.'

She grew quiet, and the melancholy on her face made him feel like he'd just killed her cat. It took an effort to stop from apologising, though he hadn't been the one to hire her. This was all due to his mother's meddling.

'I'm sorry,' she whispered. Her river-green eyes gleamed with unshed tears. 'It's just that, I had such hopes.'

'Go home, Miss Goodson. Your family can take care of you now.'

She shook her head, gripping her napkin. 'I cannot go back to them.'

'Why?' He levelled a hard stare at her.

Her expression grew strained, as if she didn't want to speak of it. After a pause, she said, 'It's complicated.'

He could tell she was trying to avoid the topic by any means necessary. But her past intrigued him, and he pressed further. 'Are they cruel to you? Or violent?'

She shook her head but kept silent. He found himself wanting to know more, despite her reluctance. At last, he offered, 'If you tell me the truth about why you don't want to return home, I will grant you a second day here.'

Hope dawned in her green eyes, and her mouth softened, almost in a smile. She said, 'As you guessed earlier, I wasn't always a governess. My father was a baron.'

'Then why would you seek employment?'

'The desire to eat,' she admitted. 'My father disappeared one afternoon with his mistress. I never saw him again, and he left us destitute.' She took a sip of water and said, 'My sisters were already married, and I had no wish to be pitied and live with them. I had a good education, and so I decided to put it to use.'

'What of your mother?' he asked. 'Why not go and live with her?'

Her expression tightened. 'Suffice it to say, I preferred supporting myself without relying upon anyone else. I might have been arrested for murder, had I stayed with my mother.'

He could understand her desire for independence and respected it. If she were sent home, it *would* make her feel like a failure, though it was through no fault of her own.

'One more day then,' he repeated. 'And I will have the coach take you wherever you wish to go, after that.'

She paused a moment and said, 'Whether you believe it or not, I *can* help you. Especially in understanding the complexities of the London ton. It's very different from Scotland.'

He was well aware of that, though he cared little about London mannerisms. 'And you know this by being here a matter of hours?'

She nodded. 'Indeed. Scotland is breathtaking. Whereas in London, I prefer to hold my breath.' A spark of humour creased her mouth with a smile. 'But all that aside, I am going to prove to you that I can be the most useful governess you've ever had.'

'You're the only governess I've ever had,' he pointed out. But in Miss Goodson's face he saw a stubbornness that revealed an inner strength. This was not a woman who would falter in the face of adversity. And though she was young, he found that he respected her mettle.

'I look forward to our lessons.' Her eyes were bright with interest, and he felt the need to correct her.

'I've offered you one day. But I'm no' going to spend hours learning about forks or God forbid, dancing.'

There was a gleam in her eyes as if she'd accepted the challenge. 'One day, Locharr. And you'll see everything I can teach you.'

'Alban will show you to your room,' he said. 'You'll want to sleep, and I may see you in the morning, after I've returned from riding.'

Her face held such wistfulness, as if she wanted to say something but held herself back.

Against his better judgement, he asked, 'Do you ride?'

'I do love it,' she admitted. 'Though it has been a few years since I've had the opportunity.' From the expression on her face, she was itching for an invitation.

'If you're wanting to go riding, I've no objection,' he said.

Although he had no desire for company, he supposed there was no harm in her taking one of the mild-tempered horses and trotting around the castle grounds. It would make it that much easier to say farewell the next day, knowing that he'd given her that consolation.

'I am so grateful, Locharr,' she breathed, a light shining in her eyes. 'Is there someone who could chaperon us?' she asked. 'Alban, perhaps?'

Us? He had no intention of riding *with* her. But he supposed he could ask his footman to accompany Miss Goodson on her ride.

'I will ask him,' he promised. 'Whenever

you're wanting to go on your ride, just ask Alban, and he'll see to it that you have a horse.'

Her face dimmed slightly. 'I thought you might accompany me. To show me the surrounding area and tell me about it.'

'Alban can do the same. I intend to leave at dawn. Alone.' He preferred riding when it was quiet outside. It gave him the chance to inspect his land and make his plans for the day.

'A true gentleman would wait upon the lady,' she chided.

Lachlan shrugged. 'Then, 'tis a good thing I am no' a gentleman yet.'

Frances awoke when it was still dark outside. The faint light of dawn illuminated the horizon, and she stretched and yawned. The laird had said he intended to ride at dawn. Well, it was nearly dawn and if she hurried, she could join him on his ride.

She said a silent prayer of thanks for this day. Though he fully intended to send her home tomorrow, Frances was determined to stay. She loved this castle, and the challenge of helping the laird was important, even if he was somewhat intimidating. But more than that, she couldn't afford to return to her boarding house in London. There was nothing for her there, and she didn't want to be a failure at something else, once again. Her mother would never stop blaming her for the sins of her past.

And so, she would do everything in her power to protect the future.

Frances lit a candle and set it down on the table. There wasn't much time, and she had only three gowns to choose from. At least she owned attire that allowed her to dress herself without the services of a maid, even if it had been mended and remade several times.

She walked over to her trunk of belongings, realising that she should have unpacked it last night. Undoubtedly her gowns would be full of wrinkles. Although she had no riding habit, she chose a serviceable blue gown that she could wear and ride side saddle.

A thrill of anticipation soared within her. She adored horses and could not wait to go outside. It was still cool and damp, so she added a warm cloak and a bonnet to her outfit.

While Frances tucked a few escaping curls back into her bonnet, her mind turned over the idea of educating the laird. He was rather…rough around the edges. Truthfully, she could not imagine Lachlan MacKinloch marrying someone like Lady Regina. The shy young woman would be terrified of such a large, brash man.

Frances, in contrast, believed that she could see beneath his fierce exterior. The laird needed softening up, but she felt confident that he would win the heart of Lady Regina with time and effort. The laird was a decent man, though his clothing was quite…vivid. And he would need his hair cut.

As for the scar…she decided that there should be a heroic story to go with it. Something that would make Lady Regina see him differently. Frances would have to think upon it.

She opened the door to leave her room and stepped into the hallway, only to bump into a maid. 'I'm so sorry,' Frances apologised. 'I didn't see you.'

The woman was elderly and plump, and she wore a grey skirt with a white blouse. A tartan arasaid was clasped beneath her chin with a brooch. The tartan left a small portion of the grey skirt uncovered, and it revealed the blouse in a similar manner of a cloak. The woman gave her a nod and a smile but did not speak.

Frances followed the maid down the hall to the staircase. Alban met her at the bottom of the stairs, and she bid the maid, 'Have a good morning.' But again, the elderly woman said nothing but only smiled.

'Elspeth doesn't hear verra well,' the footman explained, 'but she understands everything you say to her, so long as you shout. She will shout her answer, as well, when she has something to say.'

Frances nodded. 'I see.' The older footman was about to escort her outside to the stables, when she asked, 'Lady Locharr summoned me here, Alban, to help her son. Do you not think I should stay and tutor the laird?'

''Tis no' my place to say, Miss Goodson.'

It was clear that the man was refusing to take sides. Frances considered another alternative. It was an extreme measure, but she might not have a second chance.

'I truly do wish to help Locharr. He is a good man, and I want him to win Lady Regina's heart. However, if he arrives in London, he may have some difficulty. He might frighten her.'

'The laird is a fierce lad with that scar, aye.' The footman's gaze narrowed. 'What did ye have in mind?'

Frances dug into her pocket and found a penny. Though it was hardly anything, it was all she had to offer. 'Alban, all I am asking for is one week. A single day isn't enough to help him. Could you…delay the coach? Perhaps tell the laird that the axle is broken. Or something of that nature.'

'Ye want me to lie?' The footman stared at her in disbelief.

'I want you to let me give the laird lessons in

etiquette. Allow me to do my job.' She held the penny closer. 'Take it. It's all I have, but I can promise you more, if I ever receive wages.' She wasn't certain that would ever happen, but she could dream of it.

The footman sighed and took the penny. 'I will do what I can, lass.'

'Thank you.' She smiled at him and followed the older man outside towards the stables.

Morning rays of sun spilled over the horizon, and the sky was tinted grey and rose. The laird was speaking with the groom, who was bringing a stallion by the reins. Once again, MacKinloch wore a tartan with his shirt and trousers, but this time, Frances took a closer look at his physical form. He had broad shoulders and was so tall, it made her wonder if it was even possible to reach his neck if she stood on tiptoe. For that matter, he appeared strong enough to lift the horse in front of him. The laird's legs were powerful, his thighs thick as if he were ready to ride out with a conquering barbarian horde. And heaven help her, she could only wonder what it would be like to embrace such a man.

You are his governess, she reminded herself sternly. *Stop staring.*

Frances swallowed hard and gathered her composure. 'Good morning, Locharr.'

He gave her a nod in greeting. 'You're awake early.'

'You said dawn. And here I am.'

He had a slight expression of irritation. Oh, she knew full well that he'd wanted to ride alone, for he'd said so. But she wanted to accompany him, both to get a sense of the land and to gauge *him*.

The groom brought out an older mare for her, and she supposed that was a logical decision, given that he knew nothing of her riding expertise. The poor mare looked as if she would rather be grazing than cantering through a field. But perhaps there was some spark to her, beneath the surface. Frances greeted the horse, giving the animal the chance to learn her scent. 'There's a sweet girl.'

'Pip is a gentle one,' the laird said. 'You've naught to be afraid of.'

'I'm not afraid of horses,' Frances answered. 'But I would be glad if you could help me up.'

The laird caught her waist, but instead of lifting her up, he held her a moment. His hands were so large, they nearly spanned her waist. She was acutely conscious of his touch, and God help her, it was nearly an embrace.

'Could you—? That is—' Her nerves were prickled and, oh, dear, he *knew* what he was doing. There was a slight smirk at his mouth, and she felt utterly bewildered on what to do now. Should she step backwards? Push his hands back? But then again, she had asked for his help.

Before she could speak, the laird picked her up and plunked her on the side saddle. 'Er… thank you,' she said. Frances adjusted her skirts and her cloak as a distraction before she took the reins. Though she understood that he was trying to intimidate her, she refused to acknowledge it. He wanted her to leave Scotland, and she could not do anything to threaten her place here. And so, she pretended that he'd done nothing at all.

'We will need a chaperon. Shall I ask Alban or Elspeth to join us?' she suggested.

'It's no' necessary,' he said. 'It's an open field, and everyone can see us.'

She wasn't so certain if that was a wise idea. True, there were likely a dozen servants watching from the windows, but he also needed to adhere to convention. 'What about the groom?'

He didn't answer, but instead mounted his bay stallion and took the lead. Well, then. She would have to speak with him about the etiquette of not leaving the lady behind.

He didn't want you to come with him, her brain pointed out. True enough. But she was so accustomed to life as a lady instead of a governess. It was hard to remember sometimes that she was naught but a servant.

But better to be a servant than to live with her mother. Frances couldn't bear to endure Prudence's constant reproach for the sins of the past. Her stomach twisted, but she forced back the hard memories. That part of her life was in the past and it would only bring back raw grief if she allowed herself to remember it.

She urged her mare into a trot as they followed a path towards the open meadow. Then the laird nudged his horse into a canter, glancing behind to see if she would follow. Frances had the feeling that this was a test of some kind to determine her mettle. She followed at a reasonable pace—nothing too difficult for the mare, though Locharr was leaving her behind.

Instead, she chose to enjoy the brisk air. It was cool and misty, with a breath of rain lingering in the air. In the distance, the loch gleamed silver, and she spoke words of encouragement to Pip. The mare eventually perked up and managed a canter. She closed her eyes, enjoying the morning chill and the joy of being on horseback.

The laird drew his stallion into a gallop, leaving them behind. MacKinloch was a man of fierce independence, she decided. And not one who liked being told what to do. He hadn't really wanted her to come along, though she'd invited herself.

His strong will didn't bode well for their first

tutoring session. *If* he allowed her to teach him, that is. Would he trust her knowledge and recognise that her intent was not to order him around but instead, to instruct him? Or perhaps it might be better to take a different approach to teaching him. The laird struck her as an intelligent man with a competitive spirit. She frowned, turning the problem over in her mind.

When the laird rode back towards her, he remarked, 'Were you too afraid to ride fast, Miss Goodson? Pip wouldna harm you.'

'Oh, I wasn't afraid at all.' She thought up a quick excuse and said, 'But riding side saddle in this gown makes it impossible to ride fast. I decided to simply enjoy the day without the speed.' She patted Pip's back in silent reassurance to the mare.

'Why not try it astride?' he suggested. 'You'd be less likely to fall off.'

Frances shook her head. 'While that may be practical for a man wearing trousers, it is not possible for me. Not wearing this.' At least, not without showing her legs to the servants, and that simply would not do.

'Besides, if you intend to go riding with Lady Regina, she will take a slower pace.' She nudged the mare into a trot, following the rise and fall of the animal. 'And…um…you may want to be careful about leaving a lady behind. It's more dangerous in London.' She was trying to be tactful without being overly critical.

But her words *did* get his attention. His expression tightened into a shield, as if he felt embarrassed by his actions. 'My apologies. I wasna thinking of your safety.' The gruff response held a hint of remorse.

Frances wanted to lighten his dark mood, for it wasn't the greatest of catastrophes. 'It's all right, really. Nothing happened. I merely wanted to point out that it would not be wise to abandon a lady, should you be riding in Rotten Row or somewhere in town.'

He gave a single nod. When he said nothing else, Frances blurted out, 'Before we go back, would you give me a tour of the grounds?' she asked. 'I've never seen a castle of this size before, and while it's not raining, I should like to see it.'

He hesitated as if he had no wish to do so.

'Please?' she asked. 'Your home is beautiful. Especially the stained-glass windows.'

He let out a sigh and finally agreed. 'We'll leave the horses and walk. There's no' much to see out in the glen.'

When they reached the stables, he helped her down, and Frances pushed back the thrill of his hands upon her waist. She had an unfortunate weakness for strong men, and it *was* rather nice to be lifted from a horse as if she weighed no more than a spoon. Immediately, she reminded her wayward brain that the last thing she needed was to be attracted to the laird. He was her employer and was already engaged to another woman. But she could not deny that the wildness of his appearance had caught her eye. She could easily imagine being carried away, as if he were a conquering warlord.

Enough of this foolishness, she chided herself. But there was no denying that he made her nervous. And when she got nervous, she tended to talk too much.

The laird started to walk ahead, and she hurried to keep up. If he did that to Lady Regina, it could be a problem. Frances cleared her throat and called out, 'Locharr, a moment, please?'

He turned back, uncertain of what she wanted. His expression revealed impatience, of a man who had no intention of being tutored by her. Still, she wanted to help him. With a smile, she put her hand in the crook of his arm. 'I know I am only a governess, but for today, could we pretend that I am a lady? To practise.'

'You are a lady,' he answered. 'You said your father was a baron.'

Her cheeks flushed as she tried to push back the unwanted memories. 'He was, yes. But I am well aware that my station has fallen. I can only make the best of my circumstances.'

Frances straightened her posture and smiled as she walked alongside him, her gloved hand tucked in his arm. 'I have one day, and I intend to make the most of it. Shall we begin with your first lesson?'

Chapter Two

Lachlan wasn't at all certain he wanted any kind of lesson. He decided that if Miss Goodson grew too overbearing, he would return to the house. After all, she was departing in the morning. But as they walked, he saw her marvelling at Locharr. She appeared enchanted by the stone archway that led to the gardens, and he had to admit, it had been some time since he'd viewed the estate through the eyes of a stranger.

The gravel pathway meandered around the green lawn towards a stone fountain of Venus. Miss Goodson had insisted upon a chaperon during their walk, so he had asked Elspeth to follow at a close distance. He deliberately kept his pace slow, so as not to overexert the elderly maid. Even so, he couldn't understand why his governess found it necessary to be shadowed at all times.

'How lovely,' Miss Goodson breathed when

she saw the fountain. Water spilled from the hands of Venus into the small pool, and a small frog swam within the fountain. She walked alongside him, her hand pressed against his arm. The slight touch made him feel conscious of Miss Goodson's every movement, and it was strange to realise that he was enjoying her company.

Her green eyes shone with fascination and she was delighted with the garden, even though naught was blooming. 'It will be filled with roses, come the summertime.'

'There are roses, aye.' He didn't know what else to say besides that. Miss Goodson waited a moment, as if she were expecting more. When he said nothing, she stopped beside a stone urn and offered an encouraging smile. It was almost a silent battle of wills, as if she expected him to say more and he didn't want to. He had never been one for long conversations.

'Is there anything you would like to converse about, Locharr?'

He shrugged. 'Nay.' He liked the calm feeling of quiet. But from his governess's expression, she appeared concerned.

'When you are in London, be careful about long moments of silence with Lady Regina,' Miss Goodson said. 'She is the shyest young woman I've ever met, and I fear that if the conversation stops, it could be very uncomfortable for her.'

He didn't see a problem in that, but he supposed some women might feel that way. 'What are you wanting me to do?'

'If you do not know what to say, you can always ask a question. Why don't you ask me anything?' Miss Goodson waited, and when Lachlan realised she wasn't going to relent until he said something, he fumbled for a question. But came up with nothing.

He finally shrugged again and answered, 'I've no idea.'

'Let's try this. Pretend you are the lady.' She lowered her voice and said in a growling tone, 'Lady Regina, how long have you been in London?'

'That's a daft question. They come to London every Season.'

She bit back a laugh. 'Yes, you and I know that, but won't you play along for the sake of conversation? Just give it a try.'

He raised his voice to a falsetto and said, 'You already know I come to London every Season.'

Miss Goodson held back her smile, though her eyes shone with mirth. In a low tone, she said, 'The weather has been very rainy, as of late.'

Honestly, her idea of a conversation was not

that interesting. 'Why should I care about the weather?' he asked. 'Why should she?'

Miss Goodson reached out to touch his arm. 'Patience, Locharr. Just give me a moment longer, won't you?'

He couldn't conceive of how this could have any merit at all. And she was making him feel foolish by playing the part of the lady. 'Fine,' he gritted out.

'Let's try it one more time. Now that we have talked about her travels and the weather, I might venture onto a new topic to get better acquainted.' She cleared her throat and stared up at him. 'You should try to make eye contact with the lady when you are speaking to her. So much is revealed in the eyes.'

Then she straightened and said in a deep voice, 'It has been many years since we have seen one another, Lady Regina. I was wondering how you enjoy spending your time. Do you paint?'

Lachlan understood what she was trying to show him, but he couldn't resist the urge to make the conversation more interesting. In a falsetto, he said, 'No, I find painting dull. I prefer hunting.'

Miss Goodson bit her lip hard and shook her head. 'A lady might not indulge in hunting.'

'Now you're wrong in that,' he countered.

'Many ladies enjoy hunting. And I thought you were wanting to play along?'

'Fine,' she sighed. In her deep voice, she uttered, 'Fox hunting or deer?'

'Boar,' he said in the high-pitched voice. 'I enjoy gutting pigs.'

At that, Miss Goodson no longer suppressed her laughter. Her eyes filled with mirth, and her hearty laugh brought about his own smile. 'You are incorrigible, Locharr.'

He knew it, but he hadn't been able to resist the urge. 'And now you see that giving me lessons would be impossible.'

She shrugged at that. 'Actually, I believe it would be very rewarding to help you. I should be glad of the opportunity.'

They walked out of the garden and into the inner bailey of the castle. Miss Goodson glanced up the staircase and asked, 'Might we walk along the battlements so I can have a look at the sea?'

He saw no reason why not and guided her towards the stone stairs. The castle had been built so long ago, there was a walkway along the parapets where the archers used to keep guard. The wall along the edge was low enough that she could see the expanse of trees below and the sea in the distance. The morning sun was hazy, but it sparkled upon the surface of the water.

Miss Goodson's face brightened at the sight

of the water. 'You truly have the most beautiful home, Locharr. I should love a view like this. It's wonderful.'

'It is verra fine,' he agreed. 'But it's a costly view. And if I mean to keep this castle, I will need those twenty thousand pounds.'

'Lady Regina is a most fortunate woman,' Miss Goodson said. 'I would marry you myself to live in a castle like this.'

Though her words were light-hearted, his imagination conjured the vivid image of Miss Goodson walking along these parapets as Lady of Locharr. Her blonde curls framed a lovely face, and her green eyes warmed at the sight of his home. He wondered how she would look after being thoroughly kissed. Would a soft moan escape that mouth while she surrendered to his touch? Was there more to Miss Goodson beneath those prim and proper ways? A darker side of him thought about unravelling her sensibilities, tempting her into sin.

It led him to wonder why she had not married after her father had left them. Her sisters had done so. What had caused her to seek employment on her own instead of seeking help from her family? He studied the young woman, wondering what secrets she was hiding. Though Miss Goodson was cheerful and seemed glad to be teaching him, he suspected that there was more beneath the surface. Her eyes gleamed with enthusiasm as he'd shown her Locharr. It was a sharp contrast to his own weary view of the world.

'Would you like to walk a little further?' he suggested. 'There's a glasshouse in the gardens on the opposite side of the grounds.'

She brightened and took his arm again. 'I would love to continue our walk.'

He guided her through the gardens towards the structure that was inspired by a birdcage. The maid was falling further behind, but it seemed that Miss Goodson was either unaware or didn't seem to mind. As long as there was a chaperon within a certain distance, that was all she cared about.

His grandfather had built the glasshouse for his wife, and it contained some of the more exotic plants and trees that were too fragile for Scottish weather.

Miss Goodson appeared in awe of the building, and for a moment, she was quiet as she explored the plants. When she reached one of the trees, she asked, 'Is this a banana tree?'

'Aye. My mother had it brought over from the Caribbean.'

She reached up to touch the tiny green bananas as if she could not believe they were real.

'I've never seen a banana tree before. It's smaller than I thought it would be.'

'This one is,' he agreed. 'But they can grow much larger. We have to keep it inside the glasshouse.'

'I wonder what else your mother will bring back from her travels?' Miss Goodson mused. 'It sounds fascinating.'

'Ever since my father died, she has spent most of her time in different countries. She tries to bring me a gift from each country she visits.' It was part of the truth. Catrina had been devastated at Tavin's death. While Lachlan had shut himself away from the outside world, his mother had consoled herself by running away. The travel expenses were very dear, but Lachlan didn't have the heart to cut her off. It was her way of managing her own grief.

'How wonderful. She sounds like an adventurous lady.'

Adventurous was one way of describing his mother. But Catrina reminded him of a gust of wind, moving wherever she chose, heedless of whoever she knocked over along the way. It was more peaceful when she was gone. But when she returned, he intended to have words with her about her decision to hire a governess.

'When I thought you had a daughter, I imagined teaching her about botany in an environment just like this,' Miss Goodson said. 'Only there are so many plants I've never seen; your mother would likely know more than I.' She drew closer to a flower and leaned in to inhale the fragrance. 'Any child who would grow up in a home like this would be very fortunate.'

'Then you understand why I must do anything to protect it,' he said quietly.

Miss Goodson nodded. 'I do understand.' With a smile, she added, 'And I am positive that Lady Regina will be delighted to marry you.' She softened her tone and said, 'I know that you don't want me here, Locharr. But please trust that I have your best intentions in mind. I want to help you.'

'In other words, you want to tell me what to do.'

'Only to guide you. And because of it, you will become the most desirable bachelor in London.'

'You have only today,' he reminded her. 'What could you possibly teach me in that time?'

Her green eyes warmed with interest. 'Wait and see.'

Frances knew she would have to use unconventional lessons to attract the interest of the laird. He had no faith in her, and she had to prove her usefulness. She sensed that Locharr was a man of a competitive nature. And she thought of a way to win a third day at the castle.

'Do you play cards, Locharr?' she asked.

'Only when I'm planning to win money.' His gaze narrowed, and his scar stood out on his face, reminding her of a pirate. Which made her imagine being stolen away by a handsome buccaneer. Her brain really needed to stop thinking of such things.

But she squared her shoulders and forced herself to concentrate. 'I was thinking we could make a wager. What do you think?'

His expression grew interested, his pirate smile making her imagination conjure up more inappropriate visions of conquest. 'For what stakes?'

'If I win, you will complete a lesson and allow me to stay another day. If you win, I shall help you with anything you desire.'

'Anything?' he mused, and her face reddened at the sudden innuendo.

Not that. But she pretended as if there was nothing untoward about her words. 'Within reason,' she corrected.

He eyed her with interest and shrugged. 'I suppose we could play whist.'

'Where shall we have our game?' she asked. 'Elspeth can come and chaperon again.'

'In the parlour,' he said. 'But Elspeth may be

tired from her walk this afternoon. She may wish to rest in her room instead.'

No. Being unchaperoned and alone with a pirate was a Very Bad Idea. 'Or Elspeth might also welcome the chance to sit for an hour,' Frances countered.

'I don't ken why we need a chaperon. I'm no' about to try and seduce you.'

She blinked at that. Well, then. He'd made his opinion quite clear. Frances cleared her throat and said, 'It's merely a habit you must acquire, Locharr. In London, you may not go anywhere without a chaperon. Whether your intention is seduction or not.'

He frowned at that. 'It seems like a waste of time.'

It was clear that he didn't understand what she meant. 'It is always necessary to have a chaperon. It's protection for you, or else you might find yourself the target of another young lady's interest. And unless you wish to wed her, you'd best never be alone with her.' Her tone came out sharper than she'd intended, but he needed to understand the gravity of the situation. For a moment, he stared at her in a silent war of wills. Frances crossed her arms, refusing to yield.

Perhaps it was her imagination, but she thought she detected a faint note of approval from the laird. And he did call out to Alban, ordering Elspeth to join them in the parlour.

Frances tried not to gape as they walked through the halls. Although she had spent the night here, she could not resist smiling at the white columns that encircled the spiral staircase leading up. Truly, this was a magnificent castle fit for a princess.

The laird stopped in front of a smaller room and led her inside. She paused a moment to admire the parlour. 'This is lovely.'

And it was. The crimson wallpaper was cheerful, and she liked the cosy hearth, even if there was no fire in the grate.

'There are too many paintings,' Lachlan countered. 'Eight landscapes is too much for one wall.'

'It gives one the opportunity to study a different painting each time,' she said tactfully, though privately she agreed that it was indeed a lot of art for one room. A large portrait of an older nobleman hung over the fireplace, and Frances rather thought the man was leering at her.

MacKinloch led her to a smaller gaming table, and then he went to find a deck of playing cards. Frances shuffled the deck and remarked, 'We really ought to have two more players for this game. Elspeth could join us. Or possibly Alban.'

'She may not want to play,' he pointed out. 'And Alban has his duties to attend.'

'Well, we can offer.' She felt badly that the older woman had been required to traipse around the castle grounds and now had to sit in a chair.

'She's as deaf as a fence post. And I'm no' in the mood to be shouting.'

'You needn't be rude or insensitive,' Frances countered. 'She cannot help her inability to hear.'

'She's lucky to be employed,' he muttered, and Frances pretended not to notice.

When the elderly woman arrived in the parlour, Lachlan motioned for Elspeth to sit on the far side of the room. She sank gratefully into a chair, leaning back. 'Thank you, Locharr!' she shouted.

Frances was taken aback by the woman's bellowing, but she approached Elspeth. In a loud voice, she asked the maid, 'Would you care to play whist?'

The woman shook her head and put her hand to her ear. 'What was that?' she bellowed.

'Cards!' Frances shouted in return. 'Do you wish to play?'

Elspeth shook her head and waved her hand. 'Nay, lass! But thankee!'

She nodded and stepped back. To Lachlan, she said, 'I suppose if Elspeth has no wish to play, we'll just lay out the other hands after I deal them.'

Frances dealt out the cards and sorted her hand. She arranged her cards, trying not to think of how close his legs were to hers. He was staring at his cards as if he didn't like what he saw. The frown made his scar more defined, but instead of frightening her, it made him appear wild and untamed. His blue eyes narrowed a moment before he fixed his attention on her again. Was he trying to distract her by flirting? There was a slight smile playing at his mouth.

Frances took a deep breath and focused on her cards again. 'I will take the hand across from me, and you do the same. That way we will keep taking turns, and neither of us has an advantage.'

'Or we could lay the opposite hand down,' he suggested.

'If we do that, there won't be any element of surprise. I'll know what card you'll play next, and I'll know where the trump cards are.' She thought a moment. 'We could stand up and change chairs. That could be amusing.'

He looked doubtful and then shook his head. 'We'll stay where we are and switch hands.'

'Very well.' Frances examined her hand and was pleased that there were several trump cards. 'I shall lead.'

With that, she laid down the ace of hearts.

The laird countered by throwing away his lowest heart, giving her the trick. She claimed a second trick, but on the third, he trumped her.

'This one is mine.' His hand brushed against hers as he collected the cards. His touch was bold, and she tried not to think of what those hands could do to a woman.

Concentrate, Frances, she warned herself. He was trying to distract her so he could win.

As the game progressed, it soon became clear that Lachlan MacKinloch was quite competitive. He delighted in winning and grimaced at the lost tricks. They each won a game. In the corner, Elspeth was quietly snoring, her mouth open as she dozed. *So much for a chaperon,* Frances thought. And then she wondered if Lachlan had deliberately chosen the old woman for that reason.

'Do you think you can win?' he asked, his voice rough and deep. His expression taunted her, as if he held a secret.

'I know I can. But you can give up, if you wish.' Her last card was an ace. There was no doubt in her mind that she would take the game and his forfeit. She smiled at him.

'I never give up.' He tapped the card against the back of his hand. 'Ladies first.'

Frances responded by laying down the ace, smiling broadly. 'The game is mine.' Triumph spread across her face, and she was glad of the victory.

And yet, the laird had a gleam in his eyes. With that, he laid down a two, the lowliest of cards—but it was the trump suit.

'No!' Frances expelled a groan and shook her head with exasperation. 'I thought it had already been played. I must have miscounted.'

MacKinloch took the trick and leaned back in his chair, quite satisfied by the outcome. It made her wonder exactly what he wanted from her now. Her wicked brain conjured up the idea of him kissing her, though she knew the very idea was ridiculous. But she forced herself to ask, 'Well, what is my forfeit? Is there something you need help with?'

He stood from the table and drew closer until he towered over her. 'Oh, aye. There are a great many things I need help with.'

His voice was low and resonant, causing her mind to think of even more scandalous thoughts. But she pretended as if his request was ordinary. 'What do you need, Locharr?'

Oh, heavens, her voice sounded breathless, as if she was glad that their chaperon was fast asleep. When the truth was, her nerves had gathered, causing her heart to pound rapidly.

'I need you to come with me,' he said.

Into a darkened corner where he would press

her back, his warm mouth against her cheek? Her imagination went wild, and she tried to push back the scandalous visions in her mind.

Her face flamed, but she asked, 'Locharr, what is it?'

MacKinloch finally said, 'It's a task that I loathe and despise, but it must be done. My father left the estate ledgers in a terrible state. For your forfeit, I want you to help me sort through the papers.' With a wry smile, he added, 'Afterwards, you'll be wanting to flee back to London. It's horrifying.'

Relief soared through her, and her expression turned sympathetic. 'Of course, I will be glad to help you.' Without thinking, she touched his hand with her own. His eyes darkened, but not with anger. No, there was a flash of heat that rose up, tempting her towards more. Frances snatched back her hand, feeling like an idiot.

She had been burned by temptation once before, and she had sworn never to let it happen again. The mistakes of her past would remain there. And no matter how handsome and strong this man was, she would never let down her guard for a single moment.

Her future depended on it.

Lachlan opened the door to the study, steeling himself for what lay ahead. Even after the past few years, it had become a Herculean task to sort through his father's ledgers. He and his clansmen had loved Tavin, though the man was impossibly disorganised. The loss of their laird had left a hole in everyone's lives.

Lachlan had shut himself away from everyone after his father's death. Not only to heal from his wounds, but to come to terms with his guilt. He hadn't saved Tavin's life, and he blamed himself. But there was no choice except to move on. He intended to take care of the people and the estate, but first, he had to unravel where all the money had gone.

'We forgot about Elspeth,' Miss Goodson reminded him. 'She's still asleep in the parlour.'

He wouldn't say that 'forgot' was the right word. Deliberately left behind, perhaps. 'We won't need her for this. And I'll leave the door open, if it makes you feel better.'

Lachlan led her into the study, and Miss Goodson could hardly conceal her horror at the sight. 'Dear God.'

Although the room had once been Lachlan's favourite, with polished wooden panelling and rows of bookcases, there were papers on every surface. Stacks of ledgers remained on the large desk, while papers were stuffed inside books, stacked on the floor—even crammed behind a brass sconce upon the wall. He'd done his best to organise it as best he could. His father had saved every last scrap of paper, and Lachlan didn't know which ones were necessary and which could be burned.

'Oh, my,' she breathed. 'How long has it been like this?'

'Two years,' Lachlan answered. 'When I first took my father's place, there were papers so deep in places, they were up to my knees. At least I can see the floor now.'

'Did he…keep everything?'

It certainly seemed that way, though he hadn't known it at the time. 'My father stopped recording the information in the ledgers some time ago. He simply kept the bills and wrote down the amounts on scraps of paper.'

'And your mother simply allowed him to keep his books in this way?' She appeared aghast at the idea, and Lachlan privately agreed with her. Tavin had clearly been in over his head. 'Why did no one intervene?'

'He kept the room locked,' Lachlan answered. 'I believe he was ashamed and wanted no one to know about it.' And that was no surprise, for the study was a disaster. He felt slightly guilty that he had asked for her help in this, but then again, if the intent was to drive her away, this would do it.

Miss Goodson, however, didn't seem deterred

at all. Instead, she rolled up her sleeves and let out a slow breath of air, turning over the problem in her mind. 'Well, I suppose we should begin by sorting the papers by date.'

'Not all of them are dated,' he pointed out.

'Then we shall make a stack of those papers with no date and see if we can't make sense of them, in time.' She paused a moment. 'When was the last time he used a ledger to record anything at all?'

'1802.'

Miss Goodson blinked at that. Unfortunately, they were looking through at least eight years of papers. There was no way around it, except to go piece by piece.

'All right.' She steadied herself a moment and said, 'I suggest that we purchase eight ledgers. One for each year. We can sort the papers and put them inside the ledgers to be recorded later. What do you think?'

'I've already begun sorting them by year. This is 1803.' He pointed towards the stack of papers on the floor beside the desk. 'And this is 1804.' He gestured at the brass sconce. It was the best semblance of order he could achieve amid the chaos.

'Where is the pile left to be sorted?' she enquired. He didn't miss the slight note of alarm in her tone.

'In the bookcase. Behind portraits. Inside every possible hiding place you'd imagine.'

Her complexion turned sickly at his statement. 'Oh, dear.'

'Aye. I won't be asking you to sort all of it. We'll try it for an hour. That will be forfeit enough.'

Even so, he intended to speak with Alban about the extra ledgers. It was a good idea, and it would make it easier to organise the materials. The truth was, he'd been avoiding this task. A part of him thought it would be just as easy to lock the door and walk away. But he had to learn how Tavin had lost so much money over the years.

'Shall I begin gathering the papers?' Miss Goodson suggested. 'I could go through the bookcase and find them. Since you already know where your stacks are, you could put them where they belong.'

Lachlan shrugged. 'If you like.' It was as good a place to start as any. He took three pages and placed one behind the sconce and a second on the pile for 1808.

Miss Goodson glanced outside. 'What time is it, Locharr?'

He flipped open his pocket watch and answered, 'It's half past three.' He didn't know why she had asked, but he supposed it was growing later in the day.

'Should I ring for tea to be served here?'

'Aye. If you're hungry.' Now that she mentioned it, food *did* sound good right now.

She rang for Alban, and Lachlan ordered sandwiches and tea for her to drink, though he personally would have preferred whisky. Miss Goodson pulled out a slim volume from the bookshelf and found it stuffed with papers. Her eyes narrowed at his father's handwriting, but she managed to find a date. 'This one is 1805.' She passed it to him, and he stacked it beside the window.

They found a rhythm of working together that was effective. Miss Goodson went through the papers, calling out each date before she passed it to him. One date was particularly difficult, and she squinted. 'I'm terribly sorry, but I have no idea what these numbers are.' She held it out and he studied it closely with no luck.

'I'm thinking he was half-tippled when he wrote it.' But he placed it in the 1806 pile nonetheless.

'One might need to be deep in his cups to make sense of all this,' she muttered beneath her breath.

Lachlan hid a smile at that. 'In an hour, we can have a wee nip, if you're wanting something.'

'No, thank you.' Her lips pursed together in the manner of a prim governess, and he rather wondered what she would be like with her hair loosened around her shoulders, her mouth softened.

When Alban arrived with the tea, Lachlan directed him to put the refreshments on the table by the window. Before the footman could leave, Miss Goodson cleared her throat.

'Pardon me, Locharr, but do you think Alban could acquire the ledgers you need to sort through all of your father's papers?'

The elderly footman turned back with a pained look. 'How many would you be wanting, do you think?' His gaze passed over the papers as if he wanted to set them on fire.

'I should think that eight would be sufficient, don't you?' She looked back at him for confirmation.

Lachlan only shrugged. 'It doesna matter to me. Bring eight, and if we're needing more, I'll send for them.'

Miss Goodson brightened at his support. 'Good. That will help you put away what you've already sorted.' Once the footman had departed, she tucked a wayward curl behind one ear.

'Eat,' he commanded. 'You could stand to be fattened up a bit.'

She gaped and then said, 'Please don't speak

to a lady about her figure, Locharr. If you mean to offer a sandwich, then do so, but say nothing about fattening her up. I am not a pig about to be roasted for supper.'

He knew that, but he hadn't been able to resist teasing her. With a shrug, he said, 'I meant no harm.' He'd only wanted to watch her indignant reaction. Her cheeks flushed, and when she corrected him, she tended to straighten her shoulders, revealing the outline of her bosom.

Miss Goodson walked towards the window and picked up the plate. 'Well, be that as it may, it is easy enough to simply offer a sandwich.'

He took one and devoured it with a single bite. Aye, he knew it was barbaric, but he was enjoying tweaking her. 'It's no' bad. Ye should try one.'

She raised an eyebrow at him, and her expression turned into that of a prim schoolteacher. 'Were you a difficult boy in school?'

'Very. My friends and I were always avoiding our classes.' He expected her to chastise him, but there was a gleam in her eyes as if she thought it an adventure instead.

'I suppose your teachers grew frustrated,' she teased. 'You are quite a challenge. But I believe I can succeed in helping you, Locharr.'

'Why?' He set down the plate, deliberately wanting to challenge her. 'Are you forgetting that you're no' my governess, Miss Goodson? And that you're leaving tomorrow?'

Her expression dimmed at that. 'I haven't forgotten. But I want to help you as much as I am able, in whatever time I have remaining.'

'Because you believe you can change my mind about keeping you here?' He reached for another sandwich. 'It willna happen. The last thing I need is someone telling me what to do and how to do it.'

Her face flushed, and she didn't move. Those river-green eyes turned the colour of a storm cloud. 'That wasn't my intention.'

Oh, but it was. And he wanted to be quite clear that he would not allow her to give him commands.

'You're no' going to stay,' he responded. 'No matter what you say or do.'

'We'll see about that.' Her challenge brightened those cheeks, and she glared at him. It intrigued him further, and he wondered if she would keep her temper.

'Are you wanting a sandwich, Miss Goodson?' he asked. He deliberately spoke with exaggerated politeness as he pressed the bread to her mouth.

The colour deepened in her face, and she turned away. 'I'm not hungry.'

'I am.' He took the sandwich and ate half in a

single bite. Miss Goodson's expression appeared pained, but she did not correct him.

'Do you want the other half?' He held it out, knowing that she wanted to say something. But she didn't dare, knowing how that her place was tenuous.

Instead, she turned her attention to another distraction, and she poured a cup of tea for each of them. 'Do you take milk or sugar in your tea?'

'You're ignoring my question, aren't you?'

She gave no acknowledgment but held out the cup. 'Take a small sip. If you don't care for the taste, I will add milk or sugar, however you please.'

'I take whisky,' he answered. 'Without the tea.'

She eyed him and then said, 'Let me fix it for you.' He handed the cup back, and she added milk and a few nips of sugar, stirring it. 'Try it now.'

'I've never liked tea,' he told her. 'It's hardly more than boiled water.' He took a small taste. It still reminded him of water, only it was sweeter now. 'Is that how you take your tea?'

She nodded. Then, with a faint smile, she admitted, 'I don't really like tea, either. But I can tolerate it this way, if I must.'

He set it aside and suggested, 'You should try

whisky. At least if you dinna care for the taste, you won't remember that after a few glasses.'

She bit her lip. 'I will keep that in mind.'

He knew he was baiting her, but at least she wasn't being so priggish now. He mimicked a proper voice again. 'Are you certain you don't want a sandwich, Miss Goodson?'

A mischievous gleam caught her eye. 'I believe I've changed my mind. Thank you.' He handed her the plate, and she stuffed the entire sandwich in her mouth, puffing out her cheeks as she did.

An unexpected burst of laughter caught him, but he suppressed it, coughing instead. His governess was shaking with her own mirth as she tried to chew. When she finally swallowed, she was still beaming. 'That's what you looked like, Locharr. Trust me when I say it would not be attractive to Lady Regina.'

When she stopped laughing, he offered her a napkin, and their fingers brushed together.

She froze instantly at his touch. The look on her face was of a woman caught in an illicit embrace, and she took the napkin before she jerked her hand back. Her cheeks flushed, and Lachlan wondered if she had ever had a suitor. Had a man ever kissed those full lips, tangling his hands in her curls?

For a moment, he found himself wanting to

push back her boundaries and discover if there was any wildness beneath the propriety of his governess. He gritted his teeth to force back the flare of unexpected need.

'Please don't touch me,' she whispered, her face flaming.

He shrugged and lied. 'You had a few crumbs on your face. I didna think you'd want to be walking about with them.'

Her shoulders lowered in relief. 'Oh. Well, if that happens again, simply tell me and I'll get my own napkin.'

Miss Goodson dabbed at her mouth and cheeks. He noticed that she was staring at him, and he couldn't think why.

'Have I crumbs on my face, then?' he asked.

She shook her head. Her gaze passed over his clothing, and she winced slightly. He saw naught wrong with his tartan, but it bothered her in some way. For a moment, he saw her pondering him, her eyes studying him as if she didn't quite know how to broach the subject troubling her.

Then at last, Miss Goodson asked, 'When was the last time you were in London, Locharr?' She reached for another sheet of paper under her chair and read aloud, '1807.'

He took the paper and filed it with the others.

'It's been nearly four years since I've travelled there. I had no wish to go.'

'Are you not required to take your seat in Parliament?'

'My father was no' one of the landowners who had a seat, by the grace of God.' He was thankful for that, for he had no wish to be part of government.

Lachlan sat back for a moment, still aware that she was stealing glances at him while pretending to search for more papers. Was she concerned about his scar? After the fire, he rarely looked at himself any more. He knew it could frighten Lady Regina, but there was naught he could do about it. Or was there another reason Miss Goodson was staring?

She handed him two more papers. 'These are 1804.' Then she bit her lip and blurted out, 'Whether or not you allow me to stay, there is one thing you ought to consider.'

He waited for her to finish, and she added, 'Before you travel to London, we should have you fitted for new clothing. Do you have a tailor you prefer?'

Lachlan frowned at that. He had no need of new clothes. What he had suited him well enough. 'Nay, I am fine as I am.'

'You cannot wear such clothing in London.'

'Why not?' He needed to save his coins, not spend them on wasteful attire.

'Because it will draw too much attention to you. It's quite different from what the other gentlemen wear.'

He knew that, but he hardly cared about what anyone else thought. The last time he'd been in London, he had remained out of the public eye, as a guest in the Worthingstone household. They hadn't cared what he wore, and it bothered him to think that he would be judged on his attire.

The truth was, he saw no reason to spend money on himself. He had no right to worry about clothes—not when his people could go hungry this winter because of his father's debts. And it wasn't as if he intended to hide his Scottish heritage. What did it matter if he wore a tartan to a gathering?

Miss Goodson's expression turned soft with sympathy. 'Some of the men will be unkind to you, because you are courting Lady Regina. They will look for any excuse to make you into a laughingstock. I don't want that to happen.'

Lachlan shrugged. He squeezed his fists together and said, 'Then I'll be having words with them. What I wear is my business.'

'You're wrong.' She stiffened and lifted her chin. 'In Scotland, I suppose your tartan is common enough. But for a shy lady such as Regina, you must try to blend in among the other gentlemen.'

Why should he care about that? Lachlan crossed his arms and glared at her. 'I'm no' going to blend in. I am a Scot, and there's nae need for me to pretend to be anything else.' He was already taller and stronger than most men. Blending in was impossible, given his size—or even the vicious scar on his cheek.

Miss Goodson's face softened with sympathy. 'Forgive me. I was not implying that you should try to be someone you're not. It's only that, Lady Regina is very shy, and she may feel uncomfortable if everyone is…staring at you.'

He shielded his thoughts, for her opinion was clear. She did not like his clothing at all, and it irritated him to think that he would have to be fitted for attire he wouldn't need. He had better ways of spending that money.

Miss Goodson offered, 'I can send for a tailor to take your measurements. It shouldn't take more than a week or two to have an appropriate wardrobe.'

'I see no reason for spending good coins when I already own clothes.' He set down another paper and leaned back. 'It seems you're wanting me to spend money I canna spare in order to wear what the other gentlemen do.'

'As you've said, there are twenty thousand

pounds at stake. Is that not worth a new jacket and breeches, if it means winning Lady Regina's hand in marriage?'

He hesitated, pondering the matter. She did have a good point that there was a great deal to consider. It wasn't worth the risk of displeasing Lady Regina over something as trivial as clothing.

'Try it,' she insisted. 'I will hire a tailor, and you need only buy one set of clothes. Consider it an investment.'

He set down the papers and regarded Miss Goodson with all seriousness. 'It may be an investment, but once I have wedded Lady Regina, she must accept my family's traditions. I wear the tartan to show my clan that I will support them until the day I die. She must ken that and accept it.'

Miss Goodson smiled. 'Of course. But know that when you go to London, you are also supporting your clan. You are winning a wealthy heiress as your wife and bringing back twenty thousand pounds to them.' She took a step closer and pleaded, 'Set aside your pride for a few weeks, and Lady Regina will not mind if you wear the tartan when you return home.'

The laird drew closer, and Frances tried to calm the stutter of her heartbeat. His masculine scent reminded her of pine trees and rain. *Careful,* she warned herself. She was on borrowed time as the laird's governess, and she could not let her admiration lead her down the wrong path. Even so, her heartbeat only quickened at his nearness.

'Was there something else you wanted, Locharr?'

'Aye.' He took another step closer, causing her to lean back to look at him. 'There was indeed something I wanted.'

Her brain turned into cotton while her pulse pounded beneath her skin. 'W-what was it?' Her face was burning as her imagination conjured up the vision of him pressing her against the bookshelves, kissing her until she could no longer stand. And she had no doubt that his husky innuendo had been spoken on purpose, simply to ruffle her feathers.

A slow smile curved across his mouth. 'I'm wanting more food.'

Oh, he was enjoying this, wasn't he? She knew he had teased her to get under her skin. And yet, for a moment, his eyes had stared at her as if he desired her. The very thought unravelled her composure, and she struggled to shore up her weakening defences.

As a distraction, Frances chose a slice of bread, delicately smearing it with raspberry jam.

'H-here you are.' She held it out to him, well aware that for a man of his size, there wasn't nearly enough food on the tray. He could have devoured everything by himself.

The laird broke off a piece and ate it. Frances tried not to stare, but as she watched him, she grew transfixed by the sight of his mouth.

Stop it, she warned herself. Right now, she ought to knock her head against the wall if that would bring back common sense. She already knew what would happen if she let a handsome man turn her head. It would only result in heartache.

Locharr reached for another slice of bread and this time broke off a small piece before he buttered it. 'What would you have chosen as your forfeit, if you'd won the game?'

'Dancing,' she confessed. 'It is a necessary skill that you must learn, whether you want to or not.'

He suppressed a grimace. 'I ken how to dance. I've no need for instruction.'

She wondered if he felt clumsy or awkward. Or worse, if anyone had ever teased him. 'If you are engaged to Lady Regina, dancing will be expected of you.'

'I dinna care what they expect.'

'No, but it will make it easier on her if you behave as other gentlemen do.' Frances took a sip of the tea she didn't want and studied him, her mood softening. 'In time, she may even fall in love with you.'

'Love isna necessary,' he pointed out.

'No, but it will convince her to marry you. If a woman loves a man, she is glad to follow him anywhere.' Once, she had been willing to do just that. A bitter pain caught her heart, and she locked it away.

The expression on his face was knowing, but he didn't ask. She had come to Scotland to forget the past, and there was no sense in talking over matters that were over and done with. The price had been paid ten times over for her folly, and she found it easier to bury the devastating memories.

'Did you ever love someone?' he asked quietly.

The air in the room seemed to grow stifling, and she felt a tightness expand in her chest. Yes, she had loved someone, more than life itself. Emotion gathered up inside her, threatening to spill into tears. But she held it back and answered, 'A long time ago I did. But it's over now.' She had no desire to even think of the past, much less converse about it. Instead, she rang for Alban to take the tray away.

'Locharr, if you don't mind, I'd like to take a walk around the grounds. By myself, that is.'

'Are you wanting an escort?'

'No, I will remain in the gardens for a time, that's all. I don't think any of your servants will harm me, and I will be visible from the windows, should I need help.' She had met his staff and thus far, she felt quite safe.

'I must caution you about London, though. Do not *ever* be alone with a young lady at a gathering without a suitable chaperon,' she warned. 'You would be forced to wed her.' He might know that already, but she felt compelled to warn him.

'And what of Lady Regina?' he suggested. 'Is that no' the point? Her father wishes us to marry.'

'True, but she would be ruined in the sight of her friends and would resent you for it.' Frances knew from personal experience, exactly what that was like. Even now, years later, it still stung to realise that her friends had turned their backs on her. Which meant they had never truly been her friends.

She stood as Alban entered the study. The footman cleared away the tray, and the laird waited until the man had gone before he spoke.

'You may go, Miss Goodson.' He escorted her from the study and closed the door behind them. Frances was quite happy to leave the papers behind. 'Thank you for your help this afternoon.'

'You're welcome.' She added, 'And…if I am being overbearing, please forgive me. I mean only to help you win the heart of Lady Regina.'

The laird accompanied her as they walked down the hallway. 'Good day, Miss Goodson. Be sure to pack your belongings. The coach will be here in the morning.'

Not likely, if Alban managed to delay it.

But she shrugged as if it were inevitable. 'There are still some etiquette rules we can discuss tonight at supper.'

'Because if I don't use the right fork, Lady Regina willna marry me, is that it?' His dry sarcasm and roguish expression made her knees turn liquid. It made her imagine his handsome face leaning in closer to steal a kiss.

Have you no shame? she warned herself. *Your imagination has gone wanton.*

'Or the proper spoon,' she shot back with her own insolence. 'One never knows the importance of cutlery.'

She flushed at his nearness, realising that it was her loneliness that caused the idle dreams. She had trained at the agency for a year, surrounded only by women. She had lived alone, without so much as a cat for company. This was the reason why she was so sensitive to a casual touch. It would go away, she was certain.

'Would you mind very much if I asked Alban

for a basket and shears?' she enquired. 'Could I choose some flowers for the house?' A good walk would clear her head and remind her of her purpose.

'There's naught blooming just now, but you can ask him, if you wish.'

'Thank you, Locharr.' She bobbed a slight curtsy and then hurried down the hall towards the retreating footman. It was only an excuse to leave, and they both knew it.

She needed to be careful when she was around Lachlan MacKinloch. He was a handsome man with a fierce smile that made her willpower crumble. Frances reminded herself that she needed to encase her heart in steel and lock it away, along with her wayward desires. He belonged to another woman, and even if he did keep her as his governess, it was only temporary. Eventually, she would never see him again.

Chapter Three

Frances returned to the house with an empty basket, for the laird had been right. The only blooming flowers were a few brave crocuses pushing through the ground, and daffodil shoots that had emerged. She hadn't minded the brisk walk, despite the misting rain. It had been wonderful to stroll through the gardens, exploring the beds. She had no doubt that the landscape would be a magnificent rainbow of colours, come the spring.

You won't be here to see it, a voice reminded her. The thought dimmed her mood, for she adored this castle. She knew that she was treading on dangerous ground already. The laird was a good man, though stubborn. And heavens, he was attractive. When he had drawn so close to her, she had imagined kissing him, pressing her hands against his broad shoulders. The very thought sent a tremor of forbidden desire within her.

Frances shoved it back and locked it away. She could not let herself imagine something that would never be. But she would enjoy every moment of whatever time she had left, even if it was only today. For the next few hours, she could pretend that this was a new life, a new beginning. The grief of the past would fade away, and she would forget it in time.

When she reached the stairs, she saw the footman, Alban, struggling. His leg appeared to be troubling him, and he lifted it to the stair tread before stepping with his other foot.

'Are you all right, Alban?' she asked quietly. 'Is your leg bothering you?'

He reddened, as if he didn't want to answer. 'It's naught of any concern, Miss Goodson.'

'Is it arthritis?' she probed. 'My grandmother suffered badly from it, but one of our maids made a poultice that helped. I could give you the ingredients to try it.'

He stopped and turned back to face her. 'I'm not needing your help, thank you. I can manage on my own.'

It was his pride talking. She suddenly thought about it and realised that all the laird's servants were elderly, save herself. And there weren't very many of them.

'How many servants are there at Locharr?' she enquired.

Alban straightened. 'Eight, Miss Goodson.'

She barely stopped herself from gaping at him. Eight? In a castle of this size? It was little wonder that the footman was struggling up the stairs. The man likely held three positions instead of one. She suddenly realised that the laird's betrothal was more than simply trying to make a good match. The livelihood of his people depended on it.

'And how many people live in the village?' She wondered how many others would be affected by the marriage.

'Seventy or so,' Alban admitted. 'They've no' been able to pay their rents this year. 'twas a hard winter, and the laird hasna asked them for aught.'

She sobered at that. 'Do they have enough to feed their families?'

'Barely.' The footman paused, leaning against the bannister. 'I dinna think he should be paying you.'

'He's not,' she answered honestly, though she hoped he would change his mind about keeping her. Despite her circumstances, she intended to make the most of each day. Living in this castle quenched her thirst for beauty, and every time she stopped to look around, she caught another detail she hadn't noticed before.

'Locharr is already betrothed,' the footman pointed out. 'He has no need for a governess to teach him.'

'I understand that,' Frances answered. Lowering her voice, she added, 'But I want the laird to be successful in London. It is *nothing* like Scotland. His clothes, his manner of speaking, none of it is the same.'

There was a moment of silence before Alban said, 'He shouldna have to change who he is.'

Frances understood his meaning, but clarified, 'He doesn't have to change anything on the inside. He only has to blend in for a few weeks.' She tried to explain it better. 'A man like Locharr could terrify some of the younger ladies. He's strong and fierce, and he takes what he wants. But if he wants to win Lady Regina's hand in marriage, he needs to…soften his manners like the other gentlemen. And on that note, could you send a tailor to the house in the morning? It must be someone who knows how to sew his lordship a wardrobe fit for London.'

The footman eyed her with a hard gaze. 'Our laird will do what he has to. But after they are wed, 'tis his bride who will have to change.'

Frances nodded but inwardly, she wondered if Lady Regina would be suited to a life in Scotland. The woman was so meek and quiet, she suspected the lady might feel intimidated by

the laird. Lady Regina had the most impeccable manners, but she never revealed her feelings.
Her face was always set in a serene smile, and
her eyes held a vast sadness. Frances had tried to
talk to her a few years ago, but to no avail. Her
imagination conjured up the image of a woman
caught within an enchantment. A lady of ice,
unable to love.

'I agree, that he should not need to change
once he returns home.' She cleared her throat
and ventured, 'Can you be certain that the coach
will not come for me tomorrow? I want to be certain that Locharr orders the correct clothing for
London. I need to speak with his tailor.'

Alban hesitated and finally shrugged. 'I will
see what I can do.' He departed to continue his
duties, and Frances returned to her own room.
Her mind was whirling with more ideas for
Locharr, and it was time to sort them out.

She pulled out paper and ink, dipping her pen
into the inkwell. First, she began writing down
a list of everything the laird needed to know.
Though it was unlikely she could teach him all of
it in the time remaining, she would prioritise her
lessons. Her mind drifted off as she continued
writing, and as her pen moved across the paper,
she thought of the laird's appearance.

She was torn between wanting to cut his wild
brown hair short and leaving it alone. Perhaps it

would be best if he pulled it back into a queue. That would be rather old-fashioned, but it meant he would not need to change his hair. There was no sense in trying to hide his scar, but she would try to discreetly let others know that it was a mark of heroism. Frances wasn't certain how, since the scandal had ensured she was banned from attending any gatherings. But perhaps a bit of gossip, strategically voiced to the right people, might be useful.

Alban's words had begun to sink in, and she recognised that he was right. When the laird returned to London, he would be playing a role. He would wear the costume, blend in as best he could, and win the lady's heart. Afterwards, the disguise would fall away, and he would return to the Highlander he was.

You like him the way he is, her head warned. She rather enjoyed their verbal sparring and his refusal to be tamed. *Don't let yourself be turned by a handsome face.*

I won't, her heart promised.

She had learned that lesson the hard way, and a fist of grief still caught her heart in fleeting moments. Frances closed her eyes, steadying herself, before she looked down at her paper.

New clothing, she had written. She had to transform the Laird of Locharr into a gentleman. Or at least, have the tailor measure him for proper attire.

She set down the pen and forced back the memories threatening to breach her calm. Her mistakes lay in the past, and only a few people knew of them.

It would remain that way.

'You aren't packed,' Lachlan remarked. From the looks of it, Miss Goodson had no intention of leaving. To Alban, he demanded, '*Where* is the coach?'

'It is not here,' his footman answered calmly.

'I know it isn't here,' he snapped. 'What I want to know is why?'

Alban shrugged. 'Might have been a broken axle. Or a problem with the wheel.' The older man shuffled towards the drawing room. 'Locharr, the tailor that Miss Goodson sent for is here.'

Lachlan suppressed a groan at the thought. If there was coin to be spent, it needed to be for his people and their food—not vanity. He strode towards the drawing room where he saw the governess speaking with the tailor. She had made a list of outfits for the tailor, and Lachlan didn't recognise the man. He was thin, with a neatly trimmed beard, and he wore clothing in the style of the English.

'Good morn to you, Locharr!' the man exclaimed. 'I am delighted to measure you for your new clothes. Miss Goodson was just telling me about you.'

The man's exuberant nature took him aback, and Lachlan glanced back at Alban, wondering where on earth they had found this tailor. 'You're no' from Scotland.'

'Mr Smythe is from Carlisle,' Miss Goodson explained. 'He has family nearby, and we are fortunate to have someone with such sartorial expertise.'

'I am happy to assist,' Mr Smythe answered. 'I can sew anything you might need. Jackets, waistcoats, breeches…anything at all.'

'I've no need for new clothing.' Regardless of what Miss Goodson claimed, the cost was simply too dear. Lachlan couldn't justify the expense, given the suffering of his clansmen. 'I can no' spend coins that I dinna have.'

'Don't worry about that,' she reassured him. 'The clothes won't be ready for another week or two, and by then, you will have the funds.'

Her cheerfulness caught his suspicion. 'Are you planning to sell off my belongings?' he demanded.

She shook her head. 'Of course, there's no need for that.'

Again, that strange, knowing look on her face.

It heightened his suspicions, but he decided she would tell him in due course.

'I will need to take your measurements, sir.' The tailor took out a measuring tape and eyed him. Locharr was irritated, but he decided it was better to get it over with. The man quickly ran the tape measure across his shoulders and then down his arms. He wrote down the numbers and then said, 'I should have the first set of evening clothes finished within a week. The rest can be completed by the end of the month.'

'That will do nicely,' Miss Goodson responded.

Mr Smythe thanked them and departed. After he'd gone, Miss Goodson turned back to him. 'Would you sit down, please?' she asked. 'I want to look at you and see what else must be done. You're so tall, it is difficult to see you properly.'

He glanced back at the doorway. 'And why would I bother with that, when you're leaving?'

She shrugged. 'It seems that I cannot leave without a coach, now, can I? I might as well make myself useful.'

He was beginning to wonder about that. It didn't seem that she had packed any of her belongings. Then again, he'd only seen three gowns, all of which were threadbare and worn. Today, she wore a fawn-coloured gown, and the light brown colour accentuated her blonde hair and river-green eyes. Her curls were pulled back into a knot on her head, and she was eyeing him with curiosity.

He did sit down, then, and she drew closer, studying him. Her gaze centred upon the scar on his cheek, and she asked, 'What happened to you, Locharr?' She reached out to touch his face, and he caught her hand.

'It's no' your concern,' he shot back. He would carry the scar for the rest of his life, but it would have been easier to bear, had he been able to save his father. Now, it was a tangible reminder of his failure.

She pulled back her hand. 'I am sorry if I offended you. I was simply wondering if you would tell me.'

'It doesna matter.' He saw no reason to reveal the past to her. 'And if it bothers Regina, it's no' something I can change.'

'I don't think it will bother her at all,' Miss Goodson countered. 'She does not seem like a woman who would judge someone's outer appearance. At least, not when I met her.'

'She has the right to refuse the engagement,' he felt compelled to point out. 'Our fathers wanted the marriage, but the choice was always hers.'

Her face turned sympathetic, and she said, 'I don't think she will turn you down—not if you are kind to her. Or if she does refuse, you will find another heiress to wed.'

He wasn't so certain about that. His expression must have revealed that to Miss Goodson, for she drew closer. 'Believe me, Locharr, when I say that the women of London will be struck speechless when they see you in those clothes.'

'Clothes don't change who I am,' he answered, then pointed to his scar. 'They will see this and turn away.'

Miss Goodson shook her head. 'I don't agree. You are—if I may say so—quite handsome, Locharr, even with the scar. Most women will find it dashing, so long as you smile instead of glower.' He didn't agree with her, but his opinion didn't matter. She seemed to guess his dissent and added, 'And if you dance with a lady, it gives you time to be better acquainted.'

He would rather be drawn and quartered. The very thought made him tense, and he refused to consider it. 'No.'

Her mouth curved in a faint smile. 'Perhaps I'll challenge you to a game of cards again. And this time, when I win, I'll discover if you know how to dance or not.'

'But you won't be here for a second game,' he reminded her.

'Won't I?' With a smile, she left the room.

* * *

After supper that night, Frances recruited Alban and Elspeth to play cards. She chose Alban as her partner, and the laird paired up with Elspeth. Although the older woman seemed reluctant to play, she eventually relented.

'Shall we play with the same stakes?' Frances suggested sweetly. 'If you lose, you will dance with me. If I lose…'

'You will return home.'

She ignored his answer and sent a sidelong glance towards Alban. 'Only if the coach arrives. I believe Alban said something about a broken axle, was that it?'

The footman looked horribly uncomfortable and gave his full attention to the cards.

'If the coach does not come, then you will help me organise my father's papers again,' Lachlan amended.

'Thankfully, I shall not lose this time.' She was confident of that. Her sisters had taught her how to cheat at whist and given that she knew nothing of the laird's dancing skills, she would do whatever was necessary. Not only that, but she suspected Alban would not stall for very much longer. Each day at Locharr was a gift she could not squander.

The glint in Lachlan's eyes suggested that he,

too, was not above cheating to get his way. For all she knew, he might have cheated the last time. She could not be certain.

Alban and Elspeth looked rather alarmed at this exchange, but the footman cleared his throat and began shuffling the cards. Diamonds were the trump suit, and she had only three of those cards. Drat it all. She eyed her hand and then risked a glance at Alban, who appeared noticeably uncomfortable. She didn't know if he was lacking trump cards or whether it was playing against his employer that made him nervous.

With her fingers, she slid one of her trump cards loose, and waited until the laird wasn't looking. Then she let the card slip down her sleeve. He led off with the ace of diamonds, and she tossed a small card away.

'Locharr, have you received any letters from Lady Regina as of late?'

Distraction was her aim now. He cleared his trick away and sent her a knowing look. 'No.' He led the queen of diamonds next, and she was delighted when Alban trumped it with the king.

'Well done,' she complimented the footman. He took the trick and then switched to spades. They played the hand with the tricks even. When the laird regained command, he led another trump, slightly higher than the one she'd hidden in her sleeve. This time, she played a low heart and distracted him when her foot bumped against his.

'Pardon me.' She covered the card and slid the trick towards him. 'That one was yours.'

'I ken that.' He played another card, but this time, his foot slid against hers. Her eyes widened when he slipped his foot free and nudged the edge of her skirt.

She nearly jerked her legs back, but the unexpected touch disrupted her own concentration. The game had shifted balance, and now it seemed that *he* was in command. Alban did his best to help, leading with a queen, but the laird trumped it. There was a gleam of satisfaction in his eyes as he took control of the game.

But he knew nothing of the trump up her sleeve. She let him win the next two tricks, waiting until he was down to his last three cards. He laid down the nine of diamonds and grinned. 'The game is mine.'

Alban had no more trump cards, but when it was her turn, Frances asked, 'Is it?' Then she laid down her ten of diamonds. The look of utter disbelief on his face brought about her own mood of triumph. There were no trumps left, and no spades left, either. With that, she led the four, and then the two.

'I believe the game is *mine*, Locharr,' she corrected. Alban hid his own smile, and Elspeth only shrugged.

'You cheated!' he exclaimed. 'You didn't follow suit earlier.'

She ignored the accusation and turned to the footman. 'I believe we won the game, didn't we, Alban? And now, Locharr, you owe me the forfeit.'

There was a sudden flare of anger on his face before he stood from the table and walked to the window. Frances eyed the servants, and Alban took a swift departure. Elspeth sent her a questioning look, but she shook her head, granting permission for the elderly woman to leave. Whatever was bothering the laird would not be shared in front of them.

This was about more than mere dancing. He was behaving as if she'd asked him to cut off his right arm. It was almost…fear.

Frances frowned and crossed the room to stand beside him. Outside, it had begun to rain, and the droplets spilled down the windows like tears. 'Is there something wrong, Locharr?'

His gaze was hardened like stone, and his body held such tension, she sensed there was a story behind his aversion to dancing. Frances wanted to ask him the reasons why, but she held back her questions. Instead, she remarked, 'You promised me a forfeit if I won.'

'You cheated. So I owe you nothing.' His voice was tight, like a dark storm cloud threatening to unleash its fury.

Frances recognised that this was not the time to push back. Instead, she tried a different strategy. 'If you will not dance, then you must let me stay another day.'

He took a step nearer, and she had to tilt her head back to look at him. 'I ken that you've done something to delay the coach. Why is it you want to stay so badly, lass? There's nothing for you here.'

'You're wrong,' she murmured. Here, there was distraction from her past and the hope for a new start. 'There is nothing for me back in London, except hopelessness and failure. But at Locharr, I have everything. I can use my knowledge to help you. I can dream for a moment that I live in a castle with splendid gardens and a view of the sea.'

He took another step, until he was so close, she could feel his heated breath against her cheek. Her willpower came crashing down, and her skin came alive with forbidden attraction. She wanted to reach out and rest her hands upon those shoulders, to feel his arms around her. And Heaven help her, she wanted his mouth on hers, to feel desire again.

'Did you cheat in our game?' he asked. He

cupped her chin in his warm palm and tilted her face up to meet his gaze.

Frances only smiled. 'I'll never tell.'

The coach didn't arrive on the second day, either. When Lachlan questioned Alban, his footman muttered again about a broken axle. There was most certainly something afoot, but no one knew anything about it. Or if they did, they said nothing.

Strangely, it seemed as if they *liked* Miss Goodson. She enquired about Alban's health, bellowed into Elspeth's ear about her granddaughter, and her air of cheerfulness was infectious. He found himself realising that the house would seem emptier without her.

But she had to go. Especially since she had not relented about the dancing. This morning, she met him in the hall downstairs and said, 'The ballroom is prepared. Will you show me that you know how to dance?'

'I have other duties that I should tend to.' He wasn't about to surrender this battle. He loathed the thought of dancing.

'It won't take long,' Miss Goodson said calmly. She startled him when she took his arm, leaning close.

'You're no' going to give up on this, are you?' She guided him towards the far end of the house. 'No. But once I am satisfied that you know the necessary steps, I won't bother you about it again.'

Lachlan wasn't about to be deterred and stood his ground. 'Why does it matter? Lady Regina can dance with someone else.'

Miss Goodson took his hands in hers. 'Dancing is about more than merriment. It helps a man and a woman cross the boundary of friendship into something more.' Then she reached up to his face and tilted it down to look at her. 'Look into my eyes, Locharr.'

He did, and he noted that they appeared a richer shade of green today. An amber circle surrounded her pupil, and he grew conscious of her hands in his. 'All I want is for you to stand here for a moment and look at me.'

That, he could do. Frances Goodson was a lovely woman, albeit with secrets of her own. 'Aren't you afraid the servants will gossip? We're holding hands in the middle of the hall.'

'If you want to be alone, the ballroom is waiting,' she said. 'Grant me fifteen minutes. Please.'

Though he knew it was unintentional, the invitation made him want to indulge in temptation. He didn't want curious eyes watching over them. And so, he led her down the long hallway towards the small ballroom. He noticed the flush of her cheeks, as if she understood how scandalous it was to be alone with him.

And yet, she was willing to take that risk.

He decided that he wasn't about to be her puppet, tugged here and there as she pleased. If she wanted something from him, then he was going to have an even exchange.

Once they were inside, she led him to the centre of the room and stood across from him. He noted how the colour in her complexion deepened. Despite her efforts to remain unaffected, she was nervous. He decided that if he proved he knew how to dance, then she would stop asking. But while he indulged her wishes, he intended to gain his own answers about her past.

'You said that only failure waited for you in London. Why?' He took her hands and waited for an answer. She was so determined to stay here, he wanted to understand what she was running away from.

As he suspected, Miss Goodson ignored his question. 'I want you to hold my hands and take one step to your right. Don't stop looking at me.'

He remained standing in place, staring at her. She waited for him to step, but he held himself motionless. 'Answer the question first.'

Indignation flashed in her face, as if she had no intention of obeying. But the longer he waited, at last she said, 'I lived in poverty when

I was in London. This is a better place for me. It's safer.'

At that, his instincts flared. He didn't want to imagine the sorts of unscrupulous men who might attack a lady. He studied her again, his gaze fixed upon her worn grey gown. She had nothing new of her own, and she was quite slender—perhaps because she'd had so little to eat.

'Did anyone harm you there?' he asked, barely keeping the shielded anger in check.

'No. But some have tried,' she confessed.

Inside, his emotions went to stone. He was starting to understand that this post was a sanctuary for her, a means of escaping harm. 'The coach was never going to come, was it?'

Miss Goodson let out a breath. 'No. I paid Alban the last penny I had, to ensure that he never sent for the coach.'

And his footman had likely understood her plight, risking his own consequences.

'I am sorry for the deception,' she said. 'But I saw no other choice. I just…can't return to London so soon.'

He didn't answer, for he needed to think about his next actions. As a distraction, he kept her hands in his and took a single step to his right. Miss Goodson relaxed and gave an approving smile. 'Good. Now take one step to your left.'

Again, he posed another question. 'If you

didna wish to live alone, why didn't you marry? You're bonny enough to catch a husband.' He noticed a small freckle on her left temple. Her lips were full and soft, and he grew conscious of her nearness.

She bit her lip and eyed him. 'Are you going to question me with every step?'

'Aye. And the sooner you answer, the sooner I'll dance with you.'

With a heavy sigh, she said, 'I didn't find any-one I wanted to marry.'

He suspected it was a lie, but he took a step to his left. 'Were they gruesome-faced, like me, with scars?'

'No, they were cruel and unforgiving,' she responded.

Something bad had happened to her in Lon-don, he was certain. Though he was starting to expose her secrets, she wasn't ready to share them just yet. And though it plagued Lachlan to think of it, neither did he want to send her away. Not when it meant exposing her to physical threats. He didn't know what to do with a governess he didn't need.

'Now we turn in a small circle,' she instructed. He drew his hands to her waist, and she tried to pull them back. 'You're not supposed to touch my waist, Locharr.'

He ignored her and turned her in the small circle. 'This is easier, you ken.'

'But it's not proper,' she corrected, pulling his hands back. She appeared flustered by his attention. He realised that if he embarrassed her, she might relent and end the dancing lesson early.

Instead, she gripped his hands and held them in hers. 'Do not touch me with such familiarity.'

There it was—the prim and proper governess. He had no doubt she would have rapped his knuckles with a fan, if she'd had one.

'Or what?' he dared her. 'Will you be giving me a thrashing?'

Her cheeks burned scarlet. 'No, of course not.' She pulled her hand back on the pretence of straightening her glove, but he could tell that she was trying to think of a suitable punishment.

'Perhaps you'll send me to bed with no supper,' he teased.

'I am certain I can think of something unpleasant,' Miss Goodson said. 'But I hope you see that what I really want is to help you.'

'Why?' he demanded. 'I'm no' paying you.'

'It's not about money,' she answered. 'I've made many mistakes in my past. If I can stop someone else from walking the same path, I want to help.'

'I've been to London before, you ken? It's no' as if I'm unaware of the rules.'

'You simply don't care about them,' she predicted.

He shrugged and nodded. 'I remember how many people were false to my father. They pretended to be his friend, but they were unkind to him. I'm wanting no part of society.'

She reached out to touch his hand. 'I understand. But there are things I've learned from my mistakes. And if I can help you in some small way, it helps me to feel as if I have some worth.'

And there was the truth between them. She might not have revealed her past, but she had laid her feelings bare. Miss Goodson, for all her proper ways, was vulnerable. She had been deeply hurt and had paid for those sins. He didn't need to ask what had happened...but he was starting to see that by allowing her to give him lessons—even lessons he didn't need—was a way of helping *her*. She needed a way of feeling that her life had a purpose.

She paused a moment. 'Will you let me stay a little longer?'

He didn't want to agree, but he also knew he couldn't send her back. It would be throwing her to the wolves, and she deserved better than that.

With a shrug, he said, 'I suppose another week willna make much of a difference.'

Her smile lit up her face. 'Thank you, Locharr. I am so grateful.' She squeezed his palms, joy emanating from her being. 'And I promise I will help you with your father's papers whenever you have the need.'

He nodded in agreement, and Miss Goodson continued her lesson. 'All right. Show me if you know the quadrille.' She began telling him about other couples who might join in the dance and how to switch partners. Lachlan listened to her, but his concentration was distracted by the happiness on her face. Over the next few minutes, it became clear that Miss Goodson loved to dance. She moved with grace, and she was patient with him when trying to teach him the steps.

He already knew them, but he deliberately moved with slowness to make her believe she was teaching him for the first time. Miss Goodson remained encouraging, offering, 'You can go as slowly as you like until you feel comfortable with the dance.'

Although he took several missteps on purpose, she did not remark on his clumsiness or berate him. Instead, she praised him when he remembered the proper direction.

He kept getting distracted by her smile. When she held his hands, his wayward imagination pictured her hands upon his bare skin. Though he'd thought her attractive, when she beamed with genuine elation, it was like being warmed by the sun.

But she was the wrong woman.

Lachlan didn't consider himself the sort of man to dally when he had made a commitment elsewhere. Miss Goodson was meant to be his governess, and it didn't matter if she was a fair-faced lass. He might admire her beauty, but he knew better than to trespass on forbidden territory.

When he stepped close to her, he didn't miss the flush of colour on her cheeks. She was aware of it, too. 'Miss Goodson,' he said in a low voice.

'Y-yes?'

'No more dancing. Our fifteen minutes are over.' With that, Lachlan released her hands. It was best to retreat from the ballroom and bury himself among the mountain of papers his father had left. Hard work was what he needed to turn his attention away from a pretty face and towards the responsibilities that were his.

He gave a slight bow, and she offered, 'You did well with your dancing, Locharr.'

The compliment startled him, but he was too distracted by *her* to know what to say. Instead, he turned on his heel and strode away from her, needing the distance.

Chapter Four

~~~

Four days later

'I dinna like them,' the laird pronounced, when he tried on the new clothing. The tailor stood back alongside Frances, and she shook her head.

'I disagree, Locharr. You cut quite a fine figure.' The new black broadcloth jacket hugged his shoulders, emphasising his immense size. The matching waistcoat had brass buttons, and the buff breeches clung to his muscled thighs. The very sight of him made her breathless.

'They're as dull as dirt.' He scowled, staring at himself in the looking glass. 'Whoever thought black was a good colour? It looks as if I'm off to a burial.'

'It's a very plain fashion,' she agreed. 'But, Locharr, you look quite dashing. Lady Regina will be pleased by your appearance.' As would any other woman with eyes in her head. Frances had no doubt that the young ladies of London would be delighted by the laird and would flirt incessantly with him. It had been difficult enough to steel herself against his charm. She didn't know why he had relented about allowing her to stay, but she would never question it. Instead, she had helped him sort through his father's papers each night. Strangely, it had become a routine where they conversed and worked together. Though he was a stubborn, strong-willed man, she had grown to like him. And that was dangerous.

'I agree.' The tailor nodded. 'The fit is excellent. The rest of the clothes will be ready within the fortnight.'

'I need naught more than these,' the laird insisted.

'You need gloves, shoes, a coat, and clothes for everyday calls,' Frances pointed out.

'I have gloves. And shoes.'

'Not ones that will be appropriate for London society,' she said. 'Think of it as a masquerade where you are wearing a costume. You must wear all of it, in order to make it believable.'

Instead, he turned to the tailor and said in a commanding voice, 'That will be all, Mr Smythe.' The tailor appeared uncomfortable, but he walked with the footman towards the hallway.

Frances turned back to the laird after the tailor had gone. 'I know that you never wanted these clothes. But I will try to find a way to pay for them.'

The laird's expression sobered. 'It's no' your responsibility,' he reminded her. 'And we ne'er discussed payment for your services, Miss Goodson.'

'I—I know that. But I don't expect a salary. You've been good enough to give me a roof over my head and meals.' She knew how dire his finances were, and she would never ask for money he didn't have.

'Aye. But you came to my house expecting wages.'

'Not any more,' she reassured him. 'If it would help, I could sell one of my gowns to pay the tailor.' He needed the new clothing, and she would do whatever was necessary.

He shook his head. 'I've some coins set aside that I can use to pay him. The rest can come later.'

She breathed a sigh of relief. 'I am glad to hear it.' He needed the attire to become a success in London.

'Lady Regina might not want to wed me, no matter what I wear,' he pointed out. But when Frances studied the laird, she saw a handsome gentleman with a good heart. He cared for his clan and was proud to be their leader. He would make any woman an excellent husband. Not to mention, he made her heart tremble with forbidden attraction. 'No woman alive would refuse you,' she said softly.

'You would,' he answered, raising an eyebrow.

No, I wouldn't, she thought, but didn't say it. The laird was the sort of man a woman dreamed of. She could easily imagine being in his arms, his mouth upon hers. Her skin flared with heat, her body softening at the idea. No. She couldn't do this.

Instead, she changed the subject. 'I—I should go.'

'Wait,' he said, drawing close. 'If you intend to stay a few more days, I'll have need of another lesson.'

Her eyes widened at the thought. Never before had he suggested that she instruct him. Wariness rose up within her at his motivation, but she managed a nod. 'I suppose we could practise what you should do when you pay a call on Lady Regina. If you think that would be useful.'

'Send for me when you are ready.'

Frances managed a nod and fled the room, closing the door behind her. For a moment, she rested against the wall, berating herself. She had mistakenly believed that she could take this position and maintain a respectful distance. But with each moment she spent with the laird, the more her heart imagined possibilities that could never come to pass. She liked Lachlan MacKinloch far more than she should.

Lachlan had spent the rest of the afternoon in his father's study when his footman interrupted by knocking on the open door and clearing his throat.

'Aye?' he asked Alban. 'What is it?'

'Miss Goodson said she is ready to see you in the parlour.' The footman handed him a small bouquet of heather, tied with a single ribbon. 'For the lesson.'

He was grateful for the interruption but was curious about the heather. 'Why do I need flowers?'

'She only said it was about paying calls upon a lady.' Alban shrugged. 'Take it, and follow me.'

Lachlan tossed the heather into the air and caught it again. 'Fine.' He stood from his chair but was surprised that Alban walked alongside him down the hallway. 'Was there something you were wanting?'

The footman sighed. 'She said she needed my help.' When they reached the small parlour, Alban knocked on the door. Lachlan noticed that the footman withdrew three calling cards from his waistcoat pocket and held them in his gloved hand. He saw his name written in Miss Good-man's handwriting.

Elspeth opened the door and held out her palm. Alban gave her all three cards, but before Lachlan could enter the parlour, the maid closed the door in his face.

'Now why would she be doing that?' he demanded. When he had paid calls with his father in the past, they had always been invited inside.

His servant shook his head. 'The first time you pay a call, we will no' see the lady. We simply give the cards.'

''Tis a waste of time,' Lachlan grumbled. 'My father ne'er did that.'

'Only because I made arrangements for him the day before,' Alban explained.

Lachlan blinked at his footman. 'You've done this often.'

Alban glanced behind him. 'It has been many years, but aye. I've done it for your mother on many an occasion. And your father.'

Elspeth opened the door a short time later and handed Alban a card. Then she closed the door again. Alban gave it to him, and Lachlan saw that Miss Goodson had written her name with ink upon a small scrap of paper.

'That means she'll receive us on our next call,' Alban explained.

The footman knocked again and offered a

fourth calling card which Elspeth took from him. In his hand, he held another calling card. 'Lachlan MacKinloch, Laird of Locharr, has asked if Miss Goodson is at home?'

Once again, the maid closed the door.

'How many times must we do this?' Lachlan muttered. His question was answered when Elspeth opened the door. Her wrinkled face stretched in a smile, and she shouted, 'Miss Goodson is at home!'

Lachlan jolted at the volume of her voice. He was about to enter when Alban stepped in front of him. 'A moment, Locharr.' Then he accepted a calling card from Elspeth and handed it back to Lachlan.

'This way!' Elspeth shouted. Then she led him to a chair on the far end of the room. Lachlan could already see Miss Goodson standing by the window. He wanted to walk towards her, but Alban said, 'Remain there until you are brought to her. Elspeth will fetch you.'

He retreated, leaving Lachlan to wait at the chair. Miss Goodson remained with her back to him, and in time, Elspeth came forward.

'Miss Goodson will see you!' She beckoned for him to follow, and when he reached the middle of the room, the governess turned to walk towards him. She sat upon the sofa and folded her hands in her lap, her back straight. Lachlan wasn't at all certain what he was supposed to be doing, but he approached slowly, studying her for some sort of hint.

A moment later, she rose from her seat and came to greet him. 'Locharr, what a pleasant surprise.'

He reached out to take her hand and kissed the back of it. He knew it was making her uncomfortable while he continued to hold her hand, but he wanted to unsettle his governess. Her complexion flushed, but she didn't pull away. Instead, she directed her attention to the flowers and asked, 'Are those for me?'

'They are.' He thrust the heather at her, and Miss Goodson accepted the bouquet.

'These are lovely. I'll just put them in some water, shall I?' She tucked them into a vase that stood on a nearby table. 'Won't you sit down?'

He followed her to a chair and sat while she rang for tea. Then she sat in the sofa towards his left. She smiled and waited.

He did the same, expecting her to begin the conversation. When she didn't speak, he realised that this was a test. What was it she'd said? Something about the weather? Or asking her questions about herself? Yes, that was it.

'It's a fine day,' he began.

'It is.' Her expression remained serene, silently challenging him to do better. But he really didn't know quite what to say.

'What do you think of Scotland so far?' he prompted.

'It's lovely. But I fear it does rain a great deal.' Again, her quiet demeanour made it hard to find common ground for conversation. She wasn't participating, and he didn't know what to try next.

Lachlan leaned in close and muttered, 'Why are you being so difficult to talk to?'

She leaned in and answered in a loud whisper, 'Because Lady Regina is shy. She won't want to talk.'

True enough. He sat back in his chair, realising that there needed to be a strategy. 'Am I supposed to pretend that you're Lady Regina?' he whispered. When she nodded, he decided to try a different tactic.

'Lady Regina, I ken it has been many years since we've seen one another. But our fathers believed we would make a good match.'

Miss Goodson paled and said, 'Locharr, this is rather sudden. We've only just spoken this evening.'

He saw no point in wasting time. 'Aye, but we were friends, years ago. Friendship is a strong basis for marriage.'

At that, his governess dropped the pretence.

'You cannot simply propose marriage the very first night. She will say no.'

'It's possible. Or she could say aye.'

'Why would she do that? She's one of the most sought-after heiresses in London. She could have any gentleman at all.'

'Or she might have been waiting for me.' He was beginning to enjoy Miss Goodson's frustration and couldn't resist tweaking her. 'Why waste time? 'tis better to get to the point.'

'But you must get to know her first,' she protested. 'There may have been good reasons why she avoided marriage.'

'As I said before, she was waiting for me.'

Miss Goodson stood from her chair and rolled her eyes. 'Good heavens. A lady does not agree to a marriage proposal simply because her father wants it. You must court her. Win her affections.' She turned her back and went to stand by the window. A soft spring rain had begun to fall, sliding down the windowpane.

Lachlan stood from his chair and went to stand behind her. 'There are other ways to court a woman, Miss Goodson, besides with words.'

She was so close, he could smell the faint aroma of flowers rising from her skin. A wayward lock of curling blonde hair had escaped her chignon, and he reached out to slide it away from her neck.

The moment he touched her, she flinched as if she'd been burned. 'Do not touch me.'

She turned so swiftly she stumbled, and he caught her before she could fall. Lachlan held her there a moment, and her hands rested against his shoulders. Her blonde curls framed a face that held the blush of a blooming rose. Her lips drifted open, and he found himself wanting to taste her. He wanted to lean in and claim that sweet mouth, to show her that courtship was more than fancy manners and words. There was desire and need.

In her green eyes, he saw a woman who yearned for a stolen kiss. Her breathing was soft and uneven, and she met his gaze as if she wanted far more. Then abruptly, she seemed to gather her senses and her expression grew stricken. 'I'm sorry, Locharr. The lesson is over.' She shoved her way past him and fled the room.

It left him to wonder exactly what had happened to her. A dark suspicion took root within him, of how a lady such as herself might be forced to take a position as a governess. And what her reasons were for running away.

Frances remained in her room for the rest of the afternoon, pleading a headache. She thought about asking Alban to bring her a tray instead of facing the laird at dinner. She didn't know if she could be in his presence tonight after all that had happened.

Lachlan MacKinloch had done nothing more than touch a lock of her hair, but she had felt his touch down to her bones. A deep hunger suffused her, a craving to feel the strength of this man's embrace. If she had stayed there, she was certain he would have kissed her.

She had felt his warm breath against her mouth, and it was all she could do not to pull him closer. Instinctively, she was certain that a man like Lachlan would be a man of deep passion. His kiss would push past her defences and tempt her back onto a path she had sworn she would never tread again.

You cannot stay here, she reminded herself. The laird was awakening a damaged part of herself that she had tried so hard to eradicate. It had taken years to push back the anguish and move on with her life. She had mistakenly believed that everything would be all right, and that time would cause her to forget the secret shame.

She was wrong.

The scars of her past might be invisible to the eye, but they were embedded within her soul. Every day she spent at the laird's side forced her to remember her sins. It had been a little over a week now, but she was falling hard for his sense of humour, his handsome face, and the deep loyalty he felt towards his people.

The wisest course of action was to leave Scotland and return home.

But the thought of going back to London brought a sour fear within her stomach. No, it was better to shield herself from wayward emotions and carry on with her task. The laird's lessons were not over. He needed to learn social etiquette so the ton wouldn't disparage him or gossip. She could not leave now. To do so would be selfish, abandoning her post because of her own fears.

You are a woman of strength, she reminded herself. She had survived the most devastating heartbreak of her life, and she could make the best of this situation. The laird would never hurt her, and she could shield her feelings until they went away.

Frances took a deep breath. Then another. It was nearly time for supper, and she had to push back her cowardice and continue his lessons in whatever time she had remaining. It was the right thing to do. She stood from her chair and smoothed her gown, steeling her courage.

When she opened the door and stepped into the hallway, she was startled by the sound of a woman's voice downstairs. Alban was struggling to lift a large trunk with the help of a younger footman, while Elspeth was carrying two valises. The older woman's face was red from exertion, and she struggled with the weight.

Frances hurried down the stairs. 'Here, let me help you.' She reached for one of the valises, when a sharp voice interrupted from the bottom of the stairs.

'And just *who* might you be?' An older matron stared up at her. She had the same brown hair as Lachlan, though there were streaks of red and grey. Her blue eyes were narrowed with curiosity and a hint of impatience. There was no doubt in Frances's mind that she was Lady Locharr.

Frances dropped into a light curtsy. 'I am Frances Goodson, my lady.'

The woman's expression turned suspicious. 'And why are you in my house? Have you been swiving my son?'

'I—I beg your pardon?' She could hardly believe what the Lady of Locharr was implying. 'I am his governess, nothing more. Well, not a governess, precisely. More of a tutor for etiquette.'

'Jesus, Mary, and Joseph, you are *not* the person I sent for,' Lady Locharr cursed. 'I wanted a matron of sixty, not a maid of sixteen.'

Frances was not about to argue about her age or experience in the middle of the hallway with all the servants watching. 'You must be weary from your travels, my lady. I would be happy to continue our conversation in the dining room during supper.'

Lady Locharr's expression thinned. Then she turned to the footman. 'Alban, see to it that my son joins me for supper in the dining room. Send this…woman a tray in her room.'

Frances felt rather like an insect crushed beneath the lady's boot, but now was not the time to argue. She sent Alban a questioning gaze, but he shook his head discreetly. It seemed that he was rather intimidated by Lachlan's mother and was not about to question orders.

But after the woman had accused her of lewd behaviour, Frances had no desire to dine with her. The laird could explain everything. She walked towards Alban on her way to the stairs and murmured, 'Have Elspeth bring my tray to the glasshouse. I intend to dine there tonight.'

She had no intention of being banished to her room like a child. Instead, she planned to enjoy candles, starlight, and the calming peace of the indoor garden.

'Mother,' Lachlan greeted Catrina and held out a chair for her. 'Did you enjoy Spain?' It was a safe enough topic for conversation, though he didn't miss her annoyed expression.

She took her seat and answered, 'I enjoyed the sun very much indeed. But you can understand how startled I was to find that the agency sent a bonny young lass instead of a spinster who could instruct you before you go to London.'

'Miss Goodson has been a great help to me.'

Catrina rolled her eyes. 'I can only imagine what sort of "help" she provided. And what would your bride be thinking about you keeping another woman at Locharr? Regina would be furious with you.'

'*You* hired her,' he pointed out. 'Who did you think they would send?'

'Not someone like her, that's for certain.' She grimaced. 'Someone old, someone who would teach you without temptation. *That* one is after a husband, and I wouldna trust her wiles.'

'She has been naught but respectful,' he said, taking a seat at the head of the table. 'I've no' been to London in years, and she has tried to teach me what I'm needing to know.'

'Hmm,' Catrina remarked. 'I've my doubts about that.'

'She is the daughter of a baron,' he clarified.

His mother narrowed her gaze. 'We should send her back.'

Lachlan didn't tell her that he had tried this on more than one occasion. Now, he'd grown accustomed to her presence. 'Although I didna want her here at first, she's proven herself verra useful. I have been trying to make sense of Da's papers in the study for the past year. Miss Goodson has been helping me sort them into ledgers.'

'Tavin never did like to throw anything out.'

'Aye. And our debts are worse than I'd thought. I canna collect rents from our tenants, because they have nothing to give. And if you're wanting to continue travelling, we need the funds for that.' He sent her a pointed look that brooked no argument. 'I need this marriage to Lady Regina, and Miss Goodson is well aware of it.'

Catrina appeared uneasy about the news. She accepted a wine glass from Alban and sipped it, her expression turning pensive. 'What can we do to help the tenants?'

'I intended to buy more grain to plant. We also may buy sheep for wool to add another source of income.' He intended to speak with his friend, Worthingstone, to learn what the duke had done to improve his own estates in Scotland.

Her expression grew sober. 'I have faith in you, Lachlan.'

He inclined his head, glad that she saw the truth. 'I will help our clan replenish their supplies and survive the winter, once I've wedded Lady Regina. And Miss Goodson will ensure that I dinna embarrass myself in London.' Although he was remembering more of the rules of society, he continued letting her 'teach' him, for he understood that she was trying to help. The card games had also been a competitive diversion that he appreciated.

He placed his napkin in his lap, and Alban stepped forward to pour the wine. 'Where is Miss Goodson, Alban? I've been wanting to introduce her to my mother.'

'We've met,' Catrina said. From the thin line of her mouth, Lachlan gathered that his mother hadn't thought much of the governess. 'I sent her to her room. I had no desire to dine with a stranger when I've not seen my lad in nearly a month.'

'You are not in command of her,' he said coolly. 'She is my employee.'

'But as you said, *I* was the one who hired her.'

He straightened and levelled a stare at her. 'I am the laird now. And the decisions are mine to make. Not yours.' He made no effort to hide his irritation.

Catrina looked as if she was about to argue with him, but she wisely kept her mouth shut. It had been a peaceful month without her. Although his mother's travels had cost a great deal, it was coin well spent. Ever since his father had died, Catrina had turned bitter and possessive. Travelling was a distraction that made her more bearable.

'You would enjoy Miss Goodson's company,

once you're acquainted,' he said. 'She's a kind woman.'

Catrina's expression narrowed upon him. 'Is she? I only saw that she was beautiful.' She sipped at a spoonful of pea soup. 'I ken what that *governess* wants. And it's no' to teach you manners. She wants a piece of all this.' She gestured towards their surroundings.

Lachlan didn't agree with her prediction that his governess was greedy. Miss Goodson had already declined any wages for the sake of his new clothing. A woman who wanted only his wealth would never do such a thing.

'Again, that is *my* decision to make,' he reminded her. 'When I return to London, I will escort her home again,' he said. 'This is only for a short time.'

He finished his soup and sipped at the wine. Alban brought out the main course, and his mother seemed pleased with the roasted chicken. She told him about her travels, but Lachlan was distracted by the absence of Miss Goodson.

'Alban, send for the governess,' he ordered the footman. 'I'm wanting to speak with her.'

'She took a tray,' Alban answered. It was a strange answer, almost as if he didn't want to fetch her.

'I realise that my mother sent her to her room. But we would like to speak with her now.'

The footman hesitated. 'I canna find her, I fear.'

From the way Alban would not meet his gaze, Lachlan was convinced the man was lying. Possibly to protect Miss Goodson. 'Is she no' in her room?'

The footman shook his head. 'She took the tray with her. I'm quite certain no one can find her.' The stubborn glint in his eye revealed that Alban was steadfastly refusing to bring her to the table. And perhaps it was his own intent to protect the young woman from Catrina's claws. It was a strange loyalty Lachlan hadn't expected. But he had no doubt that the footman knew precisely where she was. It was evident in his nervous behaviour.

'When you see her next, tell her that I'm wanting to speak to her.'

'*If* I see her, of course.' There was a determined set to the man's face, and Lachlan made a note to follow Alban later.

'She sounds like a docile, obedient sort,' his mother said wryly. 'A model of propriety.'

'She is.' It wasn't at all like Miss Goodson to defy a command. She must have had a good reason for it. And after their earlier interaction when she'd fled, he suspected that there was more on the young woman's mind.

Alban served the dessert course of a tart made

from raspberry preserves and cream. His mother sighed with appreciation, and he allowed her to continue talking about where she wanted to go next. She did love the sun and warmth of the Mediterranean.

When they had finished the meal, his mother said, 'I suppose you're going to go and find her now.' She stood and pushed in her chair.

Lachlan rose from the table, not even bothering to acknowledge her remark. 'I hope you rest well, Mother.' Then he gave her a light bow, remembering what Miss Goodson had taught him.

Once she had gone, he rang for Alban. His footman arrived, and Lachlan said. 'Take me to her. You ken where she is, I'm certain.'

The footman glanced towards the hallway, and Lachlan insisted, 'I'm only going to talk with her—not feed her to the wolves.'

Alban sighed and said, 'She took her tray to the glasshouse. Said she was wanting to spend time in the starlight.'

It was exactly the sort of romantic evening Miss Goodson would invent. She had the soul of a dreamer, and Lachlan muttered his thanks as he strode out of the dining room and towards the door on the opposite end of the castle.

Outside, the air held a chill, but the sky was clear. The stars gleamed against a deep indigo blanket of night. His shoes crunched on the gravel pathway, and as he neared the glasshouse, he saw a dozen candles gleaming. Miss Goodson was seated upon a bench beside some plant cuttings, and the sight of her stirred his senses.

She was still wearing the grey-coloured gown, but tendrils of her curling blonde hair hung against her neck. The candlelight cast a warm glow of light upon her skin, giving her the appearance of an angel. Lachlan opened the door to the glasshouse and drank in the sight of her. Aye, he knew where his obligations lay. He had no choice but to wed Lady Regina.

And yet...he admired the beauty of the woman before him. His governess deserved better than the way his mother had treated her.

'I came to apologise for my mother's words,' he began. 'She shouldna have treated you like a servant.'

'But I *am* a servant,' Miss Goodson countered. 'She is right that it truly isn't my place to dine with you.'

He pulled up a small stool and sat across from her. Upon her plate, he saw the remnants of jam and some crumbs. Her supper, such as it was, wasn't much to satisfy anyone. 'Did you get enough to eat?'

'Plenty,' she reassured him. Then she stood from her bench and took a step away. 'I suppose I'll extinguish the candles and say goodnight.'

She was clearly running away from him after their earlier encounter. He ought to simply let her go, but he didn't like to see her afraid of him. He wanted her to stay, to talk awhile. And though it was a last resort, he saw no alternative.

'I thought we might practise dancing.'

She froze, her expression uncertain. He could see her indecision, for they both knew it was a necessary tutorial, though he despised the activity.

'In the morning, perhaps,' she suggested.

In answer, he held out his hand and waited. 'No one will see us here. And I'm not wanting my mother to intrude upon us while I practise trampling your toes.'

'I don't know if this is wise,' she said. 'And truly, there's not enough space.'

Lachlan took her hands in his, refusing to let her decline. The candlelight flickered, casting reflections against the glass. She appeared fragile, and he wanted to bring back her smile.

'Dance with me, Miss Goodson.'

Frances's heartbeat quickened, while her brain warned that this was entirely too dangerous. For a man who despised dancing, she could not understand why he had come out to the glasshouse, only to insist that she continue the lesson.

'Just for a little while,' she hedged. She took

his hand, and his fingers closed around hers. Although the space was small within the glasshouse, the laird moved through the steps with only a few stumbles.

His hand moved to the small of her back and he said, 'Show me what else I need to learn.'

The warm touch of his palm made the gooseflesh rise upon her skin. She wasn't wearing gloves, and his hands laced with hers. Palm to palm, she met his gaze. His blue eyes seemed to burn through her, and she forced herself to look away.

'Y-you should learn the waltz. It was scandalous for a time, but it is coming back into fashion.' She closed her eyes and stepped back from him. 'You count to three and follow this pattern. Only you move in the opposite way of me.' She counted out the steps, moving in a circle. 'One, two, three. One, two, three.'

She could feel his gaze upon hers, and when she took his hands again, she placed her hand upon his shoulder, guiding his hand to her elbow. 'This is a more respectable way to waltz, though some gentlemen try to put their hand upon a lady's waist. I would caution you to ask permission of Lady Regina before you touch her waist.'

'Like this?' he asked, and she felt the weight of his palm against her back.

Frances nodded, and said, 'I will take a step

backwards, and you should step forward. But not on my toes, if you please.' She tried to keep her tone light and genial, but it was nearly impossible. She was entirely too aware of the nearness of his body and the caged strength in his arms.

Lachlan was a magnificent man, and she stiffened when he took the first step. 'Sorry,' she murmured. 'I wasn't quite ready.'

He waited a moment and then asked, 'Now?'

'Yes.' This time, they moved as one, and she kept their pace slow, directing him where to step. He followed her guidance, and despite a few missteps, he caught on to the pattern.

'Is it this slow?' he asked.

'Unfortunately, it's much faster. But for now, keep to this pace until you feel comfortable with it.'

He turned her in slow circles, moving amid the glasshouse benches. The candles gleamed against the darkness, and when she glanced upwards, the stars twinkled. Her heart was overcome by the moment, and a thickness caught in her throat.

'Miss Goodson,' he murmured, slowing his pace.

Frances forced herself to look at him. 'What is it?'

He reached out to rest his hand upon her shoulder. 'Someone hurt you, years ago. Who was it?'

The urge to flee came over her with a primal need. She shook her head and tried to pull away, but his hands held her fast. 'Wait. I'm only wanting to understand.' He released her and stepped away. 'You're afraid. I can see it in your eyes, though I've done naught to make you feel that way. Did someone else harm you in the past?'

She had no intention of revealing anything to the laird. It was her secret to keep, and she would never awaken those shadows of the past.

'No. Nothing happened,' she lied with a calm tone that she didn't feel. 'But it is time that our lesson ended for the night. It's getting late, and I shouldn't be out here alone with you.'

He lifted his hands in surrender. 'I would ne'er harm you, and you ken this.'

Do I? she wanted to answer. He got beneath her skin, making her long for a life she could never have. And so, she forced herself to face him. 'Goodnight, Locharr.'

He lifted her hand to his mouth. The warm breath made her skin burn with forbidden anticipation, and she felt the kiss echo in other secret places of her body. 'Sleep well.'

Heaven help her, she didn't think it would be possible to sleep at all. Especially now.

Chapter Five

Lachlan held the reins of his mount, waiting on Miss Goodson to arrive. She had continued the habit of riding with him each morning, and he'd ordered the stable lad to saddle Pip for her.

When she arrived, she wore a dark cloak that nearly covered her blue gown, gloves, and the tattered bonnet. He found himself wishing that he had ordered the tailor to take her measurements for a new gown—especially since her own clothes were worn and frayed. Inwardly, he vowed to find a way to pay her salary.

'Good morn to you.' He smiled, and she returned it, though there was wariness in her expression. 'I must ride into the village today. Would you be wanting to come along?'

Then he suddenly remembered to add, 'With a chaperon, of course.'

His offer seemed to reassure Miss Goodson,

and she asked, 'Were you thinking of having Elspeth join us?'

'Nay, better if we take one of the younger footmen, like Gavin. We'll be gone for a few hours, and it might be too hard on her.'

Miss Goodson nodded her agreement. 'Very well. I would enjoy visiting with the rest of your clan.' Her mood seemed to lift, and he helped her onto Pip. Then he asked the stable lad to send word to Gavin to join them.

The morning sun shone upon the green fields, the dew glistening in the light as they rode towards the village. Locharr stretched out for miles, and he led her down the path towards the stone buildings while Gavin followed behind. The cobblestone streets were narrow, but Lachlan kept their pace slow as he approached the village. He lifted a hand in greeting to two of his kinsmen but saw no one else.

'It's very quiet,' Miss Goodson remarked.

It was indeed—and he found it disturbing. There should have been more people out and about, or children playing at the very least. In the distance, he spied the kirk with its fresh boards and new paint. The very sight of the building brought back the memory of smoke and fire, coupled with crushing grief. He had not set foot inside the kirk since it had been destroyed, and he wouldn't start now.

He turned away and led Miss Goodson down a narrow cobblestone street. 'Follow me. There's someone I want you to meet.' He helped her dismount and gave the horses over to Gavin to care for. Then he guided her down a side street, towards Granny MacKinloch's tea shop. The old woman knew the gossip about everyone in Locharr. If he wanted to find out who needed help, Orla MacKinloch was the best source of information.

The shop had a bright red door and when he opened the door, a brass bell rang. The interior of the shop held the strong aroma of tea, and Granny MacKinloch sold several varieties. She had half a dozen barrels set around the room which she used for tables, and an odd collection of painted stools made up the seating. It was a place for gathering, for conversation and stories. They had arrived early enough that no one else was inside, and for that, Lachlan was grateful.

Miss Goodson stepped inside, and Granny MacKinloch greeted them warmly. 'Well, good morn to ye, Locharr. 'tis good to see ye.' She took both his hands, and he leaned in to kiss her wrinkled cheek. The old woman was a distant relative but had been close friends with his grandmother. He thought of Orla in the same way.

'I came to hear the news,' he told her. The old

woman squeezed his hands and smiled brightly. Lachlan stepped back, wondering how to introduce Miss Goodson. Although she was his governess, he didn't want the entire village to know about the lessons. Instead, he said, 'And this is a visiting friend of our family. Miss Goodson, meet Orla MacKinloch.'

His governess sent him a curious look, but she said nothing to deny his explanation.

'A visitor? Well, now, I can see you've a tale to tell.' Granny gestured for them to come inside and sit at the table. 'Come in and bide a wee. I'll make tea.' She went off to put on the kettle, giving them a moment alone.

As she filled it with water, Lachlan leaned in to Miss Goodson. 'Dinna tell Granny anything you're no' wanting the entire village to know.'

She smiled and ventured, 'I presume that she loves gossip, then?'

'Aye. And I am here to learn about the clan and their needs, no' to spread more rumours.' He thought she would understand, but to his surprise, she appeared concerned.

'Is that why you called me a family friend?'

He shrugged. 'Aye. Other people might not understand why I've allowed you to stay.' He didn't want Granny MacKinloch believing that they were involved in an illicit affair.

Miss Goodson frowned as she took a seat

at the table. Granny MacKinloch had a rose-coloured tablecloth and a dainty china tea set with painted pink roses. Lachlan felt awkward amid all the delicate cups, but he sat back and waited until the elderly woman returned.

'Ye look well, Locharr,' Granny remarked. 'And Miss Goodson, ye say ye are a family friend?'

'I suppose I am, yes.' She smiled at the old woman while Lachlan silently willed her to say nothing about the lessons.

Granny MacKinloch poured the tea and handed her a cup. 'I'd be glad to hear all about it. How is it that an English Sassenach would travel so far to visit our laird?' Though the woman's voice was kindly, she was practically salivating at the story.

Lachlan pushed his chair back and shook his head at his governess. *Dinna tell her the truth,* he warned.

Miss Goodson appeared uncertain about what to say. 'It was a long journey from England.' She thought a moment and said, 'Lady Locharr invited me to come and visit.'

'How is it that ye ken Catrina? A distant relative, are ye?' Granny shot Lachlan a look of interest, and a not-so-discreet wink.

'No, not exactly.' She glanced at Lachlan and said, 'I am acquainted with Lady Regina, however. She is the woman the laird is intending to marry.' Miss Goodson took a sip of tea. 'Lady Locharr asked me to share my knowledge of English mannerisms so that the laird can win her hand in marriage.'

'Did she?' Granny teased. 'And you've no wish to wed him yourself?' Her gaze turned knowing, and Lachlan felt the weight of the old woman's stare.

Miss Goodson turned crimson, but she ignored the question. 'The laird is willing to marry for the good of his clan. Lady Regina's dowry will provide for everyone.'

Granny MacKinloch studied him, her eyes narrowed as she considered the information. Lachlan wished Miss Goodson had not said a word. She made him sound like a martyr, which was the furthest thing from the truth. Aye, he would marry Regina in return for her twenty thousand pounds to help his clan. And he would try to make her life pleasant enough, but in the end, this was an arranged marriage—not one built upon love.

To change the subject, he said, 'I came to speak with you about our kinsmen, Granny. What news have you to share?'

That was all Granny needed to begin talking. She told him about each of the families, whether they could afford rent, how much food they had, and any troubles they faced. Lachlan fixed the information in his memory, making a list in his mind of who to visit first.

'Oh, and Abigail MacKinloch just had her new bairn,' Granny said. 'A braw wee lad with his father's dark hair. Ye'll be wanting to visit.'

A slight clatter caught his attention, and Miss Goodson steadied her cup. 'Sorry. I'm a bit clumsy today.'

But in the past fortnight, Lachlan had never seen her make a single mistake. Though she gave an apologetic smile, he caught a shadow beneath it.

'If ye've finished yer tea, let's have a look at the leaves,' Granny said. 'I'll tell yer fortunes.'

Lachlan passed her his cup first, and she swirled it around before dumping the leaves on the saucer. She glanced at him first, then at Miss Goodson. 'The leaves say that ye will have a very happy marriage with yer bride.'

'I am glad to hear it,' Miss Goodson said. Her face softened towards him before she passed her own cup to Granny, who turned it upside down and examined the leaves. For a moment, the old woman's smile faded. There was silence for a time, and finally Miss Goodson asked, 'Is something wrong? Will I meet with misfortune?'

Granny pursed her lips. 'Ye will face heart-break, I fear. And ye will only find yer happiness when you turn away from the path that was never meant to be.'

Miss Goodson said nothing, but in her green eyes, he saw the fleeting catch of emotion. It was almost as if the two women had exchanged an entire conversation he was not privy to.

'That's no' exactly cheerful,' Lachlan said.

'It's only fortune-telling,' his governess answered. 'We make our own futures.'

'You are a wise lass, indeed.' Granny Mac-Kinloch cleared away the cups and saucers, and Lachlan stood.

'Thank you for all the news,' he said to the old woman, leaning in to kiss her cheek before he bid her farewell.

'Ye're welcome. Come again, lad, and dinna be a stranger.' To Miss Goodson, she said, 'Lass, take courage in the path ahead. Remain strong, and ye will find what ye seek.' She squeezed the young woman's hands with reassurance.

Lachlan opened the door, holding it for Miss Goodson. 'Thank you,' she murmured as she took the first few steps outside. He walked with her towards the waiting horses, but though he tried to converse with her, she had gone unusually silent. It was as if Granny's fortune-telling had bothered her deeply.

'Dinna be troubled by Granny,' he said. 'She loves reading her tea leaves, but 'tis only in fun.'

Gavin was waiting with the animals, but Lachlan was distracted by a wailing noise. The quiet of the morning was pierced by the cries of an infant, followed by Abigail MacKinloch shushing the child. She was walking along the street, bouncing the baby and patting his back. 'There, there, my lad.'

Lachlan paused a moment and saw it as an opportunity. Most women adored babies, and it might lighten Miss Goodson's spirits to see this one.

'I've no' seen Abigail's bairn,' he said. 'Would you be wanting to come and meet her son?'

He expected her to agree and walk with him, but instead, she shook her head. Her face paled, and she murmured, 'I'll wait with Gavin by the horses. You go on.'

Her response seemed unusual, and he prodded, 'Are you certain? It will only take a moment.'

'I'm certain.' Her expression was tight and unyielding, as if she were holding back her true emotions. And though he didn't know what had happened, he decided not to push.

Instead, he let it go and told her, 'If you'll wait, I will return in a moment.' He crossed the cobblestone street to greet Abigail. The young mother brightened and came forward. An empty basket hung over one arm while she cradled the baby in the other. Lachlan saw that her tartan was threadbare, and her shoes had holes in them.

She smiled and said, 'Have you come to meet my wee one, Locharr? This is Donald, our sweet bairn. Born only a few days ago.' She cooed over the child and held him out for Lachlan to see. The child's head was barely the size of his hand, and his wrinkled face was red.

'He's a braw lad, Abigail. I wish you and your husband good fortune and joy in him.'

'Thank ye.' The young mother beamed, cuddling her infant. 'Kenneth is so glad to be a father.'

'A blessing, to be sure. How did you fare this winter?'

Her smile tightened. 'We'll make do.'

He could tell from her hollowed cheeks that they had very little remaining. 'I'll send some food to help you get by. The bairn will need his mother healthy to give him milk, aye?'

Her face coloured, but he knew she would not turn down the supplies—not when it meant providing for her son.

'Blessings to you both.' He bid Abigail farewell and turned back towards Gavin and Miss Goodson. The footman had already helped her onto her horse, but a moment later, his governess urged the horse back towards the road leading to his castle.

'Wait!' he called out. To Gavin, he called out, 'Don't let her ride off alone.'

The footman attempted to follow her, but once she was outside the village, Miss Goodson spurred the horse onward.

Lachlan expelled a curse and untied his horse, mounting swiftly to catch up to her. He nudged his stallion faster and when they reached open ground, he increased his speed.

He had never seen Miss Goodson react in this way before, but she was clearly upset by something. She was leaning hard against her mare, but when they neared the castle, she slowed the mare's pace to a walk. She continued her path towards the stables and dismounted, giving the horse over to the groom. Then Lachlan saw her walking towards the west side of the castle grounds in the direction of the gardens.

Though every instinct told him to go to her, to demand to know why she'd fled, he saw her shoulders slumped forward, her hands gripping her arms.

Lachlan caught up to Gavin at the stables. 'I'll speak with her,' he said, dismounting from his horse. 'Leave her be.'

He hurried to follow, though he knew not what had caused her despair, save the newborn infant. It must have evoked a terrible memory of some kind.

The damp earth made it easy to track her footsteps, and he saw that she had found a hidden corner near a willow tree. Miss Goodson sat upon a large stone, her face buried against her knees.

And she was sobbing with an anguish so great, he never imagined he would see her like this.

Frances knew the laird had followed her. She could sense his presence just beyond the hedgerow, but he didn't take another step. Likely, he didn't know what to say to her, now that her feelings had cracked apart.

She had been so careful over the years, pushing past the grief and building up walls around her heart. But the sight of a newborn child, the sound of his cries, had brought it all back.

Her secret shame. The devastating scandal. And then, the empty silence. She wept for the lost years, for the child she'd buried.

Granny MacKinloch's fortune-telling had been true. She *had* known heartache. Grief had torn her heart from her chest, shredding it apart. Somehow, she had made it through the first year, and then a second. She had vowed to put it all behind her, to become a governess and take command of her own life.

And the cry of a single infant had brought it all crashing down.

She closed her eyes, letting the wave of devastation roll through her. She didn't care that the laird was watching her now. He could think whatever he wanted—she would never tell him anything. It wasn't his business.

She cried until her eyes ached from exhaustion and her stomach hurt. But no amount of tears could fill up the emptiness inside her.

It surprised her that he had not intruded. She'd expected him to push his way inside the garden, to demand answers. Instead, he kept a respectful distance, waiting, though she had no desire to face him.

Frances knew she could not stay here for much longer. The air had grown heavy with moisture, and she could feel the droplets of rain starting to fall. She sighed and unclenched her knees, standing up from the large limestone boulder. There was no sense in trying to pretend as if nothing was wrong.

And so, she walked around the hedgerow and found him waiting. In his eyes, she saw concern and compassion, not rage. 'Are you all right?' he asked.

She nodded. 'But please do not ask me questions.' She would never answer them.

To his credit, he remained silent. Instead, he

walked alongside her as the light rain fell. He let her choose the path, and she walked to the far end of the garden where the stairs led to the battlements. She climbed the steps, and he followed her.

The rain dampened her hair and her gown, but she didn't care. When she reached the battlements, she stopped to look at the angry sea in the distance. The water was grey, a reflection of the heavy sky. Waves pounded against the shore, sending sprays of salt water against the rocks. There was beauty in the untamed landscape of the sea.

The laird stood behind her, and she could feel the strength of his presence. If she wanted to, she could turn around and be in his arms. How she craved that. To be in a man's embrace, taking solace from the warmth of his hard body.

Instead, she took comfort from his silence. For a while, she simply breathed in the salty air, calming herself…locking away the past again until nothing remained. She found beauty in the sea and in the rain.

After a time, she turned to face him. 'Thank you for not demanding answers of me.'

He came to stand beside her, resting his hands upon the merlons of stone. 'When I was eight, my younger sister died of a fever. She was four years old. Sometimes, even now, I imagine I hear her voice.'

There was understanding in his tone, and she realised that he had endured his own suffering. 'And your mother is very protective of you, isn't she?'

'Unfortunately.'

The rain quickened its tempo, and Frances lifted her face to it. In spite of the miserable cold weather, the spattering droplets felt good upon her skin. It was as if she were facing down the tears of the past and rising up stronger.

'I suppose you'll want to go inside,' she said at last. 'We're getting soaked.'

'Not yet.' He reached out and touched the stone merlons behind her, trapping her in his arms. 'There's something I need to do first.'

Lachlan drew one arm around her waist, and she rested her palms on his chest. Her body temperature rose up hotter, in spite of the rain. The laird gave her a moment to shove him away, but she didn't move.

'What is it you need?' she whispered.

'I need this,' he murmured, leaning in to kiss her softly. 'And so do you.'

His warm mouth covered hers, and God help her, it was everything she imagined it would be. He kissed her like a man starving for air, claiming her mouth until she clung to him for balance.

She yielded to him, kissing him back. He drew her against his body, and she felt the hard length of him. Her breasts grew sensitive, and as the rain soaked her gown, it felt as if his touch was upon them. His tongue slid into her mouth, and a moan erupted from her lips. She wanted him so badly, though she knew it was wrong.

He belonged to another woman. Lady Regina's dowry would save his castle and his clan. What did she have to offer in return? Nothing, save poverty.

The knowledge cut her to the bone, and she forced herself to break away. She felt dazed, unable to catch her breath. There were no words she could say, nothing to mend the bad choices she'd made.

Instead, she turned and ran back to her room, feeling like the greatest of fools.

Miss Goodson barely spoke to him over the next few days. Lachlan hardly blamed her. He had overstepped the boundaries, and she was undoubtedly worried that he might try to kiss her again.

Aye, he shouldn't have done it. But that day, she had been so miserable, he'd wanted to give her comfort. He wasn't good at offering sympathy by talking. And though he didn't know what it was that had set off her anguish, he had his suspicions.

It's no' your business, he reminded himself. She was here as his governess, and anything that had happened in her past was her own secret to keep. In a small way, it had been a good reminder that he should not let himself get close to her, even in friendship. Grief had brought them together like an invisible cord. He liked this woman. She had a bright spirit, like sunshine, and she found ways of making the lessons tolerable, even if he hardly cared about the proper way to address a duchess.

But for one moment, he had seen her pain. It had mirrored his own burden of death, and he understood her. He knew what it was to lose someone and for that hole to be there. He also knew what it was to feel the guilt and the weight of a thousand what-ifs ploughing through his mind. He had lost both his sister and his father— one to a fever and the other to a fire.

Absently, he rubbed the scar on his face. Though he could never go back and save Tavin's life, at least he could fulfil the man's greatest wish by marrying Regina. It was the only amends he could make after his failure.

A soft knock sounded at the door, and he called out for the person to enter. Miss Goodson stood at the door with papers in her hands. 'May I speak with you, Locharr?'

'Aye.' He stood from the small writing desk and gestured for her to sit down. 'You can take my place here.'

'I can return at another time if you are busy,' she offered.

'Nay, it can wait. I was only accepting an invitation to stay with a friend of mine. He is hosting a gathering at his townhouse for those of us who attended school together.'

'That sounds nice. Where does he live?'

'He lives in London, which is convenient. I intend to stay with him while I court Lady Regina.'

She thought a moment. 'That's very kind of him. Who is your friend?'

'Worthingstone.'

Her eyes widened, and she stared at him in disbelief. 'Do you mean His Grace, the Duke of Worthingstone?'

'Aye, that's him.' He folded the letter and set it on a table to have Alban send later. 'We've been friends for years.'

She sank down in a chair. 'Dear God.'

'Is there a problem?'

She shrugged. '*When* were you planning to mention to me that you're friends with one of the most powerful men in London?' Before he could answer her question, she continued, 'And are there other lords with whom you are already acquainted? A prince or a king, perhaps?'

'Dalton is a viscount, no' a king, but his father is as rich as one. I'm no' certain, but I believe his father, the Earl of Brevershire, owns a gold mine in Africa. Or was it diamonds in India? I canna recall.'

'How do you know these men? I thought you were isolated in Scotland all these years.' She took his pen and an inkwell.

'We were schoolmates at Eton, and we all have Scottish roots. Gabriel MacKinnon and I are Scots, but Dalton's only half-Scottish on his mother's side. Worthingstone has no Scots blood, but he owns land here.'

Lachlan was beginning to enjoy her shock. Aye, he'd ne'er mentioned his friends or the group they had formed nearly twelve years ago. At the time, he'd been furious that his mother had sent him to Eton instead of Edinburgh. He'd been in several fights, and that was how he'd met Camford, Worthingstone, and MacKinnon. The four of them had lived together, and all were notorious for getting into trouble. They had made a pact to help each other avoid punishment, and it had evolved into a lifelong friendship.

He could tell that Miss Goodson was itching to ask questions, but she refrained. 'Have you…already made arrangements to stay with His Grace?'

'Aye. Jonathan said he had plenty of rooms in his house. Camford and MacKinnon are also coming.'

Miss Goodson let out a slow breath of air. 'Locharr, please do not refer to His Grace as Jonathan.'

'It's his name,' Lachlan pointed out. 'We've been friends since we were twelve.' He couldn't resist teasing her. The pained look of exasperation made her cheeks flush, which reminded him of the afternoon when he'd kissed her. He had no regrets for what he'd done. She had needed comfort, and he had offered it.

Except that now, he found himself daydreaming about kissing her again. Miss Goodson was talking about dukes and how to properly address the nobility. Her pen was busy moving over the paper, and he saw that she'd written *duke, marquess, viscount,* and *earl.*

'Locharr, are you listening?'

'I ken how to address my friends. And in my own home, I'll call them what I like.'

She bit her lip but backed down on her corrections. Before he could say anything else, she asked, 'Tell me more about this gentleman, Camford. You said he was a viscount?'

He shrugged. 'Dalton St George, Viscount

Camford. 'tis a courtesy title. His father, the earl, is still living, and he's been wanting to make a gentleman out of his son.' With a smile, he added, 'It didna work, so far as I ken. Camford's always done as he pleased.'

'And what of MacKinnon? Who is he?'

Lachlan smirked. 'Gabriel MacKinnon is his name. He lives further to the north. He doesna have a title, but that's never stopped him from finding beautiful women.' Women tended to flutter around Gabriel's handsome face. They adored him, and there was no denying that Gabriel could win the heart of anyone he wanted. But he had been widowed two years ago and had no interest in women now.

Frances set down her pen and thought a moment. 'We must find a way to use this to our advantage. If you are friends with a duke and a viscount, it will give you invitations that not just anyone could receive.' She pursed her lips. 'And if you attended Eton, there may be others.'

Lachlan rested his hand upon the desk and eyed her. 'They tried to teach us many things at Eton. I was a lad of twelve and hardly cared what they said. The four of us were always running off and not attending class.'

'It sounds as if you were a mischievous lad.'

'I dinna like rules,' he said. 'Being rebellious is more fun, you ken?'

She slid her chair back and regarded him. 'But your mother hired me to teach you how to behave.'

He drew the chair closer. With a slow smile, he said, 'There's a time and place for misbehaviour.'

Her face turned a dark shade of red. 'Locharr, please do not speak of that time. I regret it deeply.'

He didn't believe her. She had responded willingly, and he had enjoyed the stolen moment. 'I have no regrets. You were grieving, and I kissed you to bring you comfort. That's all.'

She closed her eyes as if doing so would push away the memory. 'I should never have allowed it.'

He leaned in and cupped her cheek. Gently, he stroked her face, and she turned away as if to shut him out. Even so, her hand covered his, holding it there as if she were savouring his touch. He suspected that she *did* desire him, though her words were to the contrary.

Then her voice came in the barest whisper. 'Locharr, please. Do not ever kiss me again.'

He wasn't about to make that promise, though he understood her reasoning. 'Only if you ask me to, lass.'

Chapter Six

'What do you think you're doing?'

Frances looked up from the mountain of papers she was sorting. Catrina MacKinloch was glaring at her from the doorway. It was clear that the woman despised her for no apparent reason. Except, perhaps, her presence at Locharr.

'I am helping the laird sort through his father's papers. He asked for my help, and I do what I can from time to time.'

They had made excellent progress after Alban had bought the new ledgers. Frances had written dates above each page, and they had sorted the papers accordingly. Instead of stacks of papers all over the room, they had twelve ledgers spread out in various locations. There were papers stuffed into every ledger, but at least it was a means of sorting through them.

'Would you like to join me?' Frances suggested.

'What I *want* is for you to get out. These papers are no business of yours, and I'll thank you to leave my husband's study.'

Frances placed one of the papers in the ledger marked 1809 and turned to face Lady Locharr. Catrina's face was red, her eyes hardened with anger. Although Frances could have argued, what was the point? The laird's mother did not understand that she was only trying to help.

'As you wish.' She closed the ledger and walked calmly towards the door. But Catrina refused to step aside. Instead, the matron crossed her arms and glared at her.

'I know that I hired you to teach my son etiquette. But I want to be very clear about your position here. If it was your hope that you could get my son to fall in love with you, understand that this is not possible.'

Frances felt her cheeks burn. 'No, of course not. I am here as his governess, nothing more.'

'I see the way you look at this castle and these grounds. You want to remain here, don't you?'

She refused to get caught up in Catrina's trap. 'Who wouldn't be delighted to live in such a lovely place? I feel very lucky to be here, even if it's only for a few more weeks.'

The woman's mouth tightened. 'Come with me for a walk.'

Her command startled Frances, for the woman seemed unwilling to accept her answer. Why else would she ask her to accompany her on a walk? But then, Frances decided there was no harm in it. The laird was visiting his clansmen in the village and would not return until the afternoon. 'All right,' she agreed. With a wry smile, she added, 'So long as you aren't asking me to walk off the edge of the battlements.'

'Don't be tempting me.'

Frances wasn't entirely certain whether the woman was teasing or not, but she followed her outside. Catrina led her down the gravel path towards the glasshouse. Her stride was brisk, as if she had a purpose in mind. When she reached the doors, she opened them and gestured for Frances to enter first.

Inside the glasshouse, she noticed a new tree that she hadn't seen before. Despite the glossy green leaves, it was a young plant, and it only came up to her elbow in height. 'The laird told me that you often brought back plants from your travels. What kind is this one?'

'It's an orange tree,' Catrina answered. 'It may not survive our winters here, but I will try to keep it alive.'

'It's lovely.'

The matron nodded and gestured for Frances

to sit on one of the benches. 'I am not a fool, Miss Goodson. I saw Lachlan kiss you.'

Oh, dear. Her cheeks turned crimson, but there was nothing she could say to deny it. 'I never asked him to kiss me, Lady Locharr. And after he did, I told him not to do it again.'

The woman's stare turned discerning. 'You'll forgive me if I don't believe you.'

'Believe whatever you like. Once I have finished helping your son, you won't see me again.'

'And I will not be disappointed. We both ken that he could never marry a woman such as yourself. I'm no' even certain if you are helping him. But I will warn you—if you teach my son anything that would cause him humiliation, I swear, I will hunt you down.'

Although the words were spoken with a true threat, Frances knew that they were wrought from a mother's love. 'I would expect nothing less.'

There was a line drawn between them, an understanding and a truce. With that, Frances asked, 'Will you be travelling again?'

The matron smiled, but it was a smug expression. 'No, indeed. I think I'll be here for the next month or two. At least, until Lachlan is betrothed to Lady Regina.'

'I hope they are very happy together,' Frances offered. And she meant that, truly. Lachlan was a good man, and she hoped he would find contentment in the marriage.

'Do you?' There was a trace of disbelief in her voice.

'Don't worry,' Frances reassured her. 'I have no feelings towards your son. He is only my employer.' After her heart had been broken years ago, the last thing she wanted was to love a man again. To love the laird would be an act of utter folly.

'Good.' Lady Locharr rose from the bench. She extended her hand to Frances. 'Then we are in agreement.'

It was a strange sort of peace, but Frances believed that beneath her thorns, there was a woman who loved her son deeply. Catrina would do everything in her power to protect him.

It was something Frances understood all too well.

'I don't think this is a good idea,' Miss Goodson whispered as Lachlan offered her his arm. 'Your mother despises me.'

'I'm certain you've met worse dragons in London.' Regardless of her apprehensions, he didn't want Catrina to bully her any longer. 'And it's her fault that you're here at all. I'm glad of her interference now.'

He guided her towards the dining room, but

her nerves did not diminish. Instead, she began rattling off instructions. 'If your hostess walks with you as her supper partner, it is a great honour,' she said. 'If that happens, you must be on your very best manners.'

He paused. 'I am no' a lad of six years old, Miss Goodson. I ken that I must use good manners.'

She flushed at that. 'I'm sorry. I just—couldn't think of what else to say.'

He escorted her into the dining room and pulled out her chair. Frances sat, and then Lachlan pulled out a chair for his mother before he sat at the head of the table. Catrina was already glaring at Frances.

'And why is the governess dining with us, my son?'

'Because I asked her to join us. And because I knew it would irritate you.'

Catrina rolled her eyes and unfolded her napkin. But despite her annoyance, he had the sense that she was testing Miss Goodson. There was an undertone of challenge, and she began by saying, 'You are so very young, Miss Goodson. What qualifications do you hold as a governess?'

'My father was a baron,' she said smoothly. 'When I was younger, I attended many balls.'

Like a viper, his mother struck hard. 'Then why did you never marry? Surely a baron's daughter could achieve more than being a governess.'

Miss Goodson flushed a moment, then she squared her shoulders. 'True. But I did not care for any of the men. I preferred to live a life of independence where my happiness did not hinge upon a man's whims.'

'You chose poverty,' Catrina pointed out.

'I chose freedom. And I have no regrets.'

A flicker of approval drifted across his mother's face before she took a sip of her water. Catrina was indeed a woman who valued her freedom. Lachlan wasn't entirely certain what had passed between the two women, but he had the sense that Miss Goodson had lifted herself in his mother's eyes.

'Will you be leaving soon?' Catrina asked Miss Goodson. 'If your lessons are finished, there is no need to stay.'

'I—' She glanced at him, uncertain. 'I will stay as long as Locharr has need of me.'

In truth, he wasn't certain whether he needed her or not. He'd allowed her to stay out of pity, but in the end, they had conjured an unexpected friendship.

'I will be going to London in a month,' he said. 'I will escort you home at that time.'

She gave a nod, but he could read the sadness in her eyes. He didn't know what to say, for they both knew this day would come. But he intended to ensure her safety after she returned to London. He didn't know how yet, but he would find a way—even if it meant finding a new governess position for her.

Alban entered the dining room and brought the first course of soup. Lachlan dipped his spoon into the soup, and remarked, 'The soup is quite good, Alban.'

'It is,' Miss Goodson agreed.

His mother was staring at both of them, and finally asked, 'Have you written to Lady Regina, Lachlan?'

'Nay.' He hadn't thought of it, to be truthful.

'Did you not think that your bride might wish to hear from you?'

'She's no' heard from me in ten years,' he pointed out. Why would it matter now?

Catrina sighed. 'Lachlan, this marriage is important. What if she refuses you?'

It was possible, but he didn't want to contemplate the idea. 'Dinna worry, Mother. She'll wed me, even if I have to carry her off to Scotland.'

'I do hope it won't come to that.' Miss Goodson winced. 'If you are kind to her, I am certain all will be well.'

'But if she *does* happen to say no, kidnapping could be the answer.' He couldn't resist teasing the governess, though he had no intention of stealing Lady Regina away. The slight frown on Miss Goodson's face suggested that she wasn't certain if he was being serious or not.

'I would prefer that you don't go to prison,' she said. 'It would make it difficult for your clan. They've endured enough, don't you think?'

Though her words were teasing, it made him think about his people. They *had* endured a great deal, and perhaps he ought to do something to lift their spirits before he travelled to London. A feast…or even a *ceilidh* might do.

'You're right,' he answered. 'My kinsmen deserve an evening of entertainment before I leave for London. And it would give you the chance to enjoy a Scottish gathering.'

Miss Goodson nodded in approval. 'I think you have an excellent idea. It would also give you the opportunity to practise your etiquette.'

Lachlan exchanged a look with his mother. A *ceilidh* would not be anything like a ball. He was trying to decide how to explain that to her when Miss Goodson asked, 'Are there any titled lords who live nearby?'

He lifted his shoulders in a shrug and shook his head. 'There are lairds but no titled lords.' His father's friends were all landowners, but Lachlan barely knew them.

She thought a moment and then said, 'I suppose we'll have to make do. We can pretend it's a London ball, and you may practise your skills.'

'Nay,' he interrupted. 'This is different. It's a gathering to bring the clan together. You can join us, but it's no' about lessons or etiquette.'

She seemed to consider it and relented, 'All right. But I will help you with the preparations.'

His mother surprised him by saying, 'If you like, I shall send the invitations and arrange for the music.'

Miss Goodson smiled and said, 'Thank you, Lady Locharr. That would be a tremendous help. Let me know what I can do to assist.'

His mother eyed her with interest. 'There is naught you can do. But I think it's time that you learned about Scottish hospitality before you leave.' There was a gleam in her eyes, making Lachlan wonder exactly what she was up to.

Chapter Seven

One week later, the castle was decorated with bunting swags and greenery. Lady Locharr had arranged for a special feast and barrels of ale, as well as musicians. Frances had thrown herself into the preparations, and nearly fifty of the clansmen had responded. It would be a large gathering, but she hoped it would be useful to the laird. The guests would be arriving within the hour.

She had dressed in her blue gown and had no intention of interfering with the festivities. Instead, she planned to remain in the background with the servants, ensuring that there was plenty of food and drink.

And she would watch over him, hoping he would triumph.

Frances was about to enter the kitchen, when a voice called out, 'Miss Goodson. Come here.'

She suppressed a groan at the orders. She turned and said, 'Yes, Lady Locharr?'

The matron's face tightened. 'You're not going to wear *that* to the *ceilidh*, are you?'

'I wasn't planning to attend,' Frances answered. 'Not as a guest, anyway. It wouldn't be my place.'

'Nonsense.' Lady Locharr held out her hand and Frances was forced to take it. 'As Lachlan's governess, of course you must attend. How else will you see if he uses the wrong fork?' Her tone remained light, though Frances didn't miss the sarcasm.

'I truly could not be so bold.'

'I insist.' Lady Locharr tightened her grip and led Frances towards the stairs. 'And you cannot wear that old gown. I have just the thing for you.'

She had no choice but to follow, but every instinct went on alert. Lady Locharr had no reason to help her—and truthfully, it seemed that the laird's mother was not on her side. But Frances saw no way to politely refuse.

Lady Locharr led her into a bedroom where Elspeth was waiting. Upon the bed, Frances spied a tartan woven in the clan colours of blue and green. She hesitated. 'I'm not a Scot, Lady Locharr. It would not be appropriate for me to wear this.'

'You do not wish to stand out among the

laird's guests,' she said, closing the door and locking it. 'Elspeth and I will help you.'

Before she could protest, the pair of them started unbuttoning her gown. Frances decided it wasn't worth an argument, but it was strange to be wearing such an unfamiliar garment. Lady Locharr pinned a brooch to keep the tartan in place over her shoulder. Beneath it, she wore a cream-coloured blouse, and the skirt was formed from the folds of plaid. It felt slightly heavy and foreign, yet she was surprised at the way the bright colours lifted her mood.

'There, now. It suits you well enough,' Lady Locharr pronounced.

'Thank you,' Frances said. She didn't quite understand why they were helping her, but she was willing to accept the peace offering.

'Your hair is wrong. Let Elspeth fix it for you,' Lady Locharr continued. 'This is a Scottish *ceilidh*, not an English ball.'

'I thought it was a Scottish ball?' she ventured.

Lady Locharr only smiled. 'You'll find that we Scots don't stand on ceremony the way the English do.'

Once again, Frances found herself guided to sit down. Elspeth removed the pins from her hair and began brushing it. But instead of tucking it back into a neat chignon, the maid let it hang down her back. She took a small section of Frances's hair and braided it across her head like a crown.

When Frances saw her reflection, it felt as if a stranger were looking back at her. For a moment, it was like glimpsing the girl she had once been, and a tightness gathered in her stomach. She couldn't ever go back to that time of innocence, no matter how much she might want to.

'You look acceptable now,' Lady Locharr said. 'Now you may go and help my son greet his guests.'

She met the woman's gaze and said softly, 'I really do want to help him.' It was important to her that his mother understood this.

The matron walked with her towards the doorway. 'I believe that.' Lady Locharr's voice was calm before she met her gaze in a direct stare. 'But I also believe you have feelings for him.'

Frances shook her head, denying it. 'I know better than to walk down that path. It would only end in heartbreak.' She had already shielded herself, shutting down that impossible vision. 'He needs to marry the woman who will help him save Locharr.'

The laird's mother regarded her with solemnity. 'I am glad you understand.' She unlocked the door and opened it. 'There is only one woman for Lachlan, and it can never be you. He is not free to follow his own desires.'

The words cut deeply, but there was truth in them. Frances knew it down to her bones. She met Lady Locharr's gaze and gave a single nod. Then they walked alongside one another down the stairs to await the guests.

Lachlan stood just inside the ballroom to greet his friends as they arrived. Most of his clansmen were jovial as they arrived, laughing and clapping him on the back. His friends and family were eager for a rollicking *ceilidh*.

One of his kinsmen approached the fiddler, and within moments, a hearty reel resounded in the room. The guests lined up across from one another and began a lively dance. Lachlan began clapping along with the others, and then his attention shifted towards the door. He saw Miss Goodson dressed in a manner he'd never seen before.

Her blonde hair was a riot of curls down her shoulders, and a large braid crossed above her forehead. She wore a tartan, and the rich blue accentuated her green eyes. As she entered the room, she appeared startled by the guests, uncertain what to do. It was clear that his kinsmen were enjoying the merriment, but it was nothing at all like the sort of gathering she was used to.

Before she could take another step, one of his kinsmen—Graham MacKinloch—seized her hand and whirled her in a circle. Miss Goodson jolted at the contact and was passed from partner to partner. She appeared stunned at being handled in such a way, but to her credit, she did not spurn any of his clansmen. When she drew closer to him, Lachlan intervened and pulled her out of the dancing. Her face was flushed, and she said, 'Thank you, Locharr. That was…not what I was expecting.'

'My clan enjoys a lively *ceilidh*,' he said.

'Are they always this loud?' She was eyeing his kinsmen as if she didn't know what to think of them.

'Louder, once they're drunk. Some might begin singing. Graham loves a good tune,' he added.

'I thought it would be a quiet gathering.' She let out a sigh of air. 'I couldn't have been more wrong, could I?'

'Well, it's no' what you were expecting, but there's no reason you couldna enjoy yourself.' He reached out as Alban passed and seized two cups of cold ale, handing one to her. 'You've taught me about London balls. Now you can see a Scottish *ceilidh* for yourself and compare them. There will be stories as the night wears on.'

She took a sip of the ale and grimaced. 'I've never been to a gathering like this one.'

''Tis good for the MacKinlochs to enjoy themselves on a spring evening. It takes their mind off their troubles.' He drank deeply of the cup and drained it, handing the empty glass to another servant. 'You might learn something about Highlanders, aye?'

She glanced down at her tartan. 'Your mother gave me this to wear. She said my clothes wouldn't be appropriate.'

'She was right,' Lachlan agreed. He didn't know his mother's intent, but perhaps it was to make Miss Goodson blend in with the others.

She could never disappear into a crowd, though. Not with that golden hair. He reached out to tug at one of the locks, and the strand curled around his fingers. 'Your hair looks bonny in this way. I like it.'

She froze at his touch, and he released the curl, staring at her. Unbidden came the memory of her kiss. Her soft lips had yielded to his, and the vision provoked the desire to do it again. He wanted to take her into a darkened corner and kiss her until those lips were swollen from loving.

'Please don't touch me,' she murmured. 'We both know it would be a mistake.'

For a moment, he wondered if she'd read his

thoughts but then realised she was speaking about her hair.

'Go off then, and enjoy yourself,' he bade her. 'Try out the dancing if you like. Anyone can teach you the steps.'

With that, he bowed and took his leave. For a moment, she stood alone, staring at her surroundings like a frightened rabbit. But then, one of the women took her by the hand and guided her towards the dancing. Miss Goodson lined up beside her, and she attempted the steps, smiling as she faltered. But within moments, she learned them, and she joined with the others, laughing as she danced.

He stood and watched over her, noticing the way her reserve melted away and she began enjoying herself. Would Lady Regina ever learn to make merry among his people in the way Miss Goodson did?

Somehow, he doubted it. Regina had always been shy, and he remembered that as a girl, she had preferred to spend time in the corners, rather than joining the others.

As he watched Miss Goodson dancing, he thought of her true first name: Frances. He had always used her surname out of formality, but tonight, the barriers had shifted. And Frances Goodson was enchanting in the way she moved and in the way she smiled.

One of his kinsmen, Malcolm MacKinloch, approached and greeted him. 'Granny MacKinloch said that you had a Sassenach at Locharr.' With a wink, he added, 'She's a sweet lass, aye.'

'And she's a respectable woman,' Lachlan added. 'She does ken that I'm to marry Lady Regina.'

'So, you're not wanting her for yourself?' Malcolm sent him a sidelong look.

'She's a lady,' he said. 'And one who deserves to be treated well, that's all.' He didn't want any of his men to believe they could trifle with her.

Malcolm inclined his head. 'But we can dance with her and talk with her?'

'As long as you do not bother her in any way,' he finished.

His kinsmen flashed a grin. 'So be it.' Malcolm strode away, crossing towards the young woman. Frances was dancing in a line, and a moment later, Malcolm caught her by the waist and spun her around. He said something to her, and she laughed.

A spear of unnatural jealousy thrust through Lachlan, though he knew he had no right to feel it. After the dance was over, Malcolm brought her a cup of ale, and she drank, laughing as he told a story.

From beside him, his mother approached.

'Do you think Regina will enjoy gatherings like this?' he wondered aloud.

'I don't think so, no.' His mother nodded towards Frances. 'But Miss Goodson seems to be having a fine time.'

It was true. The men of his clan were enjoying dancing with her, and Frances was whirling in circles. Lachlan decided he wanted to join in and excused himself from Catrina's side. Before he reached Frances, she saw him approaching and hurried closer.

'Locharr, come and join in the dancing! It's wonderful.' She took his hands in hers.

'I'm no' one for dancing,' he started to say, but she pulled him into the line.

'Oh, please do.' She smiled at him, and it struck him hard, deep down in his gut. 'Just for a moment.'

Though he didn't want to dance, he couldn't pull away from her. He was caught up in her green eyes and the flush in her cheeks. Her skin was damp from exertion, and it reminded him of what she might look like after a night of passion in a man's arms.

Lachlan couldn't have left, if he'd wanted to. He caught her waist and stared into her eyes, hardly caring what happened with the music or the steps. Her lips were parted, and more than anything, he wanted to kiss her.

He knew the steps to the dance, but he stumbled over a few turns. He'd never had very good balance and it was one reason why he avoided dancing.

'This has been a wonderful night,' Frances murmured. 'I loved it.' With a slight laugh, she glanced at the refreshment table, where men, women, and children were grabbing food with their bare hands and eating with enthusiasm. 'Somehow I don't believe they even use forks, much less worry about which one is proper.' Her mouth curved in a rueful smile. 'And no one cares.'

'Many of them havena much food at all,' he confessed. 'This *ceilidh* is a welcome gift.'

'It was a gift to me, too,' she admitted. 'I'm going to miss Scotland dearly.'

Her gaze locked upon him, and he heard her unspoken words: *And you.* As he spun her in the dance, he took both of her hands and squeezed them. Though he knew he had no right to imagine dreams that would never be, he could not deny that Frances Goodson belonged in a place like this, surrounded by laughter.

And when she was gone from his life, he would miss her, too.

When the dance ended, Frances felt breathless. The laird stared into her eyes, and at his intensity, she nearly lost her breath. He looked like a conquering warrior, ready to carry her off. The very thought made her body grow pliant and liquid. She tore her gaze away, needing a distraction. 'I am thirsty.'

'I'll fetch you a drink.'

She thanked him, but instead of leaving her side, he offered his arm. The gesture softened her heart, and she took it. 'Thank you.'

She was dizzy and not just from the dancing. She'd lost count of whether she'd had two glasses of ale or three. But the spirits had lifted away her inhibitions, until she cared naught what everyone thought of her. There was only the lively music and the dancing.

When she reached the far side of the room, two large barrels stood atop a sturdy oak table. 'Are both of those filled with ale?' she asked the laird.

'Nay, there's mead in the other. Would you be wanting to try it?'

Frances nodded. 'Or water, if you have it.' But although she knew it was unwise to partake of spirits, everyone else had already done so. And in truth, she was so thirsty, she hardly cared what she drank.

He took a cup and filled it with the mead, handing it to her. She took a first sip and was startled by how sweet it was. 'It tastes like honey.'

'Do you like it?'

'I'm not certain yet.' She tested another sip, and the warmth spread throughout her body. It was rather nice. But a voice inside her head warned that she needed to regain command of herself. She had already broken several rules by dancing with such abandon.

And yet, it had been the most fun she'd had in years. She had carried the weight of grief and shame for so long, she had forgotten what it was to live without the sadness.

The rebellious side to her took another sip of mead before she reluctantly set it aside. She fanned her face, and remarked, 'It's so hot in here.'

The moment she said it, she realised her mistake. A few cups of ale, and every sense of propriety had gone out the window.

'Would you be wanting to step outside and get some air?' he offered.

She did, although it wasn't at all a good idea to go alone with the laird outside. 'I would, except that it's not proper.'

'Should I send for Elspeth and be asking her to join us?' he asked. 'That is, if you're wanting a chaperon.'

Frances brightened that he'd remembered. 'Yes, please. But even so, we should only go out to the terrace.' They waited on the outskirts of the crowd, and the oppressive heat made her lightheaded. She was grateful when Elspeth shuffled towards them. The laird kept his pace slow to account for the old woman's gait, and Frances accompanied him down the hallway.

He escorted her towards the open door leading out to the terrace. It was still cool outside, but she welcomed the chill. Though a part of her knew this was wrong, to abandon the guests, a selfish part of her wanted to claim a moment to herself.

Frances took a few steps forward into the moonlight and confessed, 'I will miss this place.' From the moment she'd arrived, she had fallen in love with the castle. The tall turrets, the lush gardens…even the cosy rooms inside the castle felt like a home. But time was slipping away from her, and she suspected she would never return.

'In what way?' he asked.

She drank in her surroundings, smiling to herself. 'It feels enchanted. The gardens…the sea…every part of this castle has a story to tell. Even you.'

His expression shifted, and he slowed his pace. In the shadowed moonlight, she was caught by his handsome face and the caged strength of his body. Her heart was pounding, for she was slipping beneath his spell. She knew the truth of their eventual parting. He was bound to another woman and could never be hers. But for now, in this moment, she could imagine that he desired her.

'I have no story to tell. And I already ken what the ending is.' His words were a warning that she intended to heed.

'So do I.' Her answer was laced with disappointment.

The laird reached for her hands, and the simple touch made her heart beat faster. She knew he was trying to respect her boundaries. And yet, a wistful part of her wanted him to trespass.

Perhaps it was the mead that was lifting away her common sense, but she knew he would be going to another woman within a matter of weeks. She would have to give him up and never see him again. The thought tangled up her emotions in a heavy cloak of regret.

Frances reinforced the steel bands around her heart. But she lifted her gaze to his, memorising the lines of his face and those deep blue eyes.

'Someday you will find the happy ending you're wanting,' he said quietly.

But she wasn't naïve enough to believe that. 'No. I already lost my heart's desire. And I won't ever get over it.' The pain was still buried deep as she remembered the tiny infant, the son who had never taken a single breath. Though she had been ashamed of herself for falling into ruin, she had loved her unborn baby with all her heart.

'Pain grows softer over the years,' he said. 'And one day, you will find a man who deserves to love you.'

'What if I don't want to find another man to love?' she asked. 'What if I want to live my own life in freedom?' She had been humiliated by the rash choice she'd made, surrendering her virginity. And because of it, she had become pregnant. Her lover had gone his way and she had gone hers. He hadn't wanted to marry her, and truthfully, after she learned that his false promises meant nothing, she hadn't wanted to marry him, either. It had been a monumental mistake.

Her mother believed that it had been a blessing to lose the baby. *No one will ever know. You can start over again.*

Her name in society was already ruined. She could never return to London or find a husband among the ton. Her shame would haunt her for the rest of her life.

'You deserve better than loneliness,' he said. But the truth was, she couldn't imagine being loved. Not any more.

But she hoped Lachlan MacKinloch would find happiness.

Not only was he handsome and kind, but there was an inner strength she admired. He would wed Lady Regina out of necessity. With her dowry, he would provide for his clan, and he would be kind and honourable towards his wife.

'You're staring at me,' he said. 'What is it?'

'It's nothing. I was only thinking of your marriage to Lady Regina. I hope you will be happy together.' Though she tried to keep her voice cheerful, she couldn't quite hide the hint of sadness.

He nodded, but there was no joy in his gaze. ''Twould be nice if we could make our own choices, would it not?'

She could only incline her head. His blue eyes pierced through her defences, making her feel a yearning deep inside. The mead was loosening her inhibitions, and she wished he would kiss her again—even though she knew it was wrong.

'I can see why you would do anything for your people. They are a fine clan.' She glanced behind them and saw that Elspeth was sitting on a low stool, leaning against a stone wall. Her eyes were closed, and she appeared to be snoring. There was no one else here, for all the guests were inside, drinking and dancing.

'Do you still want me to leave you alone, Frances?' he asked. He traced the line of her jaw with his thumb, and the heat of his touch seared her. 'Should I not touch you?'

She went motionless, knowing she should stop

him. And yet, her emotions were raw and uncertain. For so long, she had pushed away men, knowing the consequences. She had worn the heavy cloak of loneliness, punishing herself for her past mistakes.

You are ruined, her brain reminded her.

But was she to push aside every man, doing penance for the rest of her life? Or was it all right to steal a single moment?

Her heart was heavy, but she spoke the truth. 'You belong to someone else. We should not tread upon that path.'

His expression darkened with need, and he cupped her face. For a moment, she closed her eyes, indulging in the stolen moment. If only her life were different…

'Do you ken what I would do if I were not promised?' His voice was husky, and he trailed a finger down the side of her neck. Shivers erupted across her skin.

Frances could not speak a single word. Instead, she shook her head slowly, opening her eyes to look at him. *You cannot do this again,* her brain warned. But her sense of reason was softened by the mead and her own forbidden desires.

Lachlan tipped her chin up. 'I would kiss you right now. A slow kiss to learn the shape of your mouth.' He brushed his thumb against her lips, and she felt the rise of her own arousal as her skin warmed to his touch.

Only once had she lain with a man, believing his empty promises. She had felt the weight of his naked body upon her, the rough invasion, and afterwards, the sense of shame. There had been no pleasure—only the realisation that she had made a terrible mistake.

But with Lachlan, the slightest touch of his hand was enough to make her come undone. Already, she could feel her response to him, the desperate need for more.

'Would you kiss me back?' he murmured, leaning in so close, she could feel his hot breath.

'I don't know.' Her voice revealed her nervousness, though she was utterly captivated by him.

'If you kissed me back, I would draw your body close to mine, like this.' His hands moved to her waist, pulling her against him. She felt the ridge of his arousal and the hard planes of his body. She rested her hands upon his chest, and though it was wrong, she moved her hands to his shoulders. His pulse beat wildly, mimicking her own. 'I like having your hands upon me, *a ghràidh*. Go on.'

Frances answered his command by sliding her fingers through his hair. He still hadn't cut the shoulder-length locks, and she found that she rather liked the wildness of it. She knew that their time together was drawing short. He would go to London, and she would return to the life she had known before. The enchanted moments of this brief fantasy would fade away into nothingness.

'Careful,' he warned. 'I find that I'm wanting to ignore the rules.'

She felt the same way. In less than a month, she would be alone again. She would return to the drudgery of her former life in London and would have only memories of this time with Lachlan. In his eyes, she caught a glimpse of a future she would never have. She wanted this man, and it would break her heart to walk away from him.

Let him go, her brain insisted. *Do not make the same mistake again.*

But what harm was there in a single kiss? They both knew there was no future for them. And right now, she wanted the comfort of his arms around her.

She stood up on tiptoe and pulled his face closer, brushing her mouth against his. Lachlan broke away and took her by the hand. Without a word, he nearly dragged her deeper into the garden, and she didn't protest.

He led her down a gravel pathway, and she could see her breath in the cold spring air. But despite the chill, she felt only the blazing heat of desire. He pressed her back against a stone wall and framed her face with his hands.

'I will stop, any moment you say the word,' he whispered.

'I know you will.' Frances drew her hands over his, feeling the heat. She ignored the rules of propriety and wound her arms around his neck.

But still, he waited. 'Someone hurt you in the past, aye?'

She nodded, feeling embarrassed by the choices she had made. 'I was ruined. And I paid the price for it, tenfold.'

He traced the edge of her jaw, and she saw the raw need in his eyes. Yet, he would not touch her if she wanted him to hold back.

She knew he could not stay with her—he had made a commitment he would not break. And though it was wrong, she wanted to steal a glimpse of what she would never have.

'I will ne'er hurt you, Frances,' he murmured.

'I know it.' She stood on tiptoe, drawing his face down to hers. 'But for one night, I want to imagine you are mine. In the morning, we must go back to the way things were between us.' Like a magical spell, she knew the illusion would vanish at daybreak.

Lachlan kissed her deeply, this time sliding

his tongue inside her mouth. She nearly moaned at the sensation, and every inch of her skin grew hotter. Kissing this man was dangerous, for he tempted her to cast aside the very lessons of propriety she was trying to teach.

It was nothing like the kisses she had experienced in the past. Every part of her came alive, needing so much more. He kissed her until she was starving for more than his mouth. She wanted his body upon hers, to feel him skin to skin. And she knew full well that this could never happen. He belonged to another woman, and he could never be with someone like her.

He nudged his knee between her legs, untangling her skirts until she was sitting astride his heavy thigh. He moved slightly, and she dug her nails into his back as if he had caressed her intimately. This time, his kiss changed, from hard and demanding, to a softer temptation. He murmured against her lips, 'If we were promised, I would be touching you here.' He shifted the weight of his thigh, and it created a delicious pressure between her legs. She was wet, so aroused, she closed her eyes to push back the forbidden feelings.

'I would slide my fingers deep inside you, until you couldna catch your breath. And I would stroke you with my thumb.'

His words, coupled with the thick muscle of

his thigh between her legs, was enough to inten-
sify her needs. She was biting her lip, unable to
stop the moan that came forth when he rocked
his leg against her. She could feel the rising pleasure taking hold, and her breasts grew tight, her
nipples heavy beneath her blouse.

Lachlan kissed her until she felt her body
tremble. He was relentless, his tongue invad-
ing her mouth until he drew it lower against her
throat. He slid the tartan down from her shoulder and loosened her blouse until she knew what
he intended. She wasn't wearing a chemise or
stays, and the sensation of his hands was both
sinful and glorious. *Oh, God above.*

The silent words were a fervent prayer, and
she did not deny him. Her brain was warning
her to stop, but when she looked into his eyes,
she saw a man who needed her as badly as she
needed him. Both of their lives were trapped
within the boundaries of futures they didn't
want. And she could not deny that her heart was
falling hard for him.

Lachlan pushed the blouse lower, baring
her skin. He brought his mouth to the swell of
her bosom, and the sensation made her dig her
fingers into his shoulders. A moment later, he
kissed her again, and he slid his hand beneath the
fabric. The forbidden touch of his palm against
her nipple made her shudder. He kissed her hard,

gently rolling the erect tip between his thumb and forefinger.

Her body was aching, and her breathing came in a sharp rhythm. He knew how to draw out the pleasure, bringing her close to the edge before pausing. She knew that it was wrong to allow him such liberties. But her wayward heart wanted what it could not have. And for this stolen moment, she wanted to experience his touch and give him the same.

She took his face in her hands and drew her mouth along the bristled edge of his chin. Then she traced the scar that marred his cheek. Lower still, she kissed him, memorising the lines of his face as she drew her lips over his throat. He stiffened, his hands sliding into her hair. She rested her hands upon his cravat, and his gaze grew intent. 'I'm wanting your hands upon me, Frances.'

He drew his shirt out from his trousers and pulled her hands beneath it to touch his bare back. She slid her hands up his spine, feeling the powerful way his muscles strained. There was no doubt in her mind that if they were lovers, he would lift her skirts and take her right now. The thought stunned her with the vivid imagery, and she leaned in to kiss him again.

'That's it, lass,' he said against her lips, and his eyes turned feral. 'I'm going to pleasure you now. Until you're wanting to scream.' He lowered her from his thigh, and her knees nearly collapsed. But there was a tree nearby with a low branch. He lifted her to sit upon it, and then he knelt down before her. They were completely invisible to prying eyes, and this time, he lowered her garments until her breasts were bare in the moonlight.

'Look at these,' he growled, gently touching her nipples. 'They're begging for me to taste them.'

You shouldn't do this, her conscience pleaded. *Don't allow it. Or everything they said about you will be true.*

Tears pricked at her eyes, and her emotions were wrung apart at the realisation that she could only have this moment with Lachlan. And for that reason, she kept the words silent.

He took one nipple into his mouth, just as he reached beneath her skirts. Pleasure shot through her, and when his fingers reached past her petticoats, he rubbed against the seam of her opening.

'I love the way you feel,' he said, before he moved his attention to the other breast. He laved her nipple, sucking until she surged against his hand. Her breathing came in soft pants, and he made her feel beloved. His thumb stroked the hooded flesh, and she gripped his head as her body strained for more. When he slid two fingers inside her, he nipped at her breast, and she gasped at the sensation.

She was incapable of saying no, though she was trying to hold back a flood of unwanted memories. The contrast between her first lover and Lachlan was shocking, and she realised how different it was. Her Highlander was doing everything in his power to pleasure her, and her strong reactions satisfied him.

'Look at me,' he commanded, drawing back from her. 'I'm wanting to see your face when you come apart.' She forced herself to open her eyes, and in his face, she saw the desire mirroring her own.

'Let it happen,' he ordered. 'Surrender and give in to what you need.'

His fingers renewed their caresses, and she cried out when he pressed his thumb against her sensitive flesh. She revelled in the pleasure, and he drove his fingers inside, mimicking the act of lovemaking. His voice deepened, and he spoke in Gaelic, words of endearment she could not understand. She arched her back, changing the angle of his touch. Though she didn't understand what was happening, she quaked beneath his touch until the fierce release ignited, sending waves of violent sensations flooding through her. Her moan broke forth as she shuddered against him, stunned by how good he had made her feel.

She felt boneless, drained of all vigour until she could only hold him close. He kissed her while he drew up the fallen sleeves, helping her to get dressed again. She couldn't move, could hardly hold a coherent thought together.

'You're a bonny lass, Frances Goodson,' he said against her lips as he stole one last kiss. 'I only wish things were different.'

His words were a stark reminder that there would always be a line drawn between them. She could not indulge in an affair, no matter how badly she wanted this man. Not again, not after the last time had brought such heart-wrenching consequences.

'But they're not different, are they?' She extricated herself from his embrace and stepped back. 'No matter what I might feel.'

She hadn't meant to reveal her thoughts so openly. But he caught her wrist and held it a moment. 'If I had a true choice, Frances, I would be choosing a woman like you. Someone who can laugh and belong among my people. Someone who loves the clan as much as I do.'

'Locharr, I—'

'Lachlan,' he corrected. 'Call me by my name when we are alone.'

She didn't know if she could do it. It was as if the invisible walls between them were breaking down, but she knew the terrible cost of offering her heart to a man who could never accept it.

'I can't.' Frances pulled her wrist away. She needed to go back inside, to lose herself among the crowds of people and calm her racing heart.

This had been such a mistake. For as she stared at the handsome laird, she saw a man she could not have. And with every moment she spent alone in his arms, the more she began to love him.

'Enjoy the rest of the *ceilidh*,' she urged him. 'I will be in my room.' And with that, she hurried back inside.

He was almost ready for London, she told herself. Although he didn't know everything, it would be enough to survive. If he was charming and polite, she believed he would win Lady Regina's heart.

She only hoped she could stop her own heart from breaking.

Chapter Eight

Three weeks later

Instead of a sea of papers in his father's study, Lachlan surveyed the stacks of ledgers, feeling a sense of satisfaction. Frances had helped him sort through every last scrap, until they were organised by date. There was one ledger which contained the bills with no dates, and his governess was seated in a chair, studying it with a frown.

Her blonde hair was pinned up, but two stray curls hung against her ears. He tried not to stare, but he could not deny the temptation of her. Neither had ever spoken of the forbidden night in the garden, but it haunted him still. The memory lingered, and never would he forget the way she had responded to his touch. Even now, he desired her.

'Thank you for your help,' he said quietly. 'I wouldna have ever sorted through this mess of papers without you.'

She nodded absently, turning a page. 'Lachlan, there's something very wrong with these pages. There seems to be a great deal of money being spent on extra expenses. It's as if your father was trying to hide money.'

He came to stand beside her chair and leaned down to look closer. He could smell the faint aroma of flowers from her skin, and he gritted his teeth to push back the unbidden needs. He forced himself to stare at his father's handwriting, and when he added the column in his head, the debt was staggering.

'He should have three thousand pounds more than he's accounted for.' He turned the page and saw more amounts written, though his father had written no name or reason for the lost money. 'What happened to it?'

'Did you have a relative in need?' Frances suggested. 'Or was it for your mother?'

He shook his head. From the looks of it, the amounts were varied, and over several months. 'It's almost as if he paid the bills to support someone else.'

Frances closed the book and regarded him. 'I hesitate to ask this, but…could there have been someone else in your father's life? Another woman or…an illegitimate child?'

He couldn't imagine such a thing. Tavin had been utterly devoted to his wife. But he could only lift his shoulders in a shrug. 'I would have to ask Catrina. But I canna say that I'm wanting to.'

'I don't blame you.' Frances stood from the chair. 'It might be best to ask some of the clansmen who might remember those years. They might have noticed something.' It was a wise suggestion, and he intended to heed her advice. She set the ledger down on a side table. 'I hope that someday, you'll learn what happened.'

He caught the veiled meaning of her words—that she wouldn't be here to learn the truth. But then, he had no time to investigate the ledgers. Both of them had packed their belongings for the journey to London on the morrow. Alban had already included the new clothing the tailor had made for him. Although Lachlan hadn't truly wanted the clothes, he had compromised with Frances. He agreed to take them—but only if she accepted wages for her work as his governess.

'Have I learned all my lessons of etiquette, then?' he asked. 'Or was there something else I should learn?'

She ventured a soft smile. 'I believe you will

be very successful, Locharr. And I wish you all the best.'

Although her words were kind, they were tinged with sorrow. He couldn't help but blame himself for her sadness. And he wanted to lift her spirits, bringing back her joy.

'Would you care to go riding?' he suggested. 'There are a few hours left in the afternoon.'

For a brief moment, he saw the indecision in her eyes. Then she shook her head. 'I really shouldn't.'

'Why not? We've finished with the ledgers, and you've said I have no more lessons.'

Her expression held wariness. 'The ride would be too difficult for Elspeth to chaperon.'

'We'll remain in the open where everyone can see us.'

The offer appealed to her, he could tell. She was strongly considering it. And since this was their last night, he wanted to spend it with her. As soon as he reached the Duke of Worthingstone's residence, he would have to cease all contact with Frances. The thought didn't sit well with him.

'Very well. But only for an hour or so.' She walked to the door and paused. 'Locharr, I do want you to know how grateful I am that you allowed me to stay. I have thoroughly enjoyed teaching you. I hope that it will prove useful in the forthcoming weeks.'

A knot formed in his throat, but he only nodded. 'I'll make the arrangements for the horses. Meet me outside when you're ready.'

Frances rode alongside the laird into the open meadow. The afternoon light was waning, and the spring air was warmer than usual. She lifted her face to the sun, savouring these last few moments.

Lachlan rode alongside her and asked, 'Would you come with me to the village for a few moments? Just for a little while.'

Although it would cause gossip, what did that matter now? They were leaving in the morning, and the clan would not see her again. 'Of course.'

He led her down towards the cobbled streets, past Granny MacKinloch's tea shop, until they reached a small church. She wasn't certain why he had brought her here, but she dismounted and followed him.

When they drew closer, she saw that the building was fairly new, as if it had been constructed within the past year. With every step closer, she saw Lachlan's tension heighten.

For a long time, he simply stared at the church, and he made no move to go inside. Frances didn't question him, but simply waited at his side.

'He came here alone that night, you ken? To pray.' He walked along the perimeter of the church, towards the back until she saw a small graveyard.

She understood now that he was speaking of his father. 'What happened?'

He let out a slow breath. 'No one could say. But I was in the village that night with friends, and we smelled the smoke. The kirk was on fire, and we didna ken if anyone was inside. And then I saw my father's horse rearing up and struggling to get away. He'd tied it to the post outside.'

His voice was bleak, but he admitted, 'I went inside to save Tavin, but the ceiling collapsed. I wasna strong enough to move him from under the beams.'

'I'm so sorry.' She reached out to touch his shoulder, and he took her hand.

The angry scar on his face was a result of that fire, a visible reminder of the past. She squeezed his hand, wanting to offer him silent support and understanding.

'They rebuilt it last year,' he told her. 'But I've not set foot inside since. I couldna go there, remembering how he died. It feels like my fault, even now.'

'You did everything you could.'

'Aye. But it wasna enough.' He led her back to the horse, but she stopped him. He needed to let go of the guilt haunting him. Only then could he reach for his own happiness.

'You don't need to punish yourself, Lachlan. He wouldn't have wanted that.' She touched his heart, and he took her hand.

'I shut myself away for the past two years. Everything reminded me of him. And I have the scar on my face, so that I can never forget my failure.'

She stood on tiptoe and drew his face downward, kissing his cheek. 'It will take time to heal. The scar may never go away, but one day, you will remember your love for him.' Her heart bled, for she knew what it was to be broken after death. Though she had no visible scars after losing her son, she had never forgotten the love.

'Tavin loved you, and I know he would want you to go on.' She kissed him again and then allowed him to help her mount. They rode away from the village until they reached the clearing. Lachlan spurred his horse faster, riding towards the coast. The wind whipped at her bonnet, but she loved the wildness of the breeze.

It soon became clear that he was riding further than he'd promised. Frances glanced behind at the castle, wondering if she dared to go with him this far. Or was there another reason he wanted her alone? Her skin tightened at the forbidden memory of pleasure. For a moment, she questioned whether to turn back.

But then, this was their last day together. It was an unspoken promise that nothing could happen between them. She knew that he was already bound to Lady Regina, though they were not formally engaged yet.

Lachlan rode towards a clearing and dismounted. 'We'll stop here for a little while. Let the horses graze.' He helped her off her mare and hobbled their mounts before leading her towards a large limestone boulder. Frances climbed atop the stone, marvelling at the majesty of the sea.

'I could sit here all day and watch the world go by,' she mused. 'It's beautiful.'

'So it is.'

But his gaze was fixed upon her. She was careful not to look at Lachlan, trying to distance herself.

You're not good enough for him, her conscience reminded her. *He deserves an innocent heiress. Not a woman ruined by scandal without virtue. Not a woman who bore a child out of wedlock.*

She could not argue those truths, even with herself. And even if Lady Regina refused to wed Lachlan, Frances understood that she could not hold a place in the laird's life—much as she might want to. She locked away the rising hurt, reminding herself to savour these last moments.

'Do you want to walk along the sand?' he asked.

She brightened at the idea. It was a welcome distraction. 'I would, yes.' Even better, she hoped to walk barefoot in the water. It would be cold, true enough, but she was eager to feel the cool waves around her ankles.

The laird guided her down a narrow pathway that led towards the open strand. When she reached the sand, Frances informed the laird, 'Turn your back. I am going to remove my shoes and stockings so I can walk in the water.'

His eyes narrowed, and he teased, 'How scandalous, Miss Goodson. What would a governess say?'

'She would tell me to keep my shoes and stockings on and to remember my parasol. And I do not have one, I fear.' She spun her finger in a circle. 'Turn around and do not look.'

Frances hurriedly removed her shoes and stockings, only to realise that the laird was doing the same thing. She supposed there was no harm in it, though no respectable woman would do such a thing.

She lowered her skirts, hoping that her ankles were not entirely visible. The gown she wore was a serviceable grey, and it would not matter if the hem got wet.

She left the shoes and stockings in the sand and trudged towards the water's edge. The fine-grained sand was soft and damp from an earlier rain. She loved the texture as it pressed against her toes.

Lachlan joined her, and they walked towards the wet sand. The temperature took an abrupt plunge, and she gasped when the first wave struck her ankles.

'My goodness, that's cold.' It felt as if she'd been struck by a curtain of ice. She gritted her teeth and scuttled away from the water. Lachlan, on the other hand, appeared indifferent to the frigid water.

Frances took another hesitant step, and gradually she grew accustomed to the chill. For a moment, she enjoyed walking beside the laird. She was careful to shield her heart—especially after the night he had touched her intimately. Never in her life had she felt such pleasure at a man's touch. On the night she had lost her innocence, it had not been romantic in the least. She had been embarrassed and disappointed in herself that she had fallen so low. At the time, she had believed it was love. But now, she recognised that her lover had only dallied with her, playing with her feelings and her dreams.

Now, her wayward heart had fallen again for a man she could not have. It was a physical ache within her, a need to reach out for his hand and feel his fingers against hers.

'Have you thought about a gift for Lady Regina?' she asked, forcing her conversation back where it belonged.

'Nay. I've no money for baubles or such.'

'It needn't be diamonds,' Frances said. 'You could give her something more personal. Perhaps a set of watercolours. Or even a kitten?'

'Regina was ne'er one for animals,' he said. 'When we were children, she shied away from them.'

'Oh.' She supposed he would have to find something else. 'I would talk with her and learn what she likes. But you should bring a gift if you are courting her.'

'What of you?' he asked. 'If a man were courting you, what gift would you want?'

She lifted her skirts slightly to avoid one of the waves. 'Anything at all, really. Flowers or I also love cake.' For a moment, she allowed herself to daydream that Lachlan was bringing her gifts. But the vision only evoked the heartache she was trying to avoid.

Lachlan reached down and picked up a fallen shell. It was a perfect white scallop, and he offered it to her. 'Here.'

'Thank you,' she said. Though it was only a common shell, she intended to keep it among her most precious possessions. For it would always evoke her last memories of Lachlan MacKinloch.

'When I was a boy, I used to collect seashells,' he remarked. 'I havena walked along the seashore in a while.' There was a hollow tone to his voice, and she suspected the reason.

'Since your father died,' she said quietly.

'Aye.' The water sloshed across his ankles, and he stood in the midst of the freezing water. 'We used to go together, walking through the water and simply talking. It reminds me of him.'

Lachlan reached into the water and picked up two more seashells, handing one to her. 'We used to throw seashells as far as we could and make a wish.'

He pulled back his arm and threw the shell. It soared through the air before it sank beneath the waves. Then he turned back to Frances. 'Your turn.'

She held the jagged seashell and made her own wish, before she cast the shell as far as she could. Her wish, though it could never come true, was to be with this man and to love him for the rest of her life. The shell sank beneath the waves, and she felt a pang of emotion when he took her hand in his.

'We should go back now,' she murmured. 'The others will wonder where we've gone.'

'In a moment.' His hand tightened upon hers. 'There's another place I want to show you.' He pointed towards the rocks a short distance away. 'Over there.'

Frances hesitated. 'You realise how inappropriate this is, Locharr. Everyone will think that we are indulging in something we shouldn't.' Already, they had wandered past the open meadow, and she had no doubt the servants would gossip.

'But you would ken that it's only conversation.'

She glanced back at the horses again, uncertain whether he really meant that. 'We could walk back and converse along the way.'

'I want to spend a little more time with you.'

Frances hesitated, but then, it was their last day at Locharr. She might never return to this place. 'All right. But only for a moment. Afterwards, we must return.'

He led her away from the water's edge and they walked through the chilled sand. She took the arm he offered and said, 'Lady Regina is a fortunate young woman, Lachlan. I know you will be a perfect gentleman when you reach London.'

'I had a good teacher. And I believe I ken which fork is which now.' There was a trace of humour in his voice, though she knew he truly did not care about silver.

'And you know how to dance.' She smiled at him. 'In spite of your reluctance, I think you will do well.'

'So long as I only dance the quadrille or a waltz. Some of the country dances are beyond me.'

Frances slowed her pace and regarded him. 'There is something I've always wanted to know. Why did you refuse to dance when we first began our lessons? And do not say it's because you don't like it. I know there was another reason.' He had been violently opposed to the idea, not merely embarrassed. In spite of his initial refusal, he had learned the dances and could partner her with little difficulty.

'When I was a lad, my mother hosted many gatherings at Locharr. She loved to invite the clansmen and the nobles to our *ceilidhs*. She forced me to come, and the lasses used to tease me, begging for me to dance with them.'

'Was that not flattering?' She could easily imagine Lachlan being the subject of admiration. He was quite handsome, after all.

'They were mocking me, Frances.'

She didn't understand, but he climbed atop the first boulder and held out a hand for her to follow. 'What do you mean?'

'When I was young, I broke my leg when I fell down the stairs leading from the battlements. It healed badly because the doctor couldna set it in time. The lasses teased me because I could only hobble and limp.'

Her anger tightened within her at their cruelty. 'How awful for you. Someone should have put them in their place and stopped them from such rude behaviour.'

'Would you have said something to them?' he mused.

'I would have.' She took his hand and then climbed alongside him. 'But I've never seen you limp now. It healed well enough.'

His expression grew darker. 'My father sent for a physician from Edinburgh who had to re-break the bone to put it right.'

She shuddered at the thought. 'How dreadful. I cannot imagine such a thing.'

'Whenever I think of dancing, it reminds me of having my leg broken again.' His face revealed a tight pain at the memory. 'It took a long time until I could walk, much less dance.'

'But you are a fine dancer now, Lachlan. All the women wanted to dance with you at the *ceilidh*.'

He stopped to look at her. 'It's been many years since I danced. I avoided it because it brought me back to those years when I was a lad.

I didna want to remember people staring.' His mouth twisted in a mock smile, and he tapped his scarred cheek. 'I suppose they'll always stare now, won't they?'

She would not allow him to denigrate himself. 'When I see your scar, I see a heroic man who nearly lost his own life trying to save his father. I admire your bravery.'

'It still feels like failure,' he admitted.

'When you forgive yourself, it won't feel that way any more.' She caressed his cheek again. 'Time heals the wounds of the heart.' She held steady a moment, hoping he could see the truth. 'Your people do not pity you, Lachlan. They care a great deal for their laird. No one will laugh again.'

Lachlan squeezed her palm. 'Come with me,' he said, leading her towards a large pile of limestone rocks. 'This was what I wanted to show you.'

When they reached the stones, she realised that there was a darkened opening at the top of the rock pile. A secret cave, so it seemed. Perhaps one that had been used by smugglers in times gone by.

Frances marvelled at the cavern. 'It's fascinating. I only wish we could see what's inside.'

'Another time, perhaps.'

But she knew she would never see it again. The thought brought an ache to her feelings, and she reached out to take his hand. 'Lachlan, I am grateful for having the opportunity to give you lessons. You are a fine dancer and a gentleman.'

He squeezed her fingers. 'You have taught me well, Frances.'

'I wish I could be there to watch their reaction when the young ladies see you for the first time.' She smiled, imagining Lady Regina's response. Would she find the laird handsome? Would she know how hard he had worked to learn the right etiquette?

'You should be there,' he answered. 'I will see to it that you receive an invitation.'

She flushed at the thought. 'Oh, no. I couldn't.' The scandal was too fresh, and she didn't want to risk any damage to the laird's reputation. Not to mention, he could not be seen talking to her. 'I wouldn't want any distractions for you.'

'It's no trouble at all.'

Though she knew he thought he was being helpful, he did not know of her scandal. It was better for Lachlan if she remained far away. 'No, I don't think so.'

He motioned for her to sit down on the rocks. Frances did, and he asked, 'Why don't you want to come to the ball?'

She searched desperately for a reason he would understand without revealing too much about her past. Finally, she realised that there was one truth she could give him. 'Lachlan, it would hurt me to see you with her.'

His expression transformed, and he sat down beside her. He reached for her palm and drew it to his mouth. The heat of his lips spiralled within her skin, awakening the feelings she wanted to suppress. 'I canna say that I'm wanting to wed Lady Regina. But I've no choice, and you ken this.'

'I do.'

When he leaned in to take her mouth in a deep kiss, she gave no protest at all. This man had captured her heart, despite her attempts to guard it. She surrendered to him, clinging hard as he kissed her. It was a kiss of farewell, one that would be the last. And when his tongue entered her mouth, she opened to him, feeling the echo of sensation between her legs. She was crying in silence, even as she kissed him back.

When he pulled away, his blue eyes burned into hers. His stare held unrequited longing, blended with stony resignation. He wiped her tears away with his thumbs, never taking his gaze from hers.

And she knew it was the last time she would ever be in his arms.

London—one week later

The coach rumbled through the streets of London, and Lachlan's mood darkened with every mile. Frances had given the driver her address, but he soon realised that her neighbourhood was near the outskirts of St Giles in the Fields. The idea of leaving Frances Goodson behind in this part of London was unthinkable. How could a baron's daughter even consider it? How could her family allow it?

The stench of the streets was rancid, and he didn't like to think of what caused it. The coach pulled to a stop in front of a narrow street. The houses were so close together, Lachlan had no doubt that a single fire could catch hold and destroy them.

'I canna leave you here,' he said, eyeing the stairs leading towards the boarding house. 'It's no' safe.'

'It's where I live, Lachlan,' she said gently. 'I have nowhere else to go.'

'You have sisters. A mother, too.'

But at his mention of her family, Frances stiffened. 'I am fine on my own.'

But he couldn't imagine abandoning her in a place like this. 'Who will protect you? Anyone could break down the doors.'

She opened the door to the coach and reached

for her valise. 'While I appreciate your concern, I will be fine. I've lived here for the past three years. Nothing has ever happened.'

'Then you were fortunate.' He could only imagine cutthroats or blackguards shadowing her, or worse, forcing themselves upon her.

'Fortune had nothing to do with it. I have good friends who are strong and well-armed.' She pointed towards the lower level where he saw a large man hulking in front of the window. 'Mr Belfast rarely leaves, and he has frightened away a few unsavoury callers.' She lifted a hand and waved.

Lachlan could almost imagine how many unsavoury callers had lurked upon these streets. Still, he had a mind to meet this Mr Belfast and decide for himself. He took the valise from Frances and helped her outside the coach. Every instinct roared for him to bring her back inside the coach. She lived in utter poverty, and he'd never realised it. Her fate was worse than that of his own clan.

'I still think you should return to the coach,' he said quietly. 'Worthingstone can find a place for you. He has a son now. You could be the child's nursemaid.'

She shook her head, dismissing the idea. 'Don't you realise that word will get back to Lady Regina? I cannot live in the same residence as you. The scandal would ruin your chances with her.' She took a step back from him and glanced at the narrow stairs. 'I will not be here for very long, Locharr. The agency will find me a new position as a governess soon.' She reached for his hand and squeezed it. 'I wish you well.'

There was a heavy knot in his throat, but he managed to nod. 'I will miss you, Frances.'

'And I will miss you.' She braved a smile and released his hand. 'You may write to me and tell me about your first ball. I am happy to answer your letters. At least until you are betrothed.'

It was the hardest thing he'd ever done, leaving her behind. He had come to care about Frances, and he couldn't stand the thought of someone harming her. 'Be safe,' he said. But as he returned to the coach, he promised himself that he would find a way to keep watch over her.

He waited until she was safely inside before he gave the order for the coachman to drive on. The Duke of Worthingstone was expecting his arrival, and Lachlan needed to put aside his personal feelings and attend to his duties.

He rested his hands on the dark breeches Frances had insisted that he wear. Gone was the blue and green tartan, replaced by the boring clothes he disliked. But despite his desire to save money, he knew Frances had been right. The last time he'd come to London, he had donned clothing like this. He'd been shut away for so long after his father's death, he'd forgotten the necessity of looking like everyone else. It meant putting aside his own ways and becoming the man others wanted him to be.

They arrived at the duke's residence in Mayfair within the hour, and Lachlan was impressed by the elegant townhouse. The exterior façade was constructed of red brick, and it stretched three storeys high. Arches framed the stone windows, and the residence held an understated air of wealth.

Lachlan waited inside the coach while Gavin went to knock at the door. He wasn't concerned about greeting his friend, but he had to make the right impression on everyone else.

You've done this before, he reminded himself. But years ago, he was a different man. He had followed in his family's footsteps, hardly caring about what anyone thought of him. Lady Regina had still been away at school, so he hadn't seen her.

And now, it felt as if he were conscious of every move. A litany of rules flooded through his brain, all the training Frances had given him. *The most important thing to remember is that you should behave like a king. Be kind to the servants, but when you are in public, you must behave as if you are above the world.*

A footman waited at the door and Gavin returned, opening the coach door. 'His Grace, the Duke of Worthingstone, is not at home, Locharr, but Her Grace is expecting you.'

Lachlan hid his reaction, though he'd hoped to enjoy a meal with Worthingstone. Now, it seemed, he would have to be even more careful with his manners, in order to please the duchess.

He followed Gavin up the stairs and remembered to give his hat and coat to the footman. The man stiffened at the sight of his scar, but Lachlan pretended he hadn't seen the reaction. He'd been isolated in Scotland for so long, his people were accustomed to the sight of him. 'If you'll just follow me, Locharr, Her Grace, the duchess, will receive you in the drawing room.'

Although he had received letters from Worthingstone with news of the duke's marriage to Victoria Andrews, Lachlan had never made her acquaintance before. He followed the footman down the hallway and up the stairs until the servant led him into the drawing room. The walls were a delicate blue, and tall windows allowed a great deal of light into the space. The duchess had not yet arrived, and Lachlan was not entirely disappointed to have a moment to himself. He tried to imagine what sort of manners he would need. Should he stand in her presence? Sit? Frances would have known.

She would adore a room like this. He could imagine her exclaiming over the colours and the light spilling into the drawing room. The wingback chairs were arranged near the hearth where a warm glow emanated from the coals.

Lachlan waited for a time before the footman returned with a beautiful blonde lady and her young son. The footman cleared his throat and introduced his mistress. 'Your Grace, may I present Lachlan MacKinloch, Laird of Locharr?' The duchess nodded her head in greeting, and then the footman said, 'Locharr, Her Grace, the Duchess of Worthingstone, and his lordship, the Marquess of Thornwyck.'

The duchess wore a soft green gown with her hair tucked up at her nape. She smiled at Lachlan, and she was holding the hand of a young toddler. The boy seized his mother's skirts and buried his face in them.

'Good morning, Locharr. My husband was called away, but he should return this evening. I know he is glad to have you visit, along with the others.'

He bowed in greeting and took her extended hand, kissing the duchess's knuckles. 'I am pleased to meet you, Your Grace.'

'And this is Christopher,' she said, turning the boy around to face him.

Lachlan guessed that the child could be no more than two years of age, at most. He crouched down and extended his hand. 'How do you do, lad?'

The boy hid his face in the duchess's gown once again. 'I fear he is very shy,' she said. 'Please sit down. I will send for tea and refreshments.' She rang for a servant and gave the orders, but Lachlan remained standing. He remembered that Frances had warned him to always await the lady. After the servant departed, he gestured for her to take a seat before he did. The warm smile from the duchess made him feel more at ease.

'My husband told me that you intend to court Lady Regina. I will be hosting a ball in a few days, and she and her father have accepted the invitation.'

He inclined his head. 'Yes, we knew each other as children. Our fathers wanted us to marry.'

The duchess pulled Christopher onto her lap and regarded Lachlan with a soft smile. 'And is it your wish to marry her?'

He was about to answer aye, of course. But something in her expression stopped him. 'It's been years since I've seen Lady Regina. But I ken my duty.'

In her eyes, he saw the trace of regret. 'Was there someone else you wanted to wed?'

He could only shrug. 'My own wishes dinna matter.' But he realised that Her Grace might be able to help him with Miss Goodson's welfare.

'There was someone, wasn't there?' she ventured quietly.

He nodded. 'There is a friend of mine who has fallen into hardship. I'm wanting to help her, but my own funds are lacking.' He met her gaze evenly. 'She is a governess who could use a new position.' His gaze centred upon young Christopher, wondering if that would suit.

The duchess seemed to see through his words. 'Who is she?'

'Frances Goodson,' he answered. 'Her father was a baron, I believe.' The pained expression on her face surprised him, and he asked, 'Do you ken what happened to their family? Is there aught we could do?'

The duchess's expression turned sympathetic. 'I would like to help you, Locharr. But I heard that Miss Goodson suffered through a great scandal and went into seclusion. Even if I did offer to help her, she would undoubtedly refuse.'

'What scandal was this?' He waited, but she only shook her head.

'For her sake, I would rather not speak of it.' The duchess tousled her son's hair and held him close. A frown creased her face, as if she were thinking of an alternative. 'But then, it has been many years now. I will speak with my husband and ask his opinion.'

Although Lachlan wanted to know what had happened, he did not press for more. Instead, he murmured his thanks, though his mood darkened with the possessive need to shield Frances. He didn't doubt that she had been some man's victim, and it wasn't right or fair that she should pay the price of scandal for the rest of her life. He intended to help her escape the past and forge a new future.

Though he didn't know how he could ever give her up to someone else.

Chapter Nine

It had been many years since Regina Crewe had seen Lachlan MacKinloch. Though she had heard about the fire, it was a shock to see his scarred face. Everything about the laird made her nervous. He was larger than life, bold and daring. And while some women claimed that he was exciting, Regina found him intimidating. The very sight of him—even from across the room—frightened her. Her father, Lord Havershire, was eager for her to marry, but she had never understood why he was so adamant that she should wed Lachlan.

She smoothed the invisible wrinkles from her white silk gown, feeling like a sacrificial lamb. Her father was beaming, as if his greatest wish was about to come true. As for herself, she would rather be shackled in an underground dungeon than become any man's wife.

'You look beautiful, Lady Regina,' came a man's voice.

She turned and saw Dalton St George, Viscount Camford, bowing before her. The man had dark blond hair and eyes that seemed green one moment and blue the next. Women sighed whenever he was nearby, and he had an easy smile for them. Over the past week, he had shown her kindness, and he had become a friend of sorts.

'Thank you.' Her voice came out softer than she'd meant it to, but raw nerves were gathering in her stomach.

'Have you spoken with MacKinloch yet?' Lord Camford asked.

'Not yet.' Even so, she had overheard all the gossip about him. How tall and strong he was, almost barbaric in size—and the scar made him positively wicked. While other women seemed enthralled by the Highlander's immense physical size, it only heightened Regina's fears.

'Would you care to dance?' the viscount offered.

'No, thank you.' She didn't feel like dancing with anyone just now. To be truthful, she didn't even want to be here. If it weren't for her father's insistence, she would have begged off with a headache.

But her father had made his wishes clear. She was to be obedient and subservient, no matter what her own fears might be. Even so, she would rather be hanged, drawn, and quartered before she would agree to marriage. The idea of being a man's physical property, to use as he chose, was unbearable.

Before she could find an excuse to leave, the crowds of people parted. There was no mistaking Lachlan MacKinloch, though he was wearing English clothing instead of his Scottish tartan. His long hair was tied back in a queue, and his gaze searched the throng until it settled upon her.

Regina forced herself not to turn away, though her cheeks were burning. Everything about the laird made her uncomfortable. His size, his personality—it made her feel as if she wanted to disappear into the wall.

Lachlan approached, but Lord Camford didn't leave her side. She was grateful for the viscount's presence, though she knew he and Lachlan were friends.

'Lady Regina,' the laird greeted her. 'It has been many years, has it no'? Do you remember me at all?'

She nodded, suddenly unable to speak. Though his words were polite, she was overwhelmed by his physical presence. He was so tall and strong, it terrified her to think of how easily he could subdue her.

What could she say to him? *Yes, I remember how you tried to cut my hair? How you chased me until I stumbled and tore my gown?* None of that was suitable conversation. But the laird appeared not to notice and greeted the viscount. 'I see you've been keeping the lady company, Camford.'

'Protecting her from the blackguards and rakes.' He gave a mischievous smile. 'Though some might put me in that category.'

Lachlan's expression turned wary. 'If you bother her, Camford, I'll skin your hide and leave it for the crows.' Then a moment later, he cleared his throat. 'I suppose that wasna a very polite thing to say. I beg your pardon, Lady Regina.'

She was saved from having to answer, when the duchess approached. Both gentlemen bowed to Her Grace, and Regina sank into a deep curtsy. She liked Victoria Nottoway, for the duchess was quiet, like herself.

'Are you enjoying yourself?' Her Grace asked Lachlan.

'I've only just arrived, but I am, aye,' he agreed.

'Good. There is someone I've been wanting you to meet. Forgive me, Lady Regina, but I must steal the laird away for just a moment.'

'It's no trouble at all,' she heard herself say. Though really, was there any other answer?

The laird bowed to her and said, 'I will only be a moment.' To the viscount, he added, 'You should ask the lady to dance.'

Regina waited until he had left before she turned back to Lord Camford. 'Thank you, but I still don't wish to dance.' Instead, she preferred to return to her father's side and pretend as if she were having a good time.

'Are you all right, Lady Regina?' the viscount asked gently. His voice held a warmth that invited her to share her fears. Though, of course, that was impossible.

She felt like such an outsider here, and no matter how she tried to fit in, it would never happen. Instead, she braved a smile, and answered, 'I am fine.'

Even though she wasn't.

Lachlan followed the duchess, but as he strode through the ballroom, he could not ignore the open stares from women or worse, a few who sighed and smiled at him. It felt as if there were prying eyes upon him at every moment, and he tensed at all the attention. He tried to think of what Frances would say, and the memory of her calm voice seemed to cut through his apprehension.

Behave as if you are above them all.

He took that to heart and straightened his posture, staring straight ahead as he continued down the hallway. The duchess led him to the far end of the ballroom. 'You asked me to help Frances Goodson. I spoke with my husband to see what could be done. At first, I was not certain, especially given her past circumstances.'

'She needs a second chance,' he said softly. 'Someone should give her the life she deserves.' Even if it could never be him.

'I agree. And so, I decided to honour your request. Though she cannot truly join the guests, I invited her to the house. I found a temporary position for her with my aunt. Miss Goodson wanted to see you tonight, and she is waiting in the music room.' The duchess gestured towards one of the open doors.

Her declaration brought an unexpected tightness to his throat, mingled with longing. Though it had only been a few days since he'd seen Frances, it had bothered him to leave her alone.

'The door is open, so I would not advise you to stay with her for very long, for anyone could come by.'

He thanked her and walked to the threshold while the duchess returned to the ballroom. Frances was wearing a faded gown the colour of red wine, with short puffed sleeves and a high waistline. She wore no jewels, and her curling blonde hair was swept into an elaborate arrangement, twined with a matching ribbon. Though her poverty was obvious, the sight of her stole his breath.

The moment she saw him, her face lit up with joy. 'Locharr, you do look dashing. Is the ball-room floor lined with swooning ladies?' Her tone was teasing, but he caught the trace of sincerity in her compliment.

'I had to step over their bodies,' he quipped. Then he turned serious. 'How have you been?'

'Very well, thank you.' Her voice was cheerful, and yet he thought he detected a note of falsehood about it. 'I noticed that you sent your footman to enquire after my welfare several times.'

'I dinna care for where you're staying, Frances. It's no' verra safe.' If he could have afforded the expense, he would have bought her another house in a better part of town. Instead, he could only send a servant to watch over her from time to time.

'I won't be there for much longer. Her Grace has helped me to find a new post. I understand that you asked her on my behalf.' She squared her shoulders as if to end the subject, but it didn't make him feel any better. It occurred to him that she could face even more danger in a new household. What if her employer tried to force himself upon her? She would have no means of defending herself.

But you did the same, his conscience chided. His mood darkened at the realisation that other men could behave in the same way he had. Stealing kisses from an innocent woman, tempting her towards sin.

'Where will you stay?' he forced himself to ask.

'I will be acting as nursemaid to a little boy. I believe he is a year old.' The colour rose on her cheeks, and she added, 'His parents, Lord and Lady Arnsbury, are travelling. It's only for a short while, but I will stay and look after him.'

'That's good.' The words were the correct answer, though he didn't believe them at all. With a glance back at the ballroom, he asked, 'Will you come and join the guests?'

She shook her head. 'I fear too many people know me. It would cause a great scandal, and that is the last thing you or the duchess needs right now.'

'And so you intend to skulk in the shadows.'

'Happily.' She smiled at him, and her eyes softened. 'I can hear the music from here and dance alone where no one will trouble me. And sometimes I can catch a glimpse of the gowns and imagine stories about the men and women.'

It sounded unbearably lonely, but he didn't

tell her that. Instead, he remained where he was, memorising the curve of her face, the beauty of her eyes.

'You have to go back, Locharr,' she told him.

'I ken that.' And still, he didn't move.

Her smile faded, and she finally said, 'Don't make this any more difficult than it has to be, Lachlan.' Her river-green eyes held yearning, as if she wanted nothing more than to take his hand.

His heart stumbled at the thought of leaving her behind and courting another woman. It was the hardest thing in the world to turn and walk away.

Frances kept her gaze fixed upon the laird's shoulders as he returned to the ballroom. *You don't belong here,* her conscience warned. If anyone discovered her presence, she would be shunned. After her ruin in society, the guests would be horrified to find her here.

But the truth was, she had wanted to come. After Her Grace had spoken of the nursemaid position for her aunt, she had invited Frances to return later during the ball. Though she'd known it was wrong, Frances had wanted to witness Lachlan's triumphant return to society from the shadows.

She had worn her best gown, though she had no intention of being seen by anyone. She had also entered the house through the servants' quarters, hours before the other guests had arrived. The duchess had allowed her to sit in a small room near the kitchens. It had been pleasant, listening to the servants talking amongst themselves while delicious aromas wafted through the air.

And now, she was hidden in the music room, away from the guests. She ventured towards the doorway, peering out at the ball. There was no one nearby, so she took a step forward. Then another. It was only because she wanted a better view of the guests, she told herself. Not because she was wishing to be part of the celebration.

Frances stood a few feet away from the doorway, remembering when she had been a welcome guest at gatherings such as this. She had danced with gentlemen and conversed with friends, and she had enjoyed sumptuous food and delicious strained juices. As the music played, she entertained herself by swaying and performing the steps alone.

The dancers spun, and she saw Lachlan among them. Several women were eyeing him with interest, and she was startled to realise that it bothered her. Lady Regina was not there, but the other ladies smiled openly at the laird. Frances studied the ballroom, searching for the heiress. Then, without warning, a woman came up behind her. She was startled to see Lady Rumford, the duke's aunt.

'My dear, whatever are you doing, hiding in the shadows?' She pressed her hand to Frances's spine and pushed her forward. 'You simply must join in, as one of the guests.'

'Oh, no, I couldn't. I was only here because—'

'Nonsense. Come with me.' Lady Rumford linked her arm in hers, and she led her into the ballroom. Had the matron forgotten about the scandal? It had been four years since Frances had suffered the humiliation of her ruin. Was it possible that it was all in the past?

'Lady Rumford, please. I cannot.'

But the matron would hear nothing of it and guided her into the room. The moment Frances stepped among the guests, people began to stare and whisper. She felt her cheeks burn with embarrassment, knowing she'd been right all along. No one had forgotten the shame or the scandal.

'Put your chin up, my dear, and behave as if you don't care a whit what they think.'

Despite the matron's insistence that she join the others, Frances had no intention of doing so. 'I need to leave,' she said to Lady Rumford. 'I shouldn't even be here.'

Lady Rumford stopped and held her arm, preventing her from fleeing. 'Stand and face them down, Miss Goodson. You are an invited guest, and if you are good enough for His Grace, the Duke of Worthingstone, then you belong here.'

She didn't believe that at all, regardless of what the matron had said. Instead, Frances was fully conscious of the smirks and the women leaning in to gossip with one another. 'I wasn't truly invited, Lady Rumford. I'm sorry, but this was a mistake.'

She had never expected to be among the guests, and she wasn't ready for it. But before she could tear herself away from the woman's grasp, she saw Lady Regina standing near the refreshment table. Beside the young woman was Dalton St George, Viscount Camford. And from her demeanour, Lady Regina appeared fascinated by their conversation. There was a slight smile upon her face.

At once, Frances's embarrassment faded as she recognised the potential problem. Was Lord Camford courting Lady Regina? And, worse, was Lady Regina interested in the viscount? She searched the crowd for a glimpse of the laird, hoping he would return to the lady's side. But when she finally spied Lachlan, he was surrounded by matrons and their daughters.

Lady Rumford brought Frances towards the Duke of Worthingstone. She knew the man but had never been formally introduced. He had dark blond hair and intelligent green eyes that missed nothing. His wife, the duchess, appeared concerned at her presence, but remained silent.

'Your Grace, may I introduce Miss Frances Goodson?' Lady Rumford said to the duke. To Frances, she said, 'Please meet my nephew, Jonathan Nottoway, His Grace the Duke of Worthingstone. And, of course, you've already met his wife Victoria, Her Grace the Duchess.'

Frances sank into a deep curtsy and then murmured, 'Your Grace.'

Her face felt hot, and she knew the guests were staring at her with disapproval. But she understood what Lady Rumford was trying to do. If the Duke of Worthingstone accepted her, then it was a mark of public forgiveness for her past transgressions.

But before he could acknowledge her, there came a screeching sound from the opposite side of the ballroom. A matron was calling out for help, while her daughter had fainted at Lachlan's feet.

Frances saw the shock in his eyes and predicted what he would do. He was going to behave like a gallant knight, sweeping her into his arms and carrying her to safety.

Don't do it, she thought silently. It would mean utter disaster for his courtship of Lady Regina.

'Pardon me, Your Grace,' Frances said, hurrying towards them. She knew it was a serious breach of etiquette to abandon a duke, but Lachlan was about to do something even worse. She hardly cared that she was shoving her way past the guests until she reached his side.

She took the laird's arm and pulled him backwards. In a low voice, she warned, 'Do not touch her.'

'She fainted,' he replied, as if that weren't obvious enough.

'It's a ploy. You were about to lift her into your arms and carry her off, weren't you?'

Lachlan eyed her as if he saw nothing wrong with this. 'Well, I wasna about to leave her lying on the floor.'

'If you touch her, you'll have to wed her.'

His gaze narrowed. 'Why would I have to be doing that?'

'For touching her in public.' Frances eyed him in all seriousness. 'You must never touch a lady you don't intend to wed.' She led him another step back. 'Look. Her mother has smelling salts.'

His mouth set in a hard line. 'Would a lady truly do such a thing to trap a man?'

'If she wants him badly enough.' Frances let her shoulders relax, now that the danger was over. 'I must go now. People are already talking about me.'

She didn't allow him the chance to argue, but instead hurried towards the door. As she passed the duke and duchess, she quietly begged their forgiveness for the intrusion.

There hadn't been any other choice. Her presence was damaging, and it was far better to depart and leave them to enjoy the ball. She had helped Lachlan avoid a devastating pitfall, and that was enough to satisfy her.

Frances took one last longing glance at the ballroom and resigned herself to the reality that she would never be part of society again. None of that mattered any more. She would move heaven and earth to help Lachlan gain the means to protect his clan.

Even if that meant marrying someone else.

It was late in the morning when Lachlan knocked at the door of the boarding house where Frances was staying. He wanted to ensure that she was all right, after she'd left last night. She had seemed embarrassed and uncertain at the ball, and he understood that it had not been her choice to join the guests. But then, she hadn't wanted to offend Lady Rumford, the duke's aunt.

Lachlan had been grateful for Frances's intervention after the young debutante had fainted. He hadn't thought there would be any harm in carrying her over to a chair. But now, he was beginning to understand that society rules were more intricate than he'd imagined. He had barely avoided a mess he'd never anticipated.

An older woman with white hair pulled into a topknot answered the door. She took one look at Lachlan, and he saw her eyes brighten with interest.

'Can I help you, milord?' She opened the door wider.

'I came to pay a call upon Miss Goodson.' He handed her his card. 'Would you be so good as to see if she is receiving?'

'Receiving? Well, aren't we high and mighty? Who are you, then?'

He was about to point out that she was holding the calling card with his name but realised she likely couldn't read. 'Just tell her that the Laird of Locharr is here.'

'Tell her yourself. She lives just up those stairs.'

Lachlan was taken aback by the woman's lack of manners. She mocked him with a curtsy as he passed, and he wondered if anyone else had attempted to visit Frances. He took a single step on the wooden stairs, and the board sagged beneath his weight. It seemed that he was risking his life with each step upward. The interior of the boarding house smelled rancid, with a hint of old fish.

Three years, Frances had said. She had lived

here for three years. He couldn't fathom such a thing. Just as he was about to knock on her door, another door opened down the hall.

'Don't move,' came a man's voice. Lachlan raised his hands and turned slowly. A burly man with a brown beard was holding a revolver. His clothing was faded, but it appeared to have been a sailor's uniform from years ago.

'You must be Mr Belfast,' Lachlan predicted. 'Miss Goodson spoke of you.'

'She's not here,' the man said. 'Now be on your way.'

The man's eyes were shadowed, and he had a nervous twitch. Lachlan wasn't about to make a wrong move, for he had no doubt Mr Belfast would pull the trigger.

'She doesna belong in a place like this,' Lachlan said. 'You ken this as well as I.'

There was a faint nod. 'Were you going to marry her, then?'

The man's question startled Lachlan. A sudden vision took hold, of what it would be like to live each day with Frances at his side. To see her smile, to hear her laughter. To tease her and draw her into his arms at night. The image was so real, he wished his choices were different. It felt as if he were chained into another man's life, one where he had to marry for the sake of his people. His own feelings didn't matter. Frances had no dowry, and he needed to wed an heiress for his people to survive. And more than that, he owed it to his father's memory.

'I would be happy to wed a woman like Miss Goodson,' Lachlan answered truthfully. And at that, Mr Belfast lowered his revolver.

'Good. She deserves better.'

'Aye, she does.' He lowered his hands, now that the danger of being shot was past. 'I am trying to make arrangements for her,' he said. 'Until I can get her out of this place, what does she need? Blankets or food?'

Mr Belfast eyed her door. 'Blankets, coal. Better food. She's hardly more than a wisp of grass, as little as she is.'

Lachlan nodded, intending to send supplies to the older gentleman, as well as Frances. It was clear that Belfast considered himself to be her guardian of sorts. He thanked the man and returned down the stairs, thankful that he hadn't fallen through the treads. But a dark frustration pulled at his conscience. He couldn't just walk away from Frances Goodson and abandon her. Not after all she had done for him.

His mind turned over the problem as he returned to his coach. Tonight, he intended to meet with his friends—Dalton, Jonathan, and Gabriel. A bottle of brandy might help them sort matters out. Or perhaps the duchess might have a means of helping Frances.

And when the time came, Lachlan would find a better place for her.

Frances turned the key to her room, and her heart nearly stopped. A warm fire was burning at the hearth, and there was a small table covered with a white cloth and laden with delicious food. She blinked, wondering if she had only imagined it. When the vision did not fade, she stepped inside and pushed back the rush of emotion gathering within. The thin mattress and blanket upon her bed had been replaced with a feather bed, pillows, and several warm quilts.

She walked towards the table and saw a card with a simple note upon it.

From Lachlan

Frances sank into a chair, feeling as if her emotions were about to break. Why had he done this? The gift was something she had never expected…and yet, she was so grateful. She slipped off her worn shoes and sat on a stool beside the table. For a moment, she savoured the sight of the food, imagining how delicious it would be.

She reached for a hot bun and bit into it, tasting the soft bread. There was even a small container of butter and another of raspberry jam. He had remembered her fondness for jam. As she ate, she ignored the tears welling up in her eyes.

She had been so very stupid. She had *known* better than to lower her defences. And yet, her foolish heart had dreamed of being with the laird. She had fallen in love with a man she couldn't have.

Even if he were not promised to Lady Regina, she could not wed him. She was ruined, her life ridden with scandal. He deserved a virtuous woman with no shadows to mar the future.

No one had forgotten her past, and she could not show her face in public again. Her ears had burned with the gossip, and she'd wanted nothing more than to run away. Which, she had, as soon as she had warned Lachlan about the young miss's ploy. She didn't regret her warning, even if it had earned her an enemy.

Frances wrapped up the leftover food and cleared it away. Her elbow accidentally knocked a fork to the floor, and when she got down on her knees to pick it up, she spied something beneath the bed. She reached for it and pulled out a worn scrap of flannel.

The moment she touched it, it felt as if an invisible blade had stabbed her in the heart. She crumpled the flannel against her breast and sat against the bed on the floor. This was the blanket that had held the body of her child. The tiny son, born months too soon. The midwife had wrapped the infant in this flannel and given the baby to her.

The pain struck her down with a grief so fierce, she could scarcely breathe. The morning of her son's death, she had wept ragged tears. After an hour, the midwife had taken the child away. Later that day, they had buried him atop a hillside overlooking the river. A piece of her heart was buried with the infant, and never again would she be the same.

Frances folded the cloth and placed it within a trunk amid her clothes, wishing she could shut away the memories so easily. But she would never forget the slight weight in her arms or the fragile angel's face that haunted her, even now.

It was as if God had punished her for her sins with the death of her child.

Were it not for her seduction and loss of innocence, she could have been among the debutantes flirting with Lachlan. She could have danced with him without fear of bringing shame upon his good name. Instead, she had succumbed to temptation and had paid a devastating price.

She sat down on the feather bed and was enfolded in delicious warmth. For a moment, she imagined what it would be like to sleep next to Lachlan. She closed her eyes, wishing he were here.

Why had he brought her all these gifts? It was a crushing blow that hurt even worse than she could have imagined. For it meant that he cared about her. Perhaps he even loved her, though he had sworn to wed Lady Regina.

It was a physical ache to love a man she could never have. And as she fell into a deep slumber, she let the tears fall.

Chapter Ten

Lachlan sat among his friends, a glass of brandy at his side. Worthingstone had a glint in his eyes, like a man who held a winning hand of cards. MacKinnon was frowning, as if he didn't like what he'd been dealt, but he shrugged. Camford sorted through his own hand, but he appeared distracted.

'So this…marriage was arranged when you were children, is that it?' Camford asked.

Lachlan nodded. 'Our fathers were friends for years, you ken? Regina's father told mine that he wanted us to wed, but she had to agree to the marriage. In return, her dowry will help my clan.'

'Does she want to marry you?' MacKinnon asked, leading off with an ace.

Lachlan dropped a low three, following suit. 'I dinna think she wants to wed anyone, truth to tell. She doesna seem like any of the other ladies. It's almost as if she's scared of something.'

'Scared of you?' Camford teased. 'With that scar, I can't think why.'

'There's no reason to be.' He'd tried to be kind to Regina, bringing her lemonade. He had even danced with her once, though she had put him off several times. Even then, she would barely meet his gaze. He had no idea how he would gain her consent—not when she seemed so reluctant.

'What of your governess?' MacKinnon prompted. 'She's a bonny one.'

His grip tightened upon his cards. 'Leave her alone, Gabe. She's no' for you.'

His friend sent him a mocking smile. Though Gabriel MacKinnon had been widowed years ago, Lachlan wasn't entirely certain whether the man had got over his wife's death. It seemed as if he flirted with women and that was all. But Lachlan didn't want the man to dally with Frances.

The duke took the next trick and then admitted, 'Toria asked me to find a post for her. I am sorry if Miss Goodson was embarrassed the other night by idle gossip.'

Lachlan was torn between wanting to know the truth and wanting them to hold silent about the past. But at last, he met the duke's gaze. 'What happened to her?'

Worthingstone arranged his cards and thought a moment. 'It was years ago. She made her debut, and Viscount Nelson was quite taken with her beauty. He gave her all his attention, and she was overcome by it. He seduced her and disappeared.'

Ice spread through Lachlan's veins. He wished he could tear Lord Nelson apart for what he'd done to Frances. It was a mercy that the viscount was not in London.

'Where did she go afterwards?' Lachlan asked.

'I cannot say,' Worthingstone finished. 'She never showed her face in society again. Her father left, and I don't believe she's had any contact with her family.' He cleared his throat. 'There was a rumour of a child, but no one knows.'

Lachlan shouldn't care. It wasn't truly his concern. And yet, he remembered Frances's devastating grief after she had seen Abigail and Kenneth's baby boy. She had cried like a mother whose child had been torn from her arms. The pieces fit, and it startled him that he felt the echo of her grief. No parent should have to surrender her child.

'She deserves better than the life she has now,' Lachlan told the duke. 'Thank you for finding a post for her.'

Worthingstone nodded and laid down a card.

They played another round, and when Camford took the next trick, he asked, 'Will you ask for Lady Regina's hand in marriage?'

'Soon,' Lachlan answered. He needed to make a better connection with Regina, to overcome her fears and gain her consent.

But he sensed that a ball was not the way to win Regina's consent. She held herself apart from everyone else. Instead, he wondered if she might enjoy an outing of some kind. Perhaps a carriage ride along Rotten Row or a picnic.

His conscience warned that he was courting two women. It wasn't right to give gifts to Frances while he was trying to gain Lady Regina's hand in marriage. But then, he couldn't bear to see his governess living in such poverty.

More than all else, he intended to get her out of the boarding house—by any means necessary.

'I cannot tell you how grateful I am for your help.' Charlotte Larkspur, the Countess of Arnsbury, bounced her son on one hip. 'Matthew has been crying for the last hour. My husband and I are trying to pack for our journey, and he won't settle down.'

The young boy was stuffing his fist in his mouth and sobbing. He seemed to be about a year old or perhaps a few months older. Frances couldn't tell if he had all his teeth, but it was possible that he was in pain from an earache.

'Would you like me to hold him for a while?' she offered. 'That would allow you to make your preparations.'

The countess handed over the boy, who wailed when he was taken from his mother's arms. Frances patted him on the back and bounced him. She asked, 'May I take him outside into your garden for a little while? A change in his surroundings may help.'

The countess nodded. 'Of course.'

Frances thanked her and brought the crying boy with her downstairs. Once he was away from his mother, he arched his back and screamed.

'I know you're having a hard day,' Frances soothed. 'Let's go outside and see the flowers, shall we? Oh, I know there aren't many in bloom, but perhaps we'll see a crocus or two. Let's go and have a look.'

She continued bouncing him and after a time, his screams turned into more crying. It was like a knife digging into her heart with every step— not only because of his pain, but because of her own grief. This could have been her own baby, had he lived.

Her position as a nursemaid was only for a week while the earl and countess visited Brighton on holiday. It was their anniversary, and they wanted some quiet time alone. And although Frances had accepted the post, she had been unprepared for the heartache. Enduring the past few years should have been enough to silence the grief of losing her son. Now, she was beginning to realise that the pain would never fully end. She would remember him every time she saw another infant.

When she looked at Matthew's reddened, crying face, she saw Oliver's pale, white cheeks. Instead of cold, still flesh, the boy's body was warm and squirming with pain as he sobbed.

Tears swelled within her eyes, but Frances pressed a kiss against his forehead, talking to him all the way. She made her way into the kitchens and asked the cook for a crust of bread. Then she offered it to the young boy, who grabbed it and began gnawing. Almost immediately, his crying quieted, and she took him with her.

'There now. That feels better, doesn't it?' It must have been teething, then. She walked with him towards the far end of the hall that led into the small courtyard. Then she opened the door and took him outside into the garden. The air was cool, but the sunshine lifted her mood. As she walked with the child, her grief quieted. She sat with him on a stone bench, talking about the delicious crust of bread and how good it must feel against his gums.

She glanced up and saw the earl and the countess watching her from the window. The earl put his arm around Lady Arnsbury, and Frances looked away to give them privacy. This was the sort of life she had always imagined for herself. A nobleman as a husband. A townhouse in Mayfair. A child in her arms.

Tears welled up in her eyes, for this was what she had wanted for her own life. She wished she could start over, somewhere no one knew her. Although she had ruined her reputation in London, was that any reason to resign herself to a life with no children of her own? She cuddled baby Matthew, wondering if she dared to reach for a new dream. She could pretend to be a widow. Or perhaps she could move far away and begin again.

An invisible blade thrust into her heart, for the man she wanted was Lachlan. She had always known he could never be hers. And yet, she had fallen in love with him. She wanted to spend every moment of every day at his side. She wanted to make a home for him and bear him children. But in her heart, she knew he deserved better than a fallen woman. He should wed a woman like Regina, a virtuous lady who could hold her head up in society.

The baby had fallen asleep in her arms, and Frances cradled him close. If only she had twenty thousand pounds as a dowry. The thought was so ridiculous, she almost smiled through her tears. She barely had twenty pounds, much less twenty thousand. And even if she did, the money would not erase the sins of her past.

No, she had to walk away from the man she loved and try to go on without him. No matter how much it hurt.

Lachlan had tried his best to gain Lady Regina's interest, but she seemed distracted during tea. He had followed Frances's instructions precisely, giving a calling card to the footman and being careful not to spill the tea or break china.

Despite his best efforts, Regina had paid him little heed. At the moment, her gaze was transfixed upon the window as if she couldn't wait for Lachlan to depart.

'The weather seems fair enough,' he remarked.

She nodded but gave no reply. It was exactly as Frances had predicted. The woman appeared to be a frozen statue of ice, with nothing at all to say. He tried again, 'What do you enjoy doing in your spare time?'

She blinked a moment and said, 'I'm sorry, what did you say?'

'I asked if there was anything you enjoyed in your spare time. Whist, perhaps?' He had enjoyed cheating at cards with his governess and wondered if Regina would have a competitive nature, as well.

She took a sip of her tea. 'Cards aren't my favourite pastime, I fear.'

'Then what? Watercolours? Reading? Hunting boar?' The last one slipped out before he could stop himself.

She choked, and for the first time, he saw a spark of life within her eyes. 'I cannot say that I've ever hunted boar.'

He decided to press it further. 'Wolves, then? Or dragons, perhaps.'

The amusement deepened, and her lips curved in a smile. 'I have been known to hunt down my cat when she refuses to come in at night. Unfortunately, Belinda believes in staying out all night when she finds mice as her prey.'

'Is she here now?'

Regina shrugged. 'I imagine she is asleep on my father's papers in the study.'

For the first time, he saw a slight ease in her cool demeanour, as if there were a flesh-and-blood woman behind her shyness. And though Frances had warned against it, he decided to be open with Lady Regina.

'I thought we could have a word about our meddling fathers.' There was no reason to delay the conversation, for it was his entire reason for coming to London. He sensed that Regina would prefer openness and honesty, rather than a drawn-out courtship.

The truth was, he doubted if he could ever have feelings for her, the way he felt for Frances. Theirs would be an arrangement, nothing more.

Regina's rigidity returned, along with the façade of ice. 'What do you mean?'

'You ken that our fathers wanted to arrange a match between us,' Lachlan said. 'They were good friends, and it was my father's dying wish that we be married.'

'No,' she answered hastily. 'I do not intend to marry.'

The anxiety on her face raised his suspicions about her aversion. She appeared frightened, which made him wonder what had happened to evoke such a response. He thought about prying, but Frances had warned him not to be too forceful.

Instead, he tried a different tact. 'I ken that you have your life here and that you dinna wish to change it. But if you would consider a life in Scotland, I swear to you that I would make no demands upon you as a wife. We would live as friends, and you'd have your own room.'

That got her attention, and she stared at him. 'What about children? What if I don't wish to— that is, what if—?' Her cheeks burned scarlet, but he understood her meaning.

'It could wait several years,' he promised. 'We are both young enough, and my first concern is to my clan. The winter was harsh, and they've no' had verra much food. I need to provide for them.' It was a veiled hint at her dowry, but she did not seem offended. Rather, her face turned thoughtful.

'Are you saying that it would be a marriage where you would…allow me to be alone?'

'No' precisely,' he answered. 'You would live with me at Locharr and help me look after the people. I would expect you to be mistress of the household and take on those duties. But consummating our marriage could wait until later.'

It was the best he could do. And if she agreed, it would satisfy his father's last wishes and save Locharr.

This time, she seemed to consider his offer. 'I will think about it.' Then she added, 'Would you care for more tea?'

He shook his head. 'In truth, I dinna care for tea. But I'll have another sandwich.'

She offered him the plate, and he took a sandwich with buttered bread and minced ham. It wasn't nearly enough to satisfy his appetite, but he followed the manners Frances had taught him. Lady Regina poured herself another cup of tea and took a biscuit from the tray. She nibbled at it, and admitted, 'I must say, I was not expecting this conversation. At least, not so soon. And not from someone who used to play such terrible tricks on me.'

'I was an angel,' he lied with a teasing grin. 'I dinna ken what you are talking about.'

'You tied my hair in knots. My maid spent most of the day trying to untangle it. You were a horrid boy.'

I still am, he thought, but didn't say it. He was struck by the differences between the two women. Frances with her curling blonde hair and Regina with her straight red hair. The young woman seated across from him had impeccable manners, just as Frances had. But his governess had charmed him with her friendly smile and encouragement. Being with Frances made him feel whole and capable of overcoming any obstacle. Regina, in contrast, had an invisible wall surrounding her. Only today had he glimpsed any warmth at all. And while he knew she was considering the marriage, another part of him rebelled against it. He knew, in his gut, that she would be unhappy in Scotland. This poised lady would be appalled at a Scottish *ceilidh*, and he couldn't imagine her riding out to visit with his clansmen in the way Frances would.

He should have been thankful that Lady Regina was considering his suit. Instead, his conscience pricked him with the realisation that this was wrong. They didn't belong together.

Yet, what choice did he have? He needed her dowry to save his people. Twenty thousand pounds was life-changing for everyone. He owed it to his father's memory to fulfil Tavin's last wishes and unite their families.

It rather felt like he was selling his soul in exchange. He would live with Lady Regina, although they would remain in separate rooms. There would be little interaction between them, beyond meals together. The idea of such a marriage was cold and not at all welcome.

Lachlan finished his sandwich, aware of the awkward silence stretching between them. But what else could he say? In the end, he said, 'Thank you for the tea. I would be glad if you'd think about my offer of marriage.'

Lady Regina rose from her chair, and he did the same. She held out her hand, but he did not lean down to kiss it. It felt wrong to do so. Instead, he squeezed it gently and muttered a farewell.

'I will send word when I have made a decision,' she said.

He nodded but found it strange that he had no sense of triumph. As he departed, he could not help but think that he was betraying Frances.

Yet, he could not afford to be selfish and make decisions based on desire rather than duty.

He returned to the hackney cab and rode back to Worthingstone's townhouse in brooding silence.

After a week of caring for young Matthew, Frances was grateful for the return of Lord and Lady Arnsbury. Not because the child had been difficult—on the contrary. She had loved every moment of caring for him. It had given her a taste of the motherhood she'd never had.

But it was strange to return to her tiny room where the remnants of Lachlan's gifts remained. She paused to stare at her surroundings. The blankets he had given her were still there, and she remembered the food and drinks he had provided.

A heaviness settled within her, but she reminded herself that at least she'd had a few months to enjoy the fairy-tale.

She heard a knock at the door and went to answer it. 'Who is it?' she called out through the door.

'Someone who doesna ken which fork to use,' came a familiar voice.

A swell of delight warmed her heart when she realised it was Lachlan. She threw open the door and couldn't suppress her smile. He wore a white shirt and black coat, a black waistcoat, and buff-coloured trousers. His cravat was slightly askew, and she welcomed him inside. 'Come in.'

He removed his hat, and she closed the door behind him.

'This is no' verra proper, is it?' he remarked, taking a step closer. The reddened scar upon his cheek made him seem even more fierce. And yet, she warmed at the sight of him.

'It's scandalous.' Her voice came out in a whisper, but she could hardly stop herself from drawing near. It had been a week since she'd seen him, and she hadn't known it was possible to miss him so much. Her brain was screeching at her to stop, for this would only deepen her heartache. But she could only drink in the sight of this man, wishing that he could be with her.

'Why are you here?' she asked.

'Because I canna let you stay in a place like this. I won't have it.' He reached for her hand. The touch of his gloved palm against hers was a thin barrier, but she could feel the heat of his skin.

'I'll be all right.'

'No.' He pulled her hand into the crook of his arm. 'This place ought to burn to the ground. It's no' fit for mice, let alone a lady.'

'I'm not your concern any more, Lachlan.' She pulled her hand free of his arm and stepped back. 'You have someone else. And I heard that you asked her to marry you.' It hadn't taken long for word to spread, especially since Lady Regina had not refused his offer. Lady Arnsbury had voiced the gossip after she had returned from her travels with her husband. Everyone in London was agog at the possibility of the Lady of Ice choosing a husband.

'You ken I have no choice. I'm no' able to have what I truly want.'

'And what do you want?' she demanded.

Lachlan crushed her into his embrace, seizing her mouth in a kiss that told her how much he'd missed her. Frances melted against him, kissing him back with all the unspoken words inside her heart. She wanted so badly to imagine that he'd come here to take her away with him, to marry her and live with her for always.

Against her mouth, he said, 'I'm bringing you to the duchess. She has friends and will find somewhere else for you to live.'

Even as he spoke, he was kissing her, his hands running down her spine. She was caught up in his touch, unable to grasp her thoughts. Warnings trickled through her mind like droplets of water, falling away.

She wanted him so badly, a wicked part of her wondered if she ought to surrender herself. Would he stay if she gave him what they both wanted? The terrible thought took root and grew. For a moment, she considered it, for she loved this man. She wanted to be with him, more than anything.

Lachlan continued his siege against her mouth, and he kissed her until she could barely breathe. A rush of sensation poured over her, and she faltered, wondering what she was doing. He could not stay with her. His clan's needs came before her own. It was a dream to be with him, nothing more.

With reluctance, she forced herself to break away. 'Lachlan,' she whispered, 'there is another reason why you are here. Tell me.'

He met her gaze, and in his eyes, she saw the hunger. 'To say goodbye.' He framed her face with his hands. 'My life is no' my own to give. It's tearing me up inside.'

A tear spilled over her cheek, and he wiped it away with his thumb. His words were both a blessing and a dagger within her heart. 'I'm in love with you, Frances Goodson. From the first moment you danced with me.'

She loved this man, and the wisest course was to send him away. They both knew that nothing could come of their feelings. And yet, she wanted to claim a few moments more.

Her heart pounded within her chest, and she

leaned in to kiss him again. 'I love you, too, Lachlan. I only wish things were different.'

His mouth worshipped hers and his hands moved to the buttons of her gown. She froze when he flicked the top button open. His blue eyes burned into hers with desire that mirrored her own. Her brain warned her to stop, for if she allowed him to touch her, it would only end in seduction. Just as before, she was overwhelmed by the physical needs rising within. But with each button, she felt her inhibitions slipping away.

'I'm needing to touch you, lass. One last time before I canna see you again.' His words were hungry against her throat, and when his hands caressed her skin, she felt the echo between her legs.

It was dangerous to surrender, but then again, she was already a fallen woman. Her mistakes had branded her for the remainder of her life. What did one more scandal matter? He was going away, and this might be the last time she ever saw him.

The stubble of his beard was rough against her bare skin when he removed her stays and chemise. Every touch was a memory sinking deeper into her heart. She yielded to him, offering herself. Lachlan kissed a path down to her bare breasts, and when his mouth closed over one nipple, she shuddered. She gripped his head, and he worshipped her.

Frances helped him remove his shirt, and when she touched his back, the heat of his skin ignited her own desires.

'Would to God that I could take you as my bride,' he murmured against her skin. He lifted her to the narrow bed and lay atop her. Their bodies fit together in a way that healed the broken pieces of her heart. She knew it was wrong to steal this part of him.

But right now, he still belonged to her. Regina had not yet accepted his suit, and there was no betrayal. Not yet. And so, Frances intended to accept his offering, giving of herself in return.

'Kiss me,' she pleaded. He did, claiming her mouth with an intensity that made her forget all reason. His tongue slid against hers in the mimicry of lovemaking, and she arched her back with a sigh. At the apex of her legs, she could feel his hard length beneath his trousers.

'I want to see all of you, Frances,' he murmured. 'Will you allow this?'

She loosened the laces of her petticoat and helped him draw it over her hips. Lachlan removed the layers of clothing, until she lay atop her narrow bed. Then he unbuttoned his trousers and removed his small clothes. For a moment, he lay beside her, his gaze heated as he drank in the sight of her. She ought to feel embarrassed, so bared before him. Instead, it was a moment of intimacy, as if the rest of the world fell away, and it was only herself and Lachlan.

He cupped her breasts, stroking her nipples and driving her wild with need. She was aching, so wet between her legs as she craved him. His head moved lower to her stomach, his hot breath making her quiver. As he kissed a path towards her womanhood, she touched his hair, feeling apprehensive about his intentions. He pressed her legs apart and groaned at the sight of her. 'Lass, I want you so badly, I canna stand it.'

'I am ready,' she breathed, opening her legs wider. But instead of thrusting inside her, he bent to kiss the seam of her opening. The moment his tongue touched her, she gasped in shock. He licked her, nibbling at the hooded flesh above her opening, and it was as if he had lit her on fire. She cried out, her hands fisting the coverlet as he feasted upon her flesh. A rising wave of arousal gathered into a pulsing shudder, and she convulsed against him when he used his tongue to stroke her. She was sobbing with need, and her release came upon her unexpectedly, a quaking sensation that possessed her and sent her over the edge. Only then did Lachlan draw back, his eyes burning into hers.

'Now you are ready, lass. And I'm going

to pleasure you again until you can no longer stand.'

With that, he poised atop her, a silent question between them. Frances flushed, for she was not an innocent. She knew the risks of giving herself to the man she loved. She could become pregnant again. And yet, she wanted this stolen moment as a memory she would hold on to for always. Even when he had gone, she would have this.

'Do you need me to stop?' he asked. His voice was rigid, on the edge of frustration. 'God help me, Frances, but I want you too much.'

'No, I don't want you to stop.' This man was everything to her, and it was nothing at all like her past shame. This moment was about healing the broken pieces of each other, surrendering her heart. Even if her worst fears came true and there was a child, she would love it because it was a part of Lachlan.

She guided him inside, raising her knees to let him go deeper. He slid into her, and the sensation was so good, she gasped and squeezed him within her body. There was no pain, only pleasure.

His own breath caught, but he continued to press deeper until their hips met. Lachlan never took his gaze from her, but he made love to her tenderly, his hands lacing with hers. Frances met his thrusts, keeping her eyes open as they joined together.

'I love you,' she whispered, and he cupped her hips, using his shaft to caress her deep inside.

'I love you, too.' He took her nipple in his mouth, and the sensation caused her to raise her hips, squeezing him again. They found a rhythm, and she met him, thrust for thrust. She wrapped her legs around his waist, and he turned her until she was seated atop him.

'I am yours, Frances Goodson. To do with as you will.'

She rose up on her knees and descended, taking him into her body. The tension on his face held suppressed need, and she decided to take command. She quickened the pace, riding him hard as he held her hips. Over and over, she took him inside, watching as his breathing came in rhythmic pants. He was on the edge, and she dragged it out longer, wanting to make it last. When he was near his own release, she withdrew and stood before him. His expression was raw with need, his eyes dark with desire.

'I am yours, Lachlan MacKinloch,' she echoed. Then she lay upon her stomach against the bed and spread her legs apart. 'To do with as you will.'

He did not resist but lifted her hips and guided his shaft inside her from behind. The new position brought him deeper, and she felt herself beginning tremble. He pumped deep inside, his breathing ragged as he took her body. His hands moved to her breasts again, and this time when he stroked the nipples, she spasmed against him. It was too much, the sensation of him claiming her, coupled with the soft caresses upon her breasts. She could not stop the sound that escaped her, the half-scream of unexpected pleasure that jolted through her.

He came inside her then, his thrusting so hard, she found another release that slammed through her. She was half crying with ecstasy, and his groans mingled with her own until he collapsed against her, satiated.

Neither spoke. Frances didn't want to move for fear that he would withdraw. Her body was rosy from lovemaking, her muscles pliant from the shattering pleasure he had given.

'Frances,' he whispered at last, his thumb drawing a circle against her nipple. She couldn't bring herself to respond. They had taken a grave risk this night, but she refused to let herself care. At this moment, he belonged to her, and she intended to savour it.

'I don't want to talk,' she said. 'Not now. Just lie with me.'

He did, cradling her body against his. He rested his mouth at the crook of her neck and then said, 'I need you to understand that I came here to take you away from this place. I didna intend to seduce you. It was never my purpose.'

'I know that.' Even so, she wrapped her arms around his neck, closing her eyes. Society would say that this was a sin, and how wrong it was to lie with the man she loved. But she knew the sands were slipping away in the hourglass. He was going to marry Lady Regina if she accepted. A part of her wished fervently that the heiress would refuse. Her heart ached at the thought of losing him.

Lachlan was kissing her softly, murmuring endearments against her skin. She turned her face to his, and he kissed her lips. 'We'll bide a wee,' he said, 'and then I'll take you to the duchess.'

She understood that he was trying to protect her, that he wanted more for her than this. But he could not. 'Lachlan, no. If anyone finds out what we've done, it will ruin your chances of marriage. You cannot take me anywhere.'

'But—'

She pressed her fingers over his mouth. 'Believe me when I say that you cannot take me to Her Grace.' She took a breath and said, 'If it bothers you this much to see me staying here, I'll return to my mother.'

He would not be deterred. 'She doesna live like this, does she?'

Frances shook her head. 'My father has a house in the country. It's very small, but she lives there.'

'Will she take you in?'

Frances nodded, even though she wasn't certain that was true. She'd had letters from her sister that their mother wasn't in the best of health. And her father was living in France with his mistress.

She had lived a life of respectability these past few years, trying to atone for her mistakes. But the truth was, she was no better than her father. If anything, she deserved to live in exile as penance, for daring to reach for a life that would never be.

'Stay a little while,' she whispered. 'And after you go, I won't see you again. It's better that way.'

Chapter Eleven

The hardest thing Lachlan ever had to do was leave her side. After he finished dressing, he said, 'I'll hire a coach to take you to your mother's house in the country.' But Frances had only given him a soft, secret smile. He didn't know if she would truly go or not.

His heart burned within his chest with a searing ache that would not diminish. And when he paused at the door, he told her again, 'I love you, Frances Goodson. I will think of you always.'

'And I you,' she answered.

The emptiness stretched out inside him with a never-ending pain. Even the simple act of closing the door was worse than he had imagined. He walked down the stairs, the guilt weighing upon him. As he left the boarding house, he wondered what in God's name he'd done. He had asked a woman he didn't love to marry him. And he'd seduced a woman he could never marry.

Frances deserved so much more than this.

You are a coward, his conscience chided. A true man would find a way to provide for his people without having to marry for money. The burden of Locharr rested squarely upon his shoulders. If only he could find another way.

He travelled back to Worthingstone's house in Mayfair, his mind turning over the situation. When he arrived, he was startled to see Lady Regina's father, Lord Havershire, disembarking from his coach. His wife, Lady Havershire, took his arm, and both appeared delighted to be there.

A sinking feeling caught his stomach at the sight of them. The driver opened his door, and Lachlan had no choice but to go and greet them. After he exited his own vehicle, he walked towards the earl and countess. 'Lord and Lady Havershire,' he said from behind them.

The earl turned, and his face brightened. 'Locharr! It is so very good to see you again. You were just the person we came to pay a call upon.'

From the man's eager greeting, Lachlan had a strong suspicion as to why. He escorted them to the door and led them inside. 'Would you be wanting to join me for tea?' he asked. He kept up the façade of polite behaviour, though he was not at all eager to receive them.

He had just come from another woman's bed—the woman he loved. How in God's name was he supposed to entertain Lord and Lady Havershire? It was unconscionable. He didn't truly want this marriage, and he ought to confess it to them. It was only fair. And yet, his common sense warned him to stay silent.

He had failed so many times in the past. He hadn't been strong enough to save his father's life. His own people were starving because he had failed to provide for them. How did he dare risk another failure because of his personal desires?

Lady Havershire took his arm as he led her upstairs to the drawing room. 'Lachlan, I cannot tell you how very pleased I was to hear of your marriage offer. It's something we've wanted for Regina for so very long. To join our families together... I know it was your father's dearest wish.'

Somehow, he summoned a smile and managed a nod. 'It was, aye.'

'We simply had to come and speak with you.' She beamed as he led them into the blue drawing room and then rang for tea.

The coldness in his gut spread out to his limbs, and he felt nothing at all when he took a chair opposite the earl and countess. It was as if he were standing outside himself, watching as he played out the role expected of him.

'Dearest, let us not speak too soon,' the earl

warned his wife. Then he turned back to Lachlan. 'We have come to discuss the arrangements. To ensure that we are in agreement about your offer.'

Again, he managed a stiff nod. 'I would be glad to speak with you.'

But he was never more grateful when Victoria Nottoway, the Duchess of Worthingstone arrived to greet them. 'I am so pleased you came to call.' Her smile was genuine, and the earl and countess echoed her sentiments as Her Grace joined them.

'Am I to understand that congratulations are in order?' the duchess began. 'Will there be a wedding soon?'

The countess laughed gaily. 'I do hope so, Your Grace. In fact, that is why we have come to speak with dear Lachlan. Regina has spoken with us, and she has agreed to marry the laird, once we have discussed the marriage settlement.'

For a moment, it seemed as if the very air in the drawing room turned to frost in his lungs. It was difficult to breathe, and there was a roaring in his ears. So fast. He had never anticipated this, and he wanted nothing more than to be honest with them.

These were good people who loved their daughter. And they were about to offer her to a man who could never love her, because his heart had already been given away.

This isn't about love, his brain reasoned. *It is a marriage agreement. You offered her a marriage where you would not ask her to share your bed. She would not be a true wife—only a lady to share your name and your home.*

But more than that, he owed it to his clan to make this sacrifice. He owed it to his father. Though he hadn't saved Tavin's life, he could save Tavin's clan by putting aside his own needs. He could atone for his failings by agreeing to this marriage.

He heard himself lie, 'I am verra glad to hear this.' To the earl, he added, 'Shall we retire to another room to speak alone for a moment? We can re-join the ladies when the tea arrives.'

The countess was eagerly describing to the duchess the wedding she wanted for her daughter, and the earl nodded. 'I believe that would be best if we speak elsewhere.'

As they excused themselves, Lachlan hardened himself to the feelings of his heart. This was about a dowry that would save Locharr, and that was all that mattered.

The earl joined him in the duke's study, and he took out paper and a pen. 'The dowry I promised to Tavin was twenty thousand pounds. In return, I will expect Regina to have a portion to use for her own spending.' He began outlining the terms, but Lachlan heard none of them. Instead, he could only think of how wrong it was to accept this dowry, when Regina deserved a better man.

He fell silent during the negotiation, feeling as if he were selling his soul in exchange for twenty thousand pounds.

Frances tossed the letter into the fire as if it didn't matter. Her mother, Prudence, looked up from her knitting and asked, 'Who was that from?'

'Just a friend,' she answered. 'It's nothing.'

'It *looked* like an invitation.' Prudence let out a huff of air. 'And, of course, you cannot go.' The unspoken words were: *Because of your ruined reputation.*

'I didn't want to go,' Frances answered. And a greater truth, she had never spoken. For it was an event hosted by Lord and Lady Havershire in honour of their daughter Regina's engagement to Lachlan MacKinloch. Why would they have invited her? It made no sense at all. Had the Duchess of Worthingstone intervened somehow? Or had Lachlan issued the invitation?

Fury boiled within her, though she knew it was irrational. Likely the earl and countess believed it was a compliment, inviting her to a gathering. But instead, it felt like a slap in the face. They might as well have invited her to the wedding. She picked up her embroidery, hardly even aware of what she was sewing.

'When I was a girl, *I* never would have allowed myself to be seduced by a handsome face. I prided myself on my innocence.' Her mother straightened and prattled on about how she had been a virgin upon her wedding night. She eyed Frances as if she were a woman of loose virtue. 'I suppose you're just like your father.'

The blow was an invisible slice that cut her down. *No, I'm not.* Yet, she knew that if she dared to argue with her mother, it would only evoke more dramatic outbursts. Her mother revelled in arguments, and the only way to win was not to engage. Instead, she managed to hide the burst of pain and asked, 'Have you heard from him?'

Prudence nodded. 'He's in France with that woman. It seems you will have a brother or a sister in the next few months.'

The news startled her, and she hardly knew how to respond. Was her father happy? Had he turned his back on them in exchange for his own desires? In her mother's face, she saw the flash of rage, the bitterness that consumed her. And for a moment, she sympathised with Prudence, knowing how it felt to be left behind by the man she loved. How would she feel if Lachlan conceived a child with Regina? The pain would be staggering.

'I'm sorry,' was all she could say.

'So am I.' Prudence tossed her knitting into a basket and stood, before she walked towards the window. She shielded her eyes against the sun and remarked, 'Your sister, Lucille, is here. She sent word that she intended to pay a call upon us. I'll put on the kettle.'

Her mother stoked the fire and started the water for tea. Years ago, a kitchen maid would have done the task for her, but they could no longer afford servants. Her husband sent no money at all, and Prudence had to survive off the meagre amount sent by Lucille's husband.

Was this a glimpse of her own future? Frances didn't want to think so. Would the loss of Lachlan turn her into a resentful old woman?

Lucille entered the kitchen, holding the hand of her four-year-old son, Nathaniel. 'Hello, Mother. Frances.' She reached out to embrace her, and Frances caught a faint note of perfume.

'There's my boy.' Prudence bent down to kiss her grandson and then said, 'You know where your animals are. Go and fetch them.' She kept a set of carved animals that Nathaniel adored. He opened a small drawer and started pulling them out, talking to a wooden horse.

Lucille sat across from Frances and eyed her. 'I'm so glad you've left London. It wasn't safe for you there.'

'I was happy,' Frances countered. And she had been. Although it was true that the boarding house was not in a good part of the city, she had always felt protected.

'How was Scotland?' Lucille asked, when their mother brought the tea.

'I loved it.' *And I loved him,* she thought. She would return to Scotland without hesitation, were it possible.

'You look weary,' her sister remarked. 'You should eat something.'

'I hadn't time to make cakes,' Prudence sniffed. 'But there's bread and butter.'

'I'm not hungry, Mother.' The thought of food made her ill. But her sister took a sip of the tea and studied her. Frances hardly knew what to say. Lucille had a respectable life as a wife and mother. Her husband was a baronet, and she had fine clothes to wear and three servants to tend the house.

Lucille had invited her to live with them, but Frances couldn't bear to bring the shadow of scandal upon her sister. Her mistakes should not cause hardships to her family or make others whisper about them. It was better to keep to herself and not cause more gossip.

'Frances received an invitation to a ball,' Prudence informed Lucille. 'It's being hosted by Lord and Lady Havershire for their daughter, Regina. She is to marry the Laird of Locharr.'

Lucille's face softened. 'That's wonderful, Frances. You should go.'

'I cannot.' Her face heated, and she said, 'After all that's happened, I just…shouldn't.'

'It's been years since you received an invitation,' Lucille argued. 'And it means that people have set aside the past. This may mean a new beginning for you. You really should not turn it down.'

But then, Lucille knew nothing about the Worthingstone ball or the whispers Frances had endured. She had never told them about that night or anything at all about Lachlan. It was a silent heartache that she endured alone. And worse, she could not imagine the pain of watching Lachlan with Lady Regina.

'I have nothing to wear,' Frances said. It was a simple excuse, and she hoped her sister would abandon the idea.

'Then I shall loan you a gown of mine, and some jewels.' Lucille regarded her intently. 'This is your second chance, Frances. You cannot ignore it.'

It was not a second chance at all. Rather, it was an invitation to disaster. She wanted to confess the truth to her sister, that she had fallen in love with Regina's bridegroom. How could she possibly attend?

'They may have invited her as a means of mocking her,' Prudence warned. 'I agree with Frances. It's better to turn it down and live a quiet life.'

'Is it?' Lucille passed Frances the sugar and tongs. 'I think she should go. You never know what opportunity might arise. Or who she might meet.' She reached out and touched Frances's hand. 'Come and stay with me for a day, and I will lend you my maid. Martha can transform you until every gentleman will fall at your feet.' She squeezed her hand. 'Say you will.'

Her sister's offer was born of love, of wanting to help her. Though Frances understood that Lucille was dreaming of a better life for her, she did not delude herself into that way of thinking. And yet…she wanted to see Lachlan. A part of her wanted to know if he would be happy with Regina.

It's a mistake, her heart argued. *You already said your farewell. It would only cause you pain.*

She knew that, deep in her heart. But even so, she answered, 'I will think about it.'

Another week passed, and Lachlan deferred all wedding plans to Regina and her mother. He thought it best to let them do as they wanted and stay out of the way.

'You're looking rather glum for a man about to be married,' MacKinnon said. His friend took a sip of brandy, eyeing him.

'He looks as if he's about to be strung up,' Camford agreed. 'Though it's wise to let the bride and her family make all the plans.'

Lachlan poured his own glass and didn't answer. It was safer that way. But MacKinnon had a more discerning glance. He eyed Lachlan and then remarked, 'I didna love my wife when I first married her. I'd never seen her before, you ken? It was arranged, and I hated the thought of wedding a stranger. But I learned to care for her.'

Lachlan sipped at his brandy and stared outside the window, though he heard every word.

MacKinnon came to stand beside him. 'Your father wanted this. And you said that you wanted the match as well, to save Locharr from ruin.'

'I did say that,' he answered absently. But the words were no longer the truth. He was barely sleeping any more, trying to think of a way out of the marriage. Yet it seemed that with each day, the invisible noose tightened.

'Have you arranged for the special licence?' MacKinnon asked. 'Or are you having the banns read?'

'Lord and Lady Havershire are wanting me

to get a special licence. I'll take care of it on the morrow.' But instead of being eager to make the preparations, he found that he was avoiding it.

His friend seemed to sense it, and he added, 'All will be well, Lachlan. You'll see.'

He wanted to believe that. But all he could feel was guilt towards the woman he loved. It wasn't right for him to marry Lady Regina when he'd practically come from Frances's bed. If he ever did lie with Regina, he would be thinking of someone else, which she didn't deserve.

He drained his glass, and the others went on their way—all except Camford. The viscount was eyeing him intently. When they were alone, he predicted, 'You don't want this marriage any more, do you?'

Lachlan shook his head. 'I thought I did. I thought I should wed her for the sake of Locharr. But it's no' the right thing to do. She doesna deserve a man like me.'

'What will you do? Withdraw your offer?'

He shrugged. 'I dinna ken what I should do. I suppose I should talk to her. Tell her the truth.'

The viscount didn't seem at all in agreement. 'It may already be too late. They've set the date, haven't they?'

'They have, aye.' He set down the brandy snifter and stared outside again.

Camford seemed to think it through, and at

last, he said, 'Write her a letter. I'll deliver it on your behalf. Tell her that you no longer wish to marry her—tell her whatever you want. Then take your woman and go to Scotland.'

'What of the engagement ball tonight? I canna just leave.'

'Go to the ball, then. And leave afterwards. Give me the letter, and I'll make sure she reads it after a day or two.'

Lachlan wasn't so certain that was the right way to manage it. 'I should tell her before the ball. I dinna want her to be humiliated.'

'It's too late to send word to all the guests,' Camford said. 'Just attend the gathering tonight and tell her afterwards.'

He thought about it. 'I suppose she could delay the wedding. The invitations have no' been sent yet.' After a time, she could simply call it off. They could pretend that his duties in Scotland had delayed him too long, and she had changed her mind. The more he thought of it, the better it sounded.

'You're right. I'll go to the ball tonight, but afterwards, I'll leave. You give her the letter, and it can end quietly.' At least then, Regina could be the one to call it off. Although he felt terrible for what he'd done, a weight lifted from Lachlan's shoulders at the thought of letting her go.

Now the only question was how to manage the financial ruin of Locharr.

Are you the laird or aren't you? his conscience prodded. *Find another way to save it.*

He let out a slow breath, and for the first time, he felt a sense of hope.

Frances had no desire to be at Lachlan's engagement ball. Her emotions were stripped to the bone, and a weariness settled upon her. But the true reason she had come was for herself. It was quite possible that others would try to humiliate her because of the past. Certainly, they would gossip. But her sister had taken her aside, and a truth had arisen from their conversation.

She was behaving like a coward, hiding from the outside world. Though she had made a terrible indiscretion when she was young and had paid the price for her folly, she needed to straighten her shoulders and change her view of the world. If she faced down her past and rose above it, she could move forward with her life. And Lachlan's ball was the worst possible test. If she could remember her years of training and rise above the whispers, then she would overcome it.

Courage, Frances reminded herself. *You were invited to be here.*

She deliberately chose to arrive during the

time when most guests did, for she wanted to blend in with the others. Lucille had come with her, for Frances had no wish to bring her mother. Prudence would have ruined the evening.

Her sister had loaned her a gown the colour of spring leaves, embroidered with pink roses. It was high-waisted with short puffed sleeves and a square neckline. There were no jewels to wear, but Frances had chosen a gold locket. Lucille's maid had arranged her hair with hot tongs, and ringlets hung at her ears while the rest was pinned up and threaded with pink silk ribbons. She hadn't worn such finery since her own debut, and when a gentleman smiled at her, she started to wonder if her sister was right. Perhaps this would be a new beginning.

When they greeted Lord and Lady Havershire, Frances curtsied. There was a trace of coolness upon Lady Havershire's face, but she welcomed her just as she had the others. Lady Regina wore a gown of deep blue which accentuated her red hair. Around her throat, she wore a matching sapphire pendant with pearls and diamonds.

'I wish you joy in your engagement,' Frances said quietly.

'Thank you,' Lady Regina whispered. 'You've done well with his training. Lachlan has always been a perfect gentleman.'

Frances smiled to hide her shock. She had never revealed herself to Lady Regina as Lachlan's governess, but it seemed as if the young heiress knew. And worst of all, at that moment, Frances saw the laird crossing through the throng of people, his gaze fixed upon hers. His expression held surprise and concern, as if he'd known nothing of her invitation.

'Lucille,' she murmured. 'I need your help.' She didn't want to speak with Lachlan just now—not when there was such a risk with so many people staring.

'Come with me.' Her sister saved her by taking her arm and guiding her towards the dancing. The gentleman who had smiled at her was near the dancers, and Lucille inclined her head. She greeted him, but Frances missed hearing the knight's name, since she was distracted by the handsome Highlander trying to reach her side.

'Miss Goodson, would you care to dance?' the knight was saying.

'Thank you, I would.' She ventured a smile, but sent a silent look towards Lucille, begging for help with Lachlan. The last thing she wanted was for her laird to cause a scene. Her sister looked ready to do battle, and Frances sensed that Lucille intended to have words with Lachlan.

'You look lovely tonight, Miss Goodson,' the knight said as he took her hand. Frances thanked him and struggled to remember his name. He led her into the country dance, and in time, Frances let herself enjoy the music. She'd always liked dancing, but even as she spun around, she was conscious of Lachlan watching. A part of her was glad of it. Although she could never have him as her own, at least she could stand up and prove to herself that she would not crumble beneath the heartache. She had faced the worst devastation possible, of losing her child. She could certainly face this.

Sir What's-His-Name spun her around, and Frances nearly lost her balance as the dance ended. She couldn't stop her laugh, and her partner appeared to enjoy her amusement. It had been so long since she'd danced in public.

'Shall I fetch you a glass of lemonade?' he asked.

'I would be most grateful,' Frances answered when her sister returned to her side. 'Thank you for the dance.'

He bowed and walked towards the refreshments while Lucille guided her towards the opposite side of the room. 'Who sent you the invitation to this ball, Frances?'

'It was from Lord and Lady Havershire,' she answered. 'I assumed that the laird was behind it.'

Lucille shook her head. 'I think it was Lady

Havershire's idea. I'm so sorry, but I fear that you were right about her sending the invitation. She is watching you, and I don't like the look on her face when she does.'

Frances wanted to deny it, for she was having fun for the first time in many years. But she trusted her sister's judgement. 'What do you want me to do?'

'Don't dance any more. We're going to become wallflowers for the rest of the night.' Her sister's hand tightened upon hers. 'I think the countess brought you here for a reason, and it wasn't to restore your reputation. Quite the contrary.'

Frances risked a glance towards the matron, and the look of vitriol on the countess's face was quickly masked by a false smile. There was no denying the open threat.

'I think she brought you here because she knows something about you and the laird,' her sister continued. 'And she wants to end it.'

At that, Frances lost her patience. 'It *has* ended, Lucille. There is nothing between us. Not any more.'

'Everyone can see the way he's looking at you, Frances.' There was a note of sadness in Lucille's voice. 'He doesn't look at Regina that way.'

'It doesn't matter.' She knew that Lachlan had set her aside. And it was futile to dwell upon dreams that could never come true. She had accepted that truth and that was all. It was better to use this ball as an opportunity to make new friends and restore the life she had known before.

'Oh, dear. She's coming this way.' Her sister took her arm and said, 'I don't think we can avoid Lady Havershire.'

Worst of all, Lachlan was at the countess's side. She was clearly leading him towards her, though for what purpose, Frances could not say. Thankfully, Lucille remained beside her as a shield.

'Miss Goodson, I was delighted to hear that you'd accepted my invitation to the ball. It has been so many years since we've spoken.' The countess smiled, but there was no warmth in her expression. 'And Regina has told me of how you travelled to Scotland to help the laird prepare for society. I know he had been absent from London for so very long. He has done very well indeed.'

Although Lady Havershire's words were complimentary, Frances didn't miss the hidden message. *Leave him alone. He belongs to Regina now.*

She met the matron's gaze openly, answering it with her own reply. *I hold no claim on him.*

But Lachlan spoke, saying, 'Were it not for

Miss Goodson, I would have found it verra difficult indeed. I owe her my deepest thanks.'

His eyes locked upon hers, and in them, she saw a man who was not at all giving up on her. There was hunger in his gaze, of a man determined to get what he wanted. And she didn't know what to think of that.

Lady Havershire's expression turned grim. Then she changed the subject, turning to Lucille. 'It was good of you to come with your sister tonight. Though we were all surprised to hear that Miss Goodson chose to become a governess after the scandal instead of choosing a husband.'

Lucille's eyes flared with anger, and Frances squeezed her sister's hand to keep her from speaking. *Don't say a word. She's trying to bait you.*

Instead, her sister said, 'I beg your pardon, Lady Havershire, but I cannot say I know what you mean by that.'

The countess's eyes widened in mock surprise. 'Oh, do forgive me. I should not have brought it up. I invited Miss Goodson here tonight to thank her for all that she's done for our dear Lachlan and to give her another opportunity to find a husband.' To Frances, she said, 'I am so sorry for bringing up bad memories.'

It was apparent that Lady Havershire had no such regrets. She had aimed her barb, and her point was made. The laird's face hardened with silent anger, and though Frances murmured something in response to the countess, her eyes met Lachlan's. *Do not say anything.*

Lucille inclined her head and answered, 'Lady Havershire, it was kind of you to send the invitation to our household. I know my sister and I were both delighted to attend.'

'It was my pleasure,' the countess answered. 'I wish that I could invite you both to the wedding, but of course, that would be out of the question.'

Because Frances was in love with Lachlan and he with her. She lifted her gaze to his and saw the unspoken yearning. No doubt it was mirrored in her own eyes. When she looked into his deep blue eyes, the rest of the world seemed to disappear. She remembered lying in his arms, loving him. It cut her deeply to feel the loss of this man, but she drank in the sight of him.

Before Lady Havershire could interrupt, Lachlan broke her stare and turned back to the countess. 'Would you care to dance, Lady Havershire?' It was a means of removing the enemy, and Frances understood this.

'Don't be foolish. A woman of my age could never dance,' she chided him. But she took his arm, nonetheless. To Frances, she left a parting blow. 'Let your sister introduce you to some of the knights and baronets, Miss Goodson. This may be your last chance to find a gentleman to marry. One who has lower standards than the others.'

Frances stood her ground as the laird took the countess away. Her sister glared at Lady Havershire's back. 'What a vicious harpy. She makes our mother look like an angel.'

Frances managed a nod. But she recognised the reason for Lady Havershire's insults. The woman was deeply afraid. No doubt she had witnessed Lachlan's heated gaze and had recognised the laird's unspoken thoughts.

'Do you want to go home?' Lucille asked.

'No.' Frances took a step forward into the crowd of guests. Lady Havershire might have won that battle, trying to put her down.

But Frances intended to overcome her past and win the war.

Chapter Twelve

Lachlan never made it past a few steps before the countess took him aside. 'Miss Goodson *did* tell you about the scandal, did she not?'

'It's in the past,' was all he said. He had pieced together a story full of holes, based on what Worthingstone had said. He knew that she'd been seduced by a rake, and there was the possibility of a child, but none of that mattered to him. There was no sense in blaming Frances for her naïveté.

'She bore a child out of wedlock,' Lady Havershire whispered. 'Her mother claimed that she was ill, but everyone knew the truth.'

The matron's sly smile started a rage boiling inside him. This woman was deliberately trying to cast shame upon Frances, in order to raise up Regina. He was furious with the countess for her cruelty, and he couldn't imagine why anyone would want to hurt a young woman.

A thousand questions pricked at him, but he spoke not a word to the countess. Instead, he led her back to her husband and extricated himself. 'Lady Havershire.' He bowed and left her presence. Right now, he needed to calm his temper and regain control of his thoughts. She had brought Frances to the ball in an effort to humiliate her—something he could never permit.

When he glanced up, he saw Lady Regina regarding him with veiled concern. She was a stunningly beautiful woman with her striking red hair and blue eyes. Any man would be eager to wed a lady such as her.

Yet, there was only one woman he wanted right now, and Frances was standing beside her sister. As he drew nearer, he heard the whispers of the guests.

'She shouldn't be here. Not after what she did.'

'He seduced her and left her pregnant. Everyone knows it.'

'She's hardly better than a lightskirt. Don't even consider talking to her.'

Lachlan sent a hard look towards one of the debutantes, who blushed prettily and stepped aside. It irritated him that these women didn't care about humiliating Frances. He ignored them and crossed to stand before the woman he loved.

He bowed and asked, 'Will you dance with me, Miss Goodson?'

Everyone was staring, but he didn't care at all. He needed her in his embrace right now, no matter what the others said.

'My ankle is feeling sore,' she lied. 'Perhaps later. I think you should dance with your bride. Lady Regina is looking beautiful tonight.' Her eyes sent him a warning that this was not right or appropriate. He knew that she was trying to redirect him back to his fiancée. But he only had eyes for Frances. He wanted her wholeheartedly, and he intended to have her as his own.

'Dance with her,' she repeated. And in her eyes, he saw that she would not be dissuaded. She was going to refuse him. There was stubbornness in her expression and a hidden strength. He had no doubt that if he asked her to marry him and go back to Scotland, she would say no. She believed that he was getting what he wanted in Regina—a twenty-thousand-pound dowry.

But the truth was, he had no desire to wed an heiress when he could have the governess he loved instead. Frances meant everything to him. She was strong-willed, beautiful, and he would walk through fire for her.

He was going to have to take matters into his own hands. Camford had promised to give Regina the letter first thing in the morning. The engagement would be broken, and although it was a cowardly act to end it in this manner, he saw no other choice.

He fully intended to take Frances with him, back to Scotland. She would refuse, but beneath her stubbornness, he knew she loved him. They belonged together, even if that meant taking extreme measures. Aye, it meant turning his back on wealth, but he would not rest until he found another way to save his clan.

He thought a moment, and an idea took root. It was scandalous and bold, but it would be effective. His governess would be furious with him, but in time, she might see reason.

For now, he acceded to her wishes and excused himself. Before he could get too far, Lord Havershire escorted his daughter to him. 'Lachlan, everyone is waiting for you to dance with your bride. I promised to bring her to you.'

Lachlan inclined his head and offered Regina his arm, though he didn't feel like dancing at all. His bride, too, appeared nervous. She faltered at one of her steps, but he covered for her.

'Are you well?' he asked.

She nodded. 'It's just that I don't like being the centre of attention. I know it's expected of me, but I would rather be a bystander than make a spectacle of myself.'

'I can understand that.' He led her in the steps

Frances had taught him, but Regina appeared stiff in his arms. She wasn't enjoying herself at all, which only added to his guilt. He was about to send a letter to break off this engagement, when the honourable act would be to speak with her in private.

'It's only one night,' she said. 'And then, we will not have to host another ball.' She looked relieved at the prospect, but Lachlan sensed unrest beneath her words. Something was bothering her, and he decided to find out what it was.

'Do you truly wish to wed me, Regina?' he questioned quietly. 'Or are you being forced into it?'

She hesitated. 'As I told you before, marriage was never something I wanted. But it's expected of me, and I do want to leave London. I thought that was part of our arrangement.'

He kept his face a mask of neutrality, but inwardly, he was sensing that extricating himself from the marriage might not be as difficult as he'd imagined. 'What if I offered you a chance to leave London at any time?' He didn't mind if she came to Locharr for a while. It might give her the peace she was searching for.

'I wish I could leave now,' she answered drily. 'I would rather not be here, if it were possible to go. But I suppose we don't have a choice, do we?'

'There is always a choice,' he answered. 'For

both of us.' He spoke the words to reassure her, but the truth was, it felt as if an invisible net was closing around them. Lady Havershire had begun planning the wedding, was writing out the invitations, and was expecting them to be married within a few weeks.

God above, he felt like a trout firmly hooked— and the skillet was already sizzling. The dance ended before he could decide what to say. Somehow, he needed to delay the wedding plans, so that Regina would not be humiliated in front of her friends and family. Then she could end the engagement.

'What if we wait?' he offered. 'The wedding is happening rather fast, don't you think?' He wanted her to agree, to push back against her family's haste.

Regina shrugged. 'Does it matter?' She walked alongside him and added, 'Better to get it over and done with, I think. And then I won't have to listen to my mother's meddling any longer. I can be free.'

Lachlan saw the hope in her ocean-blue eyes and wondered how he could bring himself to destroy her hopes.

Regina was not a fool. During the dance with Lachlan, she hadn't missed the way his eyes kept searching for Miss Goodson. He had feelings for his governess, and that was the reason why her mother had invited the young woman. Lady Havershire fully intended to reveal the scandal to the laird and remind him that any affair he might have indulged in was over now.

And yet, she couldn't help but feel a sense of remorse. This wasn't at all what a wedding should be. She had accepted the laird's proposal, recognising it for what it was—an arrangement. A means towards the freedom that she desperately needed.

She didn't love Lachlan, nor did he love her. But she did believe that they could be friends somehow. In spite of his intimidating scar, he had a nice smile, and he cared about his clan. He had made no demands on her, and she truly believed that they could find a way to make their marriage work, even if it was a celibate arrangement.

She had spoken her own lies, pretending that one day she would be his wife in body as well as in name. The truth was, she had no desire for lovemaking or children. The thought was a wrenching fear, and she never intended to share his bed.

Her heart ached as she watched him walk away. Lachlan was an honourable man, one who would make the right choice, even though it was not his wish. And that was another reason why her mother had insisted on a short engagement. *Don't give the man time to change his mind,* she had warned.

Perhaps there was some truth in that.

She stood at her father's side, listening as he told stories about her and Lachlan from when they were children. He was laughing, though there was a note of nostalgia in his voice when he told a guest, 'It was Tavin's last wish that our children be married. How could I refuse, when they have been friends all their lives?'

If, by friends, he meant that they had spoken once in the past ten years. Regina held back her amusement at his exaggeration. Then a voice said quietly from behind her, 'You are beautiful when you smile.'

Regina turned and saw Viscount Camford. Though Dalton St George's compliment was kind, it overstepped the invisible boundaries. And while she ought to be irritated, her traitorous mood warmed to the words. Which was utterly improper.

She kept her own voice low. 'Was there something you wanted, Lord Camford?'

'Oh, indeed.' His eyes heated at her words. 'But alas, we cannot always have that which we desire most.'

She blinked a moment, not knowing what to say. Her face must have revealed her alarm, but then he laughed. 'I was referring to the custard cups, Lady Regina. They're all gone.'

She relaxed at that and lowered her fan. 'You are incorrigible.'

'Did you think I was speaking of something else?' The tone of his voice, while teasing, bespoke another hidden meaning.

'In truth, I had no idea what you were talking about. But custard was not what I was expecting.' She flipped open her fan, for it was warm within the room. Lord Camford's presence was not helping. When he drew closer, she felt her cheeks growing hotter.

'I have misgivings about this marriage,' he said. 'Don't you?'

She did, but she wasn't about to reveal that to him. Instead, she feigned ignorance. 'Of course not. Lachlan and I have known each other a long time.'

'Is that enough?'

No, it wasn't. And yet, she wasn't about to tell him her true reasons for agreeing to the marriage. Instead, she simply nodded. Lord Camford's face held tension, and she could not tell whether it was jealousy or if he knew something about Lachlan. Finally, she decided to reveal her own hand.

'I am aware that he has feelings for someone else,' she said quietly. 'I've known it since the beginning. But I also know that he needs my dowry desperately. After he offered for my hand, we made an arrangement between us. It will be enough.'

'You don't think you deserve to be loved in a marriage?'

The anxious feelings swarmed within her stomach, and her mouth went dry. Lord Camford had no idea what she had endured. It was a fear that permeated every part of her, swallowing her whole.

'No,' she admitted. 'I don't.'

With that, she crossed the room and sought out Lachlan. Her fiancé was standing on the side of the room looking as if he were watching the crowd instead of being a part of the celebration. She could understand those emotions, and it was another reason why she had agreed to marry him. They had a great deal in common, and she believed he was a man of honour.

When she reached his side, she murmured, 'It's overwhelming having so many people watching us, isn't it? I would much rather be alone in my own home with a cup of tea and a cat snuggling beside me.'

His expression softened, and he agreed. 'Aye. Only my cup would be holding whisky.' For a moment, he looked as if he wanted to say something to her but then held himself back.

Regina debated whether to admit the truth and decided it might clear the air between them. 'I thought I should tell you… I know about the… *friendship* you have with Miss Goodson. I spoke with Lord Camford just now.'

She wasn't prepared for the look of utter shock on the laird's face. He appeared stunned by her revelation, as if he'd never imagined she would bring it out into the open.

'I am deeply sorry, Lady Regina. I never meant for it to happen.'

She had no doubt of that. And yet, it was only natural for him to have feelings for a young woman with whom he had spent a great deal of time. *She* certainly didn't intend to stand in his way. It might even help their situation if he took Miss Goodson as his mistress.

'Well, it did, and now we must decide what to do about it.' Her face flamed with embarrassment, and it was clear that he mistook her blush for anger. It didn't truly matter, though. The truth was, his feelings for Miss Goodson might be a solution to her problem. They could continue the farce of their marriage while the laird satisfied his physical urges elsewhere. He could even father a child by the woman, and she could raise the baby as her own.

Regina didn't doubt that her mother would

be appalled by such thoughts. But then, Arabella didn't understand the wrenching fears that haunted her. She couldn't possibly grasp the idea that her daughter wanted a loveless marriage with no consummation. It meant freedom and safety.

'What exactly did Camford say to you?' He appeared alarmed by her words. 'He was supposed to give you a letter tomorrow, explaining everything.'

She stiffened, feeling as if every bone in her body had turned to ice. 'A letter, Lachlan? Truly, you thought that would be the answer, regarding something so serious?' Her face flamed, and a prickle of rage caught her.

'Forgive me.' He reached out to touch the small of her back, and she stepped away to avoid the contact. 'May we go and speak in private?'

'I hardly think that's necessary now.' She had no desire to hear about his feelings for another woman. She preferred to keep it buried and for neither to speak of it. Best to set it aside and pretend as if it didn't exist.

'I am sorry, Lady Regina. Would that I could change it. You deserve a man who loves you with his whole heart.' His voice held a kindness that soothed her invisible wounds. And perhaps it was good that they spoke with all honesty now. They could enter into the marriage with full knowledge of what it was.

'Thank you for not trying to deny it,' she answered, keeping her voice low.

He still appeared shocked by her confession. 'I never meant to hurt you, lass. In fact, I was planning to—'

'Not at all. I think it's for the best.' She cut him off, not wanting him to say anything more. 'No marriage should be built upon a foundation of dishonesty.' It was better if they spoke with truth between them, and they would move forward without any lies.

He hesitated and then let out a deep breath. 'Well, then. You've taken me by surprise, Lady Regina. This was no' a conversation I was expecting tonight.'

'It will be all right,' she assured him. 'Honestly, I believe it is best for both of us. You will have what you want, and I will have the same.' He would leave her alone in the marriage bed, and she would have nothing to fear.

He waited a long moment, as if he wanted to say far more. His blue eyes studied hers with compassion, and he offered his arm. 'I cannot say how sorry I am. This was never what I imagined would happen.'

'I suppose not.' But she took his arm and walked alongside him. 'We will make the best of it.'

* * *

Frances watched them smiling at one another, and it was like a thousand daggers were carving up her heart. She could hardly bear to see Lachlan with Regina, and she wished she hadn't come to the ball. A hand reached out to touch her shoulder, and she flinched before she realised it was her sister.

'Do you want to leave now?' Lucille asked.

She nodded. Being here had accomplished nothing, save heartache. When she glanced at their host, Lady Havershire was beaming at her daughter. She had won, and Frances had no desire to watch her gloat. It was physically painful to watch Lachlan with Regina, and she couldn't stand it any longer.

'Let us go. I'll speak with Lady Havershire and give her our apologies.' As soon as her sister departed, the knight whose name she'd forgotten came forward with a glass of lemonade.

The man had an awkward gait and he looked ill at ease in the company of women. He offered it to her, and Frances knew it would be in poor taste to say no. 'Thank you.'

'I am sorry it took me longer than I'd expected,' he said. 'I brought it as soon as I could.'

'It's kind of you,' she told him, wishing she could remember his name. He shifted his weight from one foot to the other as if he wanted to say more but couldn't find the words. She tried to smile, but it only made him blush harder.

'Y-you are a lovely woman, Miss Goodson,' he stammered. 'I enjoyed our dance very much. I hope I may have permission to pay a call upon you.' He glanced at her sister, who had just returned from Lady Havershire's side.

A sudden thorn of guilt pricked at Frances's conscience. She could never accept callers, now that she had left the boarding house. It wouldn't do to encourage this man, for he deserved a lady, not a ruined governess.

At that, her sister intervened. 'Forgive me, Sir Roger.'

That was his name. Her guilt made her vow to remember it this time.

'I am so sorry, but I must take my sister home,' Lucille apologised. 'She has a headache, unfortunately.'

'I am very sorry to hear it.' His face creased with sympathy. 'I do hope you feel better, Miss Goodson.' To Lucille, he added, 'I was just telling your sister that I hoped to pay a call upon her. Another day, perhaps.'

Lucille glanced at Frances and read her thoughts. 'I'm afraid that won't be possible for some time. Our mother has been ill, and Frances is going to stay with her in the country while she convalesces.'

'Oh.' He looked quite disappointed, then offered, 'My condolences.' With a bow, he excused himself.

Frances walked with her sister, admitting, 'He was a kind man. I do hope he finds a good woman.'

'He was interested in you,' Lucille admitted. 'Perhaps something will come of it in time. If that's what you want.'

It wasn't. Frances cast another gaze at the ballroom, knowing that she was turning her back on what she truly wanted. Lachlan was standing beside his fiancée, and it was like a physical blow to her stomach. He saw them leaving, and immediately began crossing the room.

No. He couldn't pursue her like this—not with Lady Regina and the rest of London society watching.

'Hurry,' she urged her sister. 'We have to leave.'

Lucille did and told a footman to order a hackney cab for them. They had no choice but to wait in the hall, and soon enough, Lachlan was there. Before he could speak, her sister turned to face him. 'Leave Frances alone. You should not be here, and you know this.'

Though Frances understood her sister's warning, the raw pain in Lachlan's expression took her aback.

'I ken that, aye.' But she could read his face and see that he didn't want to watch her go. Her own feelings mirrored his, for she knew this was the last farewell and she didn't want it to be. But what other choice was there?

Lachlan asked her, 'Where are you staying?'

'I am staying with Lucille in town, tonight. After that, I will return to my mother's.'

'Good.' In his words, she heard the relief that she was no longer staying at the boarding house. But the yearning in his eyes nearly undid her. She wanted to go into his arms and bury her face against his chest.

Instead, she murmured, 'I wish you the best, Lachlan.' *I love you. I will think of you always.*

'Frances, there is something I must tell you.' He started to reach for her hand, but before she could take it, Lucille gripped her palm and pulled her back.

'This is not the time. Goodbye, Locharr.'

Lucille was practically dragging her towards the hackney cab, and Frances muttered, 'You don't have to tear my arm off.'

Her sister gave no answer until she had spoken to the driver and they were inside the vehicle. 'If I had left you there, you would have gone to him. Have you no shame?'

Not when it came to the man she loved. Her

heart was heavy with dismay, for she could see his own pain. 'I suppose not.'

'Frances, he wants you for his mistress. And you deserve so much better than that.'

She knew it, and yet, a part of her almost considered lowering herself. But no. That wasn't the sort of person she was, to steal Lachlan away.

'I miss him already, Lucille.' Her eyes filled up with tears, and she looked outside the window so her sister would not see the emotions welling up.

'Stay with Mother,' Lucille advised. 'She will keep you so busy, you won't even remember Lachlan after a time.'

'If I do that, you might as well lock me away in prison.' She shook her head. 'I cannot stay there. What I need is a permanent position as a governess. Somewhere far away.' But even then, she knew it would not be enough.

'You are always welcome to stay with me,' Lucille offered. 'Though I know it's small.'

'I am grateful to you, and I love you. But I want to stand on my own feet now and make my own future.'

Her sister reached for her hands and squeezed them. 'I understand. But I am always here for you if you need me.'

Frances tightened her grip on Lucille's hands,

so overcome with emotion, she couldn't speak. But her sister knew the truth of her feelings.

The hackney cab drove through the crowded streets until they later arrived at the home of Lucille and her husband, Tom. It was a modest residence, large enough for the two of them, their son, and three servants. For tonight, Frances would be sleeping in one of the servant's rooms near the kitchen. She didn't mind, because she would be warm at night.

It was dark when they arrived, and her sister paid the driver as they departed. After they entered the house, Lucille bid her goodnight and went to check on her son, Nathaniel.

Inside the kitchen, Frances was alone since the scullery maid was tending the hearths in each of the bedchambers. She sat in front of the kitchen fire, warming her hands. As she did, she let her tears fall, wishing she could release the pain in her heart as easily. She regretted leaving so quickly, though she knew her sister had saved her from a possible humiliating moment. It would have ruined the engagement party, if anyone had seen her touching Lachlan's hand.

One of her sister's cats entered the kitchen and rubbed against her legs, purring softly. Frances bent down to pet the cat, realising she could not change out of her gown until the scullery maid returned or unless she asked Lucille for help.

She stood before the hearth, closing her eyes as she imagined what it would be like if Lachlan were with her. She would reach up and twine her arms around his neck, feeling his mouth descend on hers. His strong arms would hold her close, and she would lose herself in his embrace.

A soft sound caught her attention, and she turned, expecting to see the scullery maid. Instead, she saw Lachlan MacKinloch, dressed in his evening finery. He stood at the entrance to the kitchen and stared at her.

'What are you doing here?' she asked. Why had he followed her?

His answer was a heated stare. For a moment, she could hardly breathe. His very presence reawakened her longing. Then he drew closer and reached for her wrap. Without asking permission, he pulled her cloak over her shoulders and fastened it. Then, before she could say a word, he lifted her into his arms.

'No, Lachlan, we cannot—' she started to say. But he cut off her words by kissing her hard. The kiss silenced her protests, and she found herself kissing him back, though she knew it was wrong.

'You asked me what I am doing,' he murmured against her lips. 'I'm doing something I should have done long ago. I'm kidnapping you.'

His answer stunned her, and she could hardly

gather the right words. But she met his gaze and demanded, 'Put me down.'

He stared at her, as if wondering if she meant it. Frances kept her gaze firm, though inwardly, she was quaking. She wanted him more than all else, but he wasn't thinking clearly. He didn't truly understand the consequences of these actions.

'Do you no' wish to go with me?' he asked quietly, setting her down again.

'Not like this. I've caused one scandal already. I don't want to start another.' She kept her voice calm, though she understood what she was giving up. Her heart was breaking at the thought of pushing him away. Especially now, when she had missed her courses. She closed her eyes, terrified that she would face the same consequences as before. It was awful enough to become pregnant and abandoned after a seduction. But this time, she had knowingly gone into his arms. It was too soon to know if their night of lovemaking had resulted in a child. Yet, she could not deny the possibility.

She was a sinful woman, a wanton who did not deserve a man like Lachlan. Lady Regina was a virtuous innocent, someone who could raise him up in society and help his clan. There was no tarnish to her name, and no one would dare whisper.

Unlike herself.

No one had forgotten her past. Instead, they took salacious delight in gossiping about her ruin. If she allowed Lachlan to take her away from London, it would make matters so much worse. Not only would he lose the means of saving his clan, but it meant he could no longer show his face in society.

'You're afraid,' he said quietly.

She nodded. 'I'm afraid that it would result in disaster. I have so many sins in my past, my name is ruined for ever. But I don't want to destroy your future or that of the MacKinloch clan. They need you, Lachlan. They need Regina's dowry.'

'And what about us? What about what *we* need?'

'It doesn't matter.' She reached for his hands and held them. 'I am content with the precious time we had together. It will have to be enough.'

He framed her face with his hands, stroking the line of her jaw. 'Do you love me, Frances?'

Tears welled up against her will. She knew she should tell him no, that she should push him away. But she could not stop herself from murmuring, 'I love you with all my heart. Enough to let you go, so you have the happiness you deserve.'

At that, something in him shifted. The pirate

gleam returned to his eye, and he reached into his waistcoat pocket. He dropped a folded note on the kitchen table.

'What was that?'

'A note for your sister.' With that, he lifted her back into his arms and began striding up the narrow stairs, outside the kitchen, to a waiting coach.

'Lachlan, don't.'

But he refused to listen to her. No longer was he playing the role of English gentleman. Instead, he had grown wild again, like a Highland barbarian carrying her off. He opened the door of the coach and lifted her inside before he entered the vehicle and closed the door behind him.

'This isn't a good idea,' she argued. Her heart was beating in a staccato rhythm, and she could not deny that it was rather exciting being carried off. But her mind knew that it was a foolish choice.

'I ken that,' he answered. 'But neither is it right to wed a woman I dinna love. Nor is it right to bind her to a life of disappointment.' He pulled her onto his lap and cradled her face in his hands. 'I love you, Frances Goodson. And damned if I'll turn my back on you for twenty thousand pounds. You're worth three times that.'

He kissed her hard, and she returned the kiss, heedless of the tears she wept. Her heart and her head warred with one another, though she knew this was wrong. *I will face the consequences later.* Being in his arms was all she wanted, and she surrendered to her feelings. She continued kissing him, and it was a desperate kiss of being apart for too long.

The coach continued the journey, and she yielded to Lachlan's embrace, his tongue sliding against hers. Her body responded to him, and the heat of desire made her long for more. He fumbled beneath her gown, and his hand caressed her bare thigh. She ached for him, and he conjured up a thousand wanton feelings. Yet, she needed to understand his intentions.

'What about Lady Regina?' she asked.

'I broke off the engagement. You are the only woman I want. If you will have me.' He kept her in his lap, and the position only tempted her more.

Her breath caught in her lungs, and she framed his face with her hands. His eyes were shadowed in the darkness, and she could only see his expression from the dim flare of the coach lantern hanging outside the vehicle.

'I love you, Frances. And Regina knows about us. It would not have been fair to her.'

He rearranged her position until she was facing him, her legs astride his lap. It brought her up against the rigid shaft of his erection, and the memory of making love to him made her grow liquid.

'What about your clan?' she breathed, gasping when his fingers moved between her legs. He stroked her intimately, and a shocking flare of desire quaked within her.

'I'll find another way to save it.' He caressed her, sliding one finger within. 'I'm going to marry *you*, if you'll have me.'

His blue eyes caught hers, and she saw the sincerity in his gaze. He meant it, down to his soul.

'And if I say no?' she asked. She feared that his people would suffer for this choice, and worse, that he would one day regret what he'd done. She couldn't bear to imagine Lachlan resenting her for her poverty.

'Then I will continue to tempt you until you say yes.' His wicked fingers stroked her, and the erotic sensations rose up within. Her breath caught in her lungs, and she moaned as he entered and withdrew. 'I will torment you until you give in to me. If you love me, it will be enough.'

With all her being, she wished that it would be enough. Although her heart rejoiced at his offer, a part of her could not let go of the apprehension. Lachlan was stubborn and demanding, a man who was sacrificing everything for her. And all he wanted was for her to try.

'I do love you, Lachlan,' she murmured, kissing his mouth. She wanted nothing more than to be his wife. But she didn't know if she could agree, not when it meant he would lose everything.

'It's a long journey to Scotland,' he warned. 'But I'll be wanting to wed you when we reach Locharr.'

She didn't answer him, though she kissed him as a distraction. At this moment, she was starting to realise all the troubles that could happen. Her sister would be horrified at what she'd done, and the scandal would taint their family name. It was bad enough that she'd been ruined before. But this was far worse.

Leaving with Lachlan would destroy his livelihood and reputation. It meant turning her back on the life she had known and giving up everything for him. There was no greater price for either of them.

And yet, she didn't have the strength to walk away.

'How long will we travel before we stop for the night?' Frances asked.

Lachlan was hardly able to keep a spare thought in his mind, for he was overcome by having her in his arms. 'A few hours,' he said. 'There's an inn outside the city, if you're wanting a bed.'

She nodded. 'It is late, and I would be grateful for a bed.'

'You could sleep in my arms,' he offered. 'I will hold you.'

For a moment, she remained on his lap, studying him. Her hair was falling from its chignon, and her skirts were tangled against her waist. He had enjoyed pleasuring her, but her face had gone serious. It made him wonder if she was regretting her decision.

He had no such regrets. Before he'd left, he'd warned Camford to deliver the note to Regina, to ensure that she knew the engagement was off. Even so, he felt certain that it wouldn't matter, especially after he'd spoken with Regina at the ball. Her confession that she was aware of his feelings towards Frances had made it clear that she did not want to marry him, either. It was better for them to go their separate ways. Lachlan was determined to wed Frances and bring Locharr out of the ashes and towards a better future.

'I have ruined you now,' she whispered. 'People will say that I have brought you low.'

'You've done nothing wrong. No one knows anything,' he reminded her.

'But they will find out that you broke off an engagement with London's most eligible heiress to marry your governess instead.'

'No.' He brushed a kiss against her mouth. 'In my letter to Regina, I told her that she was to tell everyone that she broke our engagement because we weren't suited. No one will ken that we have married in secret. They willna care that I've returned to Scotland.'

Her eyes held such hope, he was glad he'd made the arrangements. 'Then no one else knows?'

'No one, save you and me. And by morning, your sister.'

She expelled a sigh of relief. 'As long as we can keep it secret for a while, it may not harm Lady Regina too badly.' Still, her face remained furrowed with worry.

He hardly cared about that any more. 'I'm finding that I dinna care what anyone else thinks, lass. Now that I've kidnapped you, I mean to seduce you.'

'Here?' Her voice held confusion. 'But—'

'Here,' he said. 'If you'll have me.' Lachlan began unfastening the back of her gown until he reached her corset. 'We've hours yet to travel. And I canna wait that long to touch you.' He ached for her, needing to claim her in an act of possession. He wanted to reassure her that everything would be all right, that he would love her despite the problems that lay ahead.

Lachlan paused a moment, allowing her to

protest if she would. When she made no move to stop him, he untied and loosened her stays. He bent to taste the silk of her throat, and she moaned at the contact. He loved the softness of her skin, and he lowered her gown to the swell of her breasts. It took a few moments to unlace her enough to expose her nipples. In the darkness, he could not see them, but he could feel the erect tips beneath his fingertips.

She trembled, her hands clasping his head as he bent to worship her. With his mouth and tongue, he kissed each nipple, delighting in her muffled cries of desire.

He reached beneath her petticoats and found that she was wet and ready for him. When he drew circles against her hooded flesh with his thumb, she strained against him. He answered her need by suckling one breast hard, and she shuddered.

'Lachlan, I need you,' she groaned. 'Please. Come inside me.'

He unbuttoned his trousers and fumbled with his erection, while she knelt with both legs astride him. In one swift stroke, he sheathed his length inside her, and she gasped at the intrusion.

'Are you all right?' he gritted out.

Her breathing was laboured, but she began to ride him. Inside the bumpy carriage, her rhythm was awkward at first, but she started to relax against him. He continued to tend to her breasts, and she squeezed his length in response.

'Are you enjoying that, lass?' he asked, gently nipping at the erect tip.

'Yes,' she breathed. Then he moved to the edge of the seat, giving her deeper access to him. She rode him hard, and he thrust against her, loving the sinful sensation of her body claiming his. For a moment, she seemed to be nearly crying out in frustration, seeking her release but being unable to claim it.

Abruptly, he pulled back, holding only the tip of himself inside her. She was straining, trying to sheathe him again, but he prevented it. 'Wait, lass. Give me a moment.'

He reached beneath her skirts and caressed her again, finding her place of pleasure while he suckled her breasts. She had no choice but to let him fondle her, and he could tell the moment she was reaching the edge. Her breathing was laboured, her voice pitched as she gasped.

He rubbed her until she arched against him, shuddering as her release broke over her. Only then did he slide deep inside. He could feel her body squeezing his, her inner walls shuddering against his length. This time when he made love to her, her nails dug into him, and she held on as he thrust deep inside, over and over. The building pressure broke over him, and he erupted inside her, lost as their bodies became one.

She was utterly satiated, her body slack against his while he remained inside her. He continued to kiss her, and at moments, she quaked against him with aftershocks.

'Imagine every day like this,' he said gruffly.

'You might kill me,' she answered. 'But I would gladly die in your arms.'

It was the middle of the night when the coach finally stopped at the inn. Lachlan had helped her by lacing up her corset once more and buttoning her gown. She had attempted to repair the mess of her hair, but without a bonnet, it was nearly impossible.

She waited until Lachlan returned, after arranging for a room. He helped her from the coach and brought her inside. Her cheeks burned, and she tried not to look at the innkeeper while he led them to their room.

Lachlan gave the man a coin and then brought her inside, turning the lock behind him. He took her hand and led her to the bed. 'I ken that you're verra tired, lass.'

'I am,' she agreed. But even so, her mind could not be still. It darted from thought to thought like a moth fluttering against a gas lamp. She had run off with the man she loved, risking everything. And she could not relinquish her fear of the consequences.

Lachlan removed his shoes and his coat, unbuttoning his waistcoat and removing his shirt. Then he came to her and stood at her back. He unfastened the buttons of her gown while his warm mouth stole a kiss at her nape. Goosebumps erupted over her skin, and she closed her eyes at the sensation. He helped her disrobe, but this time, he left her chemise on. He removed his trousers, save for his drawers.

'Come and sleep with me, *a thasgaidh*,' he said. She warmed to the endearment and ventured a smile. Lachlan pulled back the coverlet, and she lay down on the bed, keeping near to the edge so he would have enough space.

He held her close, his arms around her waist while her backside rested against his legs. She sensed that he was tired, like she was—and yet, he had not voiced his own thoughts about what they had done.

'Do you have any regrets?' she asked at last.

'Nay. I am well pleased with my choice, Frances. I hope you dinna have any regrets, either.'

It was more worry than regret, she decided. She reached back, guiding his face to hers for a kiss. 'We will face what lies ahead together.'

'Good.' He kept her close, and she was aware of the rigid length against her spine. He gave a low laugh. 'Forgive me for wanting you too much, lass.'

'It's all right.' She tried to close her eyes, but his hands moved down to her flat stomach. Her heart ached at the memory of her lost child, and she sensed his silent question. The harsh memories came pouring through her, and she covered his hands with her own. 'You want to know what happened, don't you? My scandal, all those years ago.'

'Only when you're ready to speak of it.' He kissed her temple, and she thought about it. It had been years, though the pain would never fade. And after the baby had come too soon, she didn't know if it was possible for her to have more children. Lachlan truly ought to know before he considered marrying her. It was only right.

Slowly, she turned to face him. She traced her fingertip down his cheek and said, 'I will tell you everything. But please understand how very young I was. I was naïve and didn't know what was happening.'

She hardly knew how to begin. The emotions were tangled up within her, knotted in years of silence. At last, she said, 'I made my debut when I was seventeen years old. My father and mother had taught me all the rules of good behaviour, but I didn't listen to them. I thought they were trying to ruin my fun.'

He stroked her hair, holding her close as she spoke. 'I met a gentleman that night. Mother warned me to stay away from Viscount Nelson, but I was dazzled by him. When he gave me his attention and asked me to dance, I lost my head. And I can only say that I was too young and green to understand his purpose. I thought he wanted to marry me.'

She could sense the tension in Lachlan, in the lean strength of his body and the way his embrace grew overprotective. He chose his words carefully. 'But that wasn't what he wanted.'

'No. He flirted with me over a few weeks, and I believed that he would offer for my hand. He came to pay a call upon me, and I sent away my chaperon.' A chill suffused her skin at the memory. 'I…thought I was being worldly by letting him have my innocence. But it was painful and humiliating. He—he made it clear that he never intended to offer marriage. I was a dalliance, nothing more.'

She wasn't aware she had started crying until a gentle thumb brushed against her wet cheek. 'I learned I was with child a few months later. My mother was furious with me, and my father ordered me to leave with her. I stayed at the house in the country until the summer. But my son was stillborn. He never took a single breath.'

The wrenching pain spilled over, and she tried to suppress the sobs. 'I named him Oliver, and I buried him on a hill overlooking the river.'

'Did you ever tell Viscount Nelson?'

She shook her head. 'He left to travel abroad. I haven't seen him since, and as far as I can tell, his debts have kept him occupied.'

'I'm glad he wasna here,' Lachlan said. 'Otherwise, I might have killed him for what he did to you.'

Frances didn't quite agree. 'It was my own fault for not listening to my mother. She warned me never to be alone without a chaperon. I knew the consequences of my actions, and I paid the price.'

'You were too young to understand.'

'I was. And though it may be sinful, I wish to God that Oliver had lived. I think of him every day.' She let the tears fall freely, grieving for her son. He would have been three years old now, old enough to play and laugh. It cut her to the bone, thinking of his tiny face.

Lachlan held her close, offering her comfort in his steady presence. And in his arms, Frances felt a blend of both joy and fear. She had made the choice to run away with him, and that scandal would follow them always. She knew what it was like, being shunned from gatherings. There would be no more invitations—not after this. She only wished there was a way to shield Lachlan from the humiliation.

'I am sorry for your loss, Frances,' he said quietly. 'And I am sorry for the poverty that awaits us at home. I dinna ken if I will be able to keep Locharr after all the debts have been paid. But I will try.'

She believed him. 'So long as we are together, it will be enough.'

Chapter Thirteen

For the first three days, Lachlan buried himself in his father's study. He went over all the figures, and he had pinpointed exactly when their fortunes had taken a fall. It was nearly five years ago. As he'd discovered before, a yearly sum of three thousand pounds had gone missing. And every year, the same amount was deducted. The ledgers hid it well, for sometimes the amount was divided up as his mother's gowns. At other times, the three thousand pounds were spent on bonuses for the servants. Whoever had been taking the money had been careful to disguise it as ordinary household expenses.

Except that his mother never purchased gowns for herself. She rarely wore them. And he knew how hard the servants had worked. A bonus of several thousand pounds would have transformed their lives, had it been true.

No, his father—or someone close to his father—had been sending money elsewhere. And he could not say why.

'You look tired,' came the voice of Frances from the door. She was holding a cup of warm chocolate, a welcome sight.

'I think I've discovered how my father fell into ruin,' he admitted. 'Come and look.' He patted his leg, and she brought the hot drink over to the desk before she sat on his lap to study the papers. Lachlan sipped at the chocolate, relishing the hint of cinnamon in the flavour. He explained his findings to Frances, who studied the ledgers and ran her finger down the columns.

'You're right,' she said. 'Look. The cost of feeding the animals would not rise three thousand pounds in a single year. Grain and corn are not that dear.'

'But what can we do about it?' he said bleakly. 'The money is gone now.'

'Is it?' she wondered aloud. 'Or did he move it somewhere else?'

'I've no idea.'

Frances continued studying the ledgers, biting her lower lip. He grew distracted by the sight of her, and with her soft bottom pressed against his lap, he suddenly had all manner of daydreams flooding through his mind. None of which had to do with ledgers or desks, unless it meant laying his governess down upon it and loving her most thoroughly.

'Have you chosen a gown for our wedding yet?' he asked, leaning in to kiss her cheek. He nibbled against the line of her jaw, and she laughed softly.

'Not yet. And you're distracting me just now.'

'Good. I know other ways I could be distracting you, *a ghràidh*.' Right now, he needed to lock the door. He emphasised his point by squeezing her rounded bottom.

'Lachlan, not until we're married properly,' she insisted. 'The servants gossip enough about us as it is.'

'Then make the arrangements. We could wed on the morrow, if you like.' The details of the marriage didn't matter to him, so long as Frances became his wife. 'The sooner, the better.'

She turned to face him, resting her arms around his shoulders. 'Are you certain this is what you want, Lachlan? You're giving up everything.'

He kissed her hard. 'How can you even ask me this? I kidnapped you, did I no'?' Aye, it would be a challenge to restore their fortunes, but he would do everything in his power. He could leave Frances and his mother to look after the clan while he sought help for them. Even if it meant travelling elsewhere, like Ireland or to another part of England, he would do what was necessary.

'I don't want you to resent me one day,' she said. 'Or your clansmen.'

He embraced her. 'They like you, Frances. And we are going to invite them to our wedding. 'twill be a celebration for everyone.'

'I would like that,' she agreed. 'But I fear, we haven't enough to feed everyone.'

'We will,' he said. 'I have things I can sell, if need be. My father's pocket watch is made of gold.'

Her face fell at the mention. 'Lachlan, no. You can't sell something so precious. It holds memories for you.'

'You are worth more to me than gold,' he insisted. And while he didn't want to sell the watch, he wouldn't hesitate if it meant hosting a wedding celebration for her. He couldn't afford more than a silver ring, but she would have the best he could give.

She shook her head. 'No. We will have a simple celebration. I will wear a gown I already own, and we will do our best with what we have.'

'You deserve better,' he said. And he meant that. He wanted Frances to have a perfect gown and the wedding of her dreams. Despite all that she had lost, he wanted to give her the fairy-tale.

'I don't need better,' she insisted. 'I have you,

and it is enough.' She leaned in to kiss him, but even the sweetness of her affection could not dim the guilt he felt. It was his duty to provide for a wife and family, and he had to dig himself out of the debts his father had acquired and make it right.

Frances stood from his lap and said, 'I will speak with Alban and the other servants. It may be that we can ask everyone to bring a small dish to share, and together, it will feed many.'

'When do you want to be married?' he asked. 'On the morrow?'

She laughed. 'As much as I love the idea, a week will be soon enough. I need time to plan the gathering and see to the arrangements. Your mother has offered to help me.'

He nodded, though Catrina had privately voiced her disapproval of the marriage. Not because she disliked Frances, but rather, because he had broken the arrangement made by Tavin and Lord Havershire. He had told himself that it didn't matter now. Regina had discovered his feelings for Frances, and she had given him permission to break off the marriage. It bothered him to leave Regina behind like this, but it would have been far worse to wed her. Every time he saw her face, he would be thinking of Frances, and that wasn't fair.

He ventured a smile. 'I love you, my governess.'

Her eyes brightened. 'And I, you.'

Though he warmed to her words, he did understand that there would be unspeakable damage to his reputation and hers, after what they had done. Eventually, the truth would come to light about their marriage.

He could only hope that she would never hold any regrets.

'Where are we going?' Frances asked Catrina. The matron had arranged for them to go riding, and the groom helped her onto her horse.

'I thought you should come and meet more of the clan, since you are to be their Lady.' She straightened upon her saddle and eyed her with a silent challenge.

'I agree,' Frances answered. She suspected that Lachlan's mother had another purpose in mind, but she agreed with Catrina's proposition.

They rode alongside one another, but there was little conversation. Frances didn't mind, for she was preoccupied with other thoughts. Not only her wedding to Lachlan, but the other desperate hope that bloomed within her. Of course, it was far too early to tell, since her courses were only a few weeks late. But still…with each day that passed, it felt as if life had given her a second chance at a child.

It must have happened the first night she had given herself to Lachlan. And though she ought to be ashamed, a fierce happiness threatened to consume her with the hope that it was true.

The sunlight warmed her face, and Catrina led her into the village. The thatched houses were set close together, and the scent of peat fires permeated the air. Frances smiled at the people, though they appeared wary of her. Some of the folk returned her smile, and she recognised them from the *ceilidh*, a few months ago.

When they reached the edge of the village, Catrina dismounted and tied the reins of her horse to a post outside one of the homes. Frances did the same and followed Lachlan's mother to the doorway. Catrina knocked, and a woman's voice called out for her to enter.

They did, and Frances followed, closing the door behind her. It was dim inside, and Frances saw a young mother tending her baby. She recognised Abigail MacKinloch from several weeks ago and her young son, Donald. The infant was fretting, and Abigail was trying to feed the baby, dipping her finger into milk and letting the boy suckle against it.

'How are you, Abigail?' Catrina greeted her, touching the young mother's shoulder.

Abigail didn't return the smile. She traced the edge of her infant son's face, and Frances felt her gut clench at a reawakened memory. The boy was so pale, so fragile. Unbidden tears sprang to her eyes, but she would not let them fall.

'I lost my milk a fortnight ago,' Abigail confessed. ''Tis too soon to wean my bairn, but he's no' thriving with the goat's milk.' The fear in her voice echoed the past nightmares Frances had endured—only her baby had never taken a single breath.

She could feel the silent accusations against her. Likely Abigail had lost her milk from lack of food. A baby needed his mother's milk, and he could die if he was weaned too soon. Her skin grew cold at the thought, and Frances drew nearer to see the baby. Worry creased the lines of Abigail's face, and the child was clearly weaker.

Grief gathered up inside Frances at the memory of her son, and she could hardly bear to look at them. Catrina had made her point clearly. By wedding Lachlan, she was condemning the clan to a life of poverty.

'I will ask Lachlan to send more food to you,' Frances offered. 'Or perhaps a wet nurse can be found for the baby.' It was a feeble offer, but Abigail murmured her thanks.

Inside, she felt sick to her stomach, but there was nothing else she could do. They stayed a little while longer and left with promises to return soon.

'I hope you ken what you're doing,' Catrina said, after they mounted their horses and began the ride back to the castle. 'Twenty thousand pounds could have changed many lives.'

The words hovered over her, with the weight of the woman's disapproval. Frances knew she could never please Catrina, no matter how hard she tried. It hurt to know the truth, but she turned to face her. 'You want me to leave him.'

The matron nodded. 'It isn't too late. Let him go, and he could save his kinsmen from starvation.'

Frances knew that Catrina wanted her to give up the marriage. And though it was expected of her, she couldn't bear to walk away. For so long, she had pushed her dreams away, believing she was unworthy of being loved. Her sins of the past had resulted in heartache, one she had never thought she could overcome. But Lachlan had challenged her, forcing her to find her backbone and reach for a different life. She loved him with all her heart, and he had given up everything for her sake.

A memory came back to her, of Granny MacKinloch's fortune-telling. *Ye will only find yer happiness when you turn away from the path that was never meant to be.* Once, she believed that she was meant to turn away from Lachlan. But now, she realised that she could only be happy when she turned away from London society and her past life. Her path led into Lachlan's arms, and she would not turn cowardly and hide in the shadows. No, it was time to fight for what she wanted.

'I gave him that choice already,' she said. 'I left him once. And yet, he came back to me.'

''Tis a mistake he will come to regret,' Catrina insisted. Then she softened her tone. 'You think I despise you. But you're wrong. I think you have a good heart. Were it no' for the needs of our clan, I would welcome you as my son's wife.'

'Lachlan and I will find a way to help the people,' Frances argued. 'I may not have a twenty-thousand-pound dowry, but I do have resources of my own and a brain in my head.' She squared her shoulders and faced his mother. 'I love him. And I will stand by his side and take care of him until my last day on this earth.' It was time to defend her own dreams and find a way to help the clan.

'If you loved him that much, you would have let him marry Lady Regina. He would have saved so many. Now, when there are children dying this winter, the clan will ken who to blame.'

Her cheeks flamed, and she hardly knew what to say. If she fought back against Catrina's outburst, it would only turn her into a greater enemy.

She studied his mother's face and saw the worry in every line. Catrina loved her son and her clan. There was no question she would do anything for them.

But there was another reason why she could not turn away from Lachlan. Slowly, she let her hands drift down the gown to rest upon her womb. 'This marriage may bring blessings, as well,' she said quietly. She wanted Catrina to know the possibility, even as early as it was.

His mother's face turned stricken, and she closed her eyes in resignation. 'Och, I see how it is, then.'

Frances reached for her hand and squeezed it. Both of them shared the burden of having lost a child. Never could she forget her son. But the searing grief had changed over the years into a hollow ache of emptiness. If this was indeed her second pregnancy, and if the child lived, she would consider it nothing but a gift.

'I love Lachlan. And I will find a way to bring him happiness. I swear it.'

Catrina gripped her hand in return. 'I pray it may be so.'

One week later

On the morning of his wedding day, Lachlan walked alongside his friend Gabriel. There was not time to invite Camford from London, and he planned to celebrate with him later.

'Nervous?' Gabriel teased.

'Nay.' Lachlan was eager to make Frances his bride. Ever since they had arrived in Scotland, she had remained in a separate bedroom, closely guarded by his mother. It was an irresistible temptation, and he was frustrated by having to remain apart from the woman he loved. 'I'm wanting to marry her and end the waiting.'

Gabriel clapped his shoulder. 'I'll bid you happiness, my friend.' But Lachlan didn't miss the sudden shift in the man's mood. Undoubtedly, he was thinking of the day he had married his wife. He had lost her, years ago, in childbirth. Lachlan didn't want to even imagine his friend's pain. Losing Frances was unthinkable.

His kinsmen smiled as he passed them. They reached the kirk, and Lachlan took a deep breath, pushing back the harsh memories of the fire. It was time for a new beginning, and he wanted to imagine that his father would have liked Frances. His bride was already waiting with his mother, for it was considered lucky for her to arrive first. He had asked her if she'd wanted her sister and mother to be present, but she had declined, claiming that they might only try to stop the wedding.

His bride was breathtakingly bonny. Her blonde hair was the colour of sunlight and a crown of heather rested upon her head while the golden locks curled below her shoulders. Her river-green eyes glowed with love, and she wore a deep blue gown the colour of the sea. It clung to her waist in long lines before flaring out to the skirt. He remembered Catrina had worn it to a gathering years ago. Seeing Frances in the gown evoked the memory of the awestruck look in Tavin's eyes when he had beheld his wife in the gown.

An echo of the feeling reverberated within him. One of his kinsmen played an aching melody upon the harp, and Lachlan felt the presence of his family and clan. His mother braved a smile, but worry creased her face.

He had no such fears, for this was the right decision. Frances had come into his life, and he could not imagine living without her.

Lachlan stepped forward and took her hands in his. The minister began the words of the marriage ceremony, and he swore to love and honour her, all the days of his life. Frances repeated her own vows, and the minister wrapped the linen cloth around their hands, joining them together.

The joy in her eyes mirrored his own, and he gave her a silver ring that had belonged to his grandmother. There were loud cheers from his clansmen when he kissed her, and afterwards, they were surrounded by well-wishers. He lost count of the men and women who came to greet the new bride, until he saw the last face in the crowd.

At first, he hardly recognised the older man standing alone. It was the Earl of Havershire. The sight of the man's haggard face shocked Lachlan, for he had not expected to see him. It appeared that the earl had been travelling without stopping, for his clothing was wrinkled and stained.

'Lord Havershire,' he said. 'Is aught amiss? Has something happened to Regina—'

The very mention of his daughter's name made the earl's expression tighten into rage. His voice was quiet, but there was no doubting the accusation within it. 'You—you humiliated her. How could you do it? My sweet lamb.' His voice caught, and Lachlan motioned for Alban to come forward.

'We should speak in private,' he insisted. The man was distraught, and Lachlan couldn't quite piece together what had happened.

'I will not be silenced!' the earl called out. His

harsh tone quieted the wedding guests, who appeared as confused as Lachlan felt.

'Regina and I came to an agreement nearly a fortnight ago,' Lachlan said. 'She did not wish to marry me, and we broke off the engagement.' He tried to keep his tone calm, but his words did nothing to soothe the man's agitation.

'No. That's not true. You abandoned her.' The old man's expression revealed the pain of a father who was shattered by all that had happened. 'You left her to stand alone on her wedding day. She waited over an hour for you at the altar, but you were gone.' His face was nearly purple with rage now. 'Then she married that ne'er-do-well, that viscount.'

Lachlan had no idea what to think of any of this. The man's ravings had enough truth in them to make him wonder. 'Do you mean to say that Lady Regina married Viscount Camford?'

The earl nodded. He was twisting his hands together, the rage so strong, it bordered on madness. 'It wasn't supposed to happen. She was supposed to marry you, and then she would be safe from harm. The debt would be repaid. It was our agreement, and you broke it.'

The debt? Lachlan exchanged a glance with Frances, wondering if that meant what he thought it did. Had his father loaned money to the earl?

'Lord Havershire, let us go inside,' Frances

intervened. 'I believe we can sort all of this out.'
She turned to Alban. 'In the meantime, let the
others begin the dancing and feasting. We will
join them soon.'

The footman hurried away to do her bidding,
and within moments, the sound of music filled
the glen. Lachlan gestured for Havershire to join
them. 'If you'll just follow me and come inside.'

But the earl didn't move. 'It's your fault,' he
said quietly, staring at Frances. 'All of it.'

Lachlan didn't like the look in the earl's eyes.
Lord Havershire's demeanour was unstable, a
man bordering on madness. He didn't trust him
at all. 'My wife has done nothing wrong. And
if it was your intent to ruin our wedding, I will
not let that happen.' He took her hand in his,
wanting to guide her away. 'Wait a moment, if
you please.'

Lord Havershire quieted, gathering control of
his emotions. Lachlan met the gaze of Gabriel,
and the man silently approached. His friend
would take the earl away, if necessary.

When they reached the stairs leading to the
back of the house, Lord Havershire slowed his
pace. He stared at them and a moment of clarity
seemed to break through. 'You made the choice
to leave my daughter behind.'

'Regina wasna happy about the match, and
neither was I. I did the right thing by her. So if

you came here to put a stop to my wedding, it's too late.' He kept his tone hard, intending to stop any further conversation about it.

Frances placed her hand on his elbow and tried to soften the blow. 'I know you love your daughter very much, Lord Havershire. But I truly believe Viscount Camford has feelings for her. She may be very happy, in spite of the haste. There are worse things than to be married to man who adores her.'

And yet, Lachlan was beginning to understand the debacle. If everyone knew he had run away with Frances to be married and had left Lady Regina at the altar, they could never show their faces in London again. Moreover, if Regina had married Camford in haste, society would draw their own conclusions about why. It was also an illegal marriage, for there had been no time for a licence. Yet, if the viscount had married her, he'd done so of his own free will. Perhaps to save her from humiliation.

It was difficult to imagine what had happened, but if Havershire had travelled this far, the man was clearly casting blame upon Lachlan for all of it.

The earl regarded Frances, but there was no trace of understanding on his face. Instead, he appeared unsettled, uncertain of what to do now. 'She cannot marry Camford,' he answered at last. 'She was promised to the laird. Were it not for you, they would be married now.'

Frances grew sombre. 'I am so sorry for your daughter's suffering, Lord Havershire. Truly, I am.'

Her dismay was evident, for she fully comprehended the scandal they had caused. But Lachlan reached for her hand and caressed her fingertips. It mattered not to him what everyone else thought. What mattered was that she was now his wife, and he intended to protect her.

'Frances, I will speak further with the earl. Why don't you see to our guests? I'll join you soon.' He squeezed her hand gently, and he caught the worry in her eyes. Finally, she gave a nod and turned back towards the music and dancing.

Havershire studied her as she left, and then his gaze turned downward. 'I am sorry for my intrusion. It's just that… Regina needs to leave London. It's not safe for her there.' His hands were trembling, and he reached for a handkerchief. 'Her dowry belonged to you. Then the debt would be forgiven.'

Clarity broke through him now. Lachlan had always believed that Havershire had more wealth than most of the men in London, but now it seemed he was wrong. He chose his words carefully. 'Do you mean to say that my father loaned you money?'

The earl nodded. 'Many years ago. I swore I would pay it back, and he demanded that you marry my daughter in return. Then the money could be divided between us.'

Now it was all beginning to make sense. Tavin had successfully hidden the loan within the ledgers, keeping them in such disorder that no one would learn if it.

'Was it twenty thousand pounds?' Lachlan asked quietly.

'Fifteen thousand,' the earl corrected. 'The five thousand was Regina's true dowry.' He trudged towards the house then paused. 'Your father helped us during a difficult time. I owe him everything. It's why I promised Regina to you.'

In other words, his daughter's hand in marriage was part of the repayment. Lachlan released a breath and shook his head. 'I ken why you and my father made this bargain, but it willna happen now.'

At his words, the earl's complexion turned grey and sickly. 'It must. I will not give over twenty thousand pounds to you and that—that governess. It should remain with Regina.'

Were he able to turn away from the money, he would have. But this change in fortune meant everything to his people, and Lachlan intended to hold the earl to his promise. 'If you owed a debt to my father, then it must be repaid. We will speak of it in the morning. For now, I intend to celebrate my wedding.'

He understood that the Earl of Havershire was a distraught father seeking answers for his daughter's choices. And though Lachlan was annoyed that the man had interrupted his wedding celebration, he would not send him away. From the earl's demeanour, he appeared quite unwell. For the sake of his father's memory, he would not dishonour the friendship they had shared.

'If you would like to rest in one of the rooms at Locharr, speak with Alban, and he will find a place for you,' he offered. 'In the meantime, I must join my wife and return to our guests.'

As he walked back towards the celebration, he kept turning over the earl's revelations in his mind—Regina's humiliation and the rushed wedding; the money his father had loaned to the earl; and the debt to be paid. Perhaps it would be best if he invited Camford and Lady Regina to Locharr. They could come to an agreement about the debts between them.

'Is everything well?' his friend Gabriel asked. 'I wouldna trust Havershire, were I you.'

He agreed with the man on that point but shrugged. 'He's upset about his daughter. Camford wedded her in my place.'

The incredulous look on Gabriel's face was replaced by a sly smile. 'That devil. Should've guessed he'd do something like that.'

The rousing sound of bagpipes and drums lifted Lachlan's mood when he arrived among the guests. One of his kinsmen was dancing with Frances, and her face was rosy while she laughed. He spun her in a circle and then another man stepped up to take her hands. She danced with his clansmen, one by one, and it filled his heart with happiness to see her.

In the distance, he saw Lord Havershire approaching the guests. The man's colour had returned, but even so, Lachlan felt an instinct of unrest. It would have been better had he stayed at the house.

As the afternoon wore on, the bride blushed as each of the clansmen received a kiss. The glass bowl set upon one of the tables was filled with pennies given by his people. The coins would be used to pay the musicians, and although it was tradition for the remainder of it to be a bridal gift, Lachlan intended to use it for grain to be given back to his people.

The women took Frances away, laughing as she joined them. He knew not where they were taking her, but he guessed it was a game of sorts. While they waited for them to return, his men plied him with spirits. He drank with them but was careful not to take too much. The last thing he wanted was to be unconscious on his wedding night.

The afternoon waned into evening, though it remained lighter from the summer nights. Lachlan waited even longer, but there was still no sign of the women.

Finally, he saw his mother hurrying towards them. Her face had gone pale, and she called out, 'Lachlan! Come quickly!'

He broke into a run, and when he reached her side, she took his wrist. 'He took her before we could stop him.'

'What do you mean?'

'Havershire. He took Frances. They're on the battlements.'

He'd never before seen such wild fear in Catrina's eyes, and it evoked his own terror. His mother was never one to panic, but he doubled his speed after he heard a woman's scream. When he reached the stone stairs leading to the battlements, he took them two at a time.

On the far end of the wall, the earl held Frances against the edge of the battlements, his hands locked upon her wrists as she struggled.

Frances fought to free herself from the old man's grasp. She could smell the liquor upon his breath, and he clearly was not himself. He'd been drinking all afternoon, and in his frail mind, he believed that he was solving a problem—the problem of her marriage to Lachlan.

'It will all be over soon,' he soothed. 'You won't even feel it. It will be like going to sleep.' He gripped her waist and lifted her up, surprisingly strong for a man of his age.

'Put me down, my lord. You don't want to do this.' Though she kept her voice calm, inwardly, she was terrified. From her vantage point, she could see the drop below. The battlements rose at least twenty feet above the ground, perhaps more. There were trees and shrubs below, but if he dropped her from this height, she would die.

The madness in his gaze suggested that her death was indeed his intent.

'Then the laird will wed my Regina. All will be set to rights, I promise you.' He stroked her hair, and the insidious caress made her skin crawl. 'Don't fight it.'

At his words, she began kicking at him, twisting as he lifted her higher. When she felt the edge of the stone wall against her shoulders, she screamed as loudly as she could. From the far end of the battlements, she saw Lachlan running hard. In that moment, the world around her seemed to slow down. She saw him reaching towards the earl, and a moment later, she was on the opposite side of the battlements, her body hanging over the edge. She was holding on to the earl, gripping him with all her strength. But it was not enough. She could feel herself slipping and, oh, God, the ground was so very far away.

She could hear her own screams echoed in the voices of the women and realised that this was her moment to die. Perhaps it was punishment for daring to reach for a dream she could never have. And Lachlan had no way of saving her in time.

'Please don't do this,' she begged the earl. 'Think of your daughter and how it will hurt Regina.'

'She will have the man she was meant to marry,' he said. There was a slur to his voice, revealing how drunk he was. A moment later, he began to cough, and his eyes watered from the exertion.

'You don't want to kill me. This isn't who you are.' She tried to tighten her grip on him, but her palms were slick with perspiration, making it impossible to hold on. 'What would Regina think of you now?'

For a brief second, she saw him falter. Tears filled his eyes, and he seemed to suddenly grasp what was happening.

'Y-you're right. I shouldn't do this.' His hands began to shake, and a tremor caught his mouth. 'I—I don't know what is wrong with me. Forgive me, please.' The earl tried to pull her up, but he lacked the strength. Tears rolled down his face, and she struggled to hold on to him.

A moment later, Lachlan reached for her. His strong arms reached down, and at that very moment, Havershire's strength gave out. Frances tried to keep her grip, but her hands slid away, and she began to fall.

A scream tore from her throat before she struck something hard and everything went dark.

Chapter Fourteen

Horror washed over Lachlan as Frances slipped from his hands. He was too late.

His own roar of frustration ripped from him as she fell, and he could only blame himself. Just as before, he had been unable to stop the death of someone he loved.

This was your fault, his mind roared. *Your fault. You should have saved her. You never should have left Havershire alone.*

The pain was so devastating, Lachlan wanted to step off the battlements and join her in death. He eyed the distance, contemplating it.

Frances had struck one of the trees instead of the ground, but he doubted if it had made any difference. Her body lay unmoving in a crumpled heap against the thick branches. Her gown was torn and stained with blood.

Gabriel stood behind him with Havershire firmly in his grasp. Two other men joined him and took the old man away, who was sobbing, 'I didn't mean to. I tried to pull her back, but I wasn't strong enough. God forgive me.'

A darkness rose within him, and Lachlan pushed his way past the men, needing to be away from the earl before he did something he would regret. The truth was, the earl was not responsible for Frances's death—*he* was. He could still feel the slickness of her palms as she fell from his grasp.

If he had reached her a second sooner, she would be alive now. If he had grabbed her harder, he would not have lost her.

Lachlan's eyes blurred as he ran through the postern gate, hurrying towards his wife. He could see the vivid blue gown against the grey tree trunks, and behind him, he could hear the other men. One was shouting for a doctor, though he knew it was futile to hope that she could have survived the fall.

Lachlan climbed up the tree, trying to reach his wife. Frances was unmoving, so very still, he was certain that the worst had already come to pass. She was dead, and it was his fault, just as before when he'd been unable to save his father from the fire. A harsh ball of emotion gathered within him, and his fingers dug into the bark of the tree. The pain was an agony of frustration and grief, knowing he would never again hold her in his arms. He would never hear her laughter or dance with her. And God above, he wanted to tear the earl apart for it.

Lachlan sat upon the thick branch and braced his leg as he reached for her body, knowing he had to bring her down.

But the moment he touched her, a moan escaped her lips. Fragile hope filled him up inside, though he suspected she had only moments left. 'Frances,' he said gently. 'Lass, look at me.'

Her eyes fluttered open, and she whispered, 'Love you,' before her eyes closed again.

Three days later

Every moment was filled with indescribable pain. Frances drifted in and out of consciousness, barely hearing the commands of Dr Fraser as he tended to her. She had broken countless bones, which he had set. She'd heard him say, ''Twas a miracle she survived that fall. Were it no' for the tree that broke her fall, she'd be dead now.'

Other voices mingled with the doctor's—the voice of Catrina giving orders, the low murmur of servants, and through it all, the deep timbre of Lachlan's voice. He talked to her constantly, urging her to fight. At night, he told her stories of his boyhood, and his voice was a soothing balm to her battered body.

He lay beside her, and the warmth of his touch gave her comfort. She opened her eyes and saw her husband beside her, keeping vigil. The doctor was there on the other side of the room, his expression grim.

'Doctor,' she whispered.

'Aye.' Dr Fraser drew closer and came to her side. 'What is it, Lady Locharr?'

She reached down below her waist. 'The baby. Will it live?'

His expression blanched, and he hesitated. 'I was not aware you were with child.'

'Neither was I,' came the voice of Lachlan beside her. His expression held a blend of wonder and fear. He sat up and reached for her hand. 'Lass, are you certain?'

She nodded, for the signs had been the same. 'It has been weeks since my last courses. I thought you would be happy, but now I fear...' Her voice trailed off as the worry caught her. She had been in and out of awareness for days, and all she could think of was her baby. With such a fall, it was unlikely that the child could possibly have lived.

And yet, she needed to know. Tears filled up her eyes with the terror that she had lost another baby. The thought was unbearable, a gnawing grief that made it difficult to breathe.

The doctor exchanged a glance with Lachlan. 'I canna say what has happened, but if you were early enough in the pregnancy, there is a chance that there was no harm done. We willna ken for certain until a few more weeks have passed.'

Her husband leaned down to kiss her forehead. There was tenderness in his expression, and he said, 'Lass, while I pray our child lives, I am more worried about you.' He stroked her cheek. 'I will ever be grateful to God that you survived the fall. I could not imagine living without you.'

'It hurts,' she admitted. But far worse was the fear for their unborn child.

'The pain is a good sign,' the doctor added. 'Did you no' feel it, you might ne'er walk again. As it is, I have reason to hope you will recover.'

And so did she. If her child lived, she could bear any pain. Especially with Lachlan at her side.

'What happened to Havershire?' she asked. An unsettled feeling took hold in her gut.

'Gabriel took him back to London. I told him I would not bring charges against him, so long as he remained there for the rest of his days, and so long as he repaid the debt he owed to my father.' He let out a heavy sigh. 'He is old and I dinna think he understood what was happening. Madness overtook him.'

She agreed with his decision and was glad to hear that they would now have the money necessary for taking care of their clan. As long as the earl would never again cause them harm, she was willing to let go of the past. 'Good.'

Her husband leaned down to claim her lips in a kiss, and a surge of love filled her at the affection. She heard the sound of the door closing as the doctor left them alone. When Lachlan drew back, she ventured a smile. 'Your kiss took my mind off the pain.'

'Then I'll have to be kissing you often,' he said.

'Every day,' she answered. 'If you can spare the time.'

He claimed her mouth again, and in his kiss, she tasted the healing love. There was no doubt in her mind that they belonged together.

'Every day,' he repeated against her mouth. 'For the rest of our lives.'

One year later

Autumn came, and with it, the chill of a new season. Lachlan walked through the garden with Frances, and though everything was barren, there was still the frail promise of new life.

Only this time, it was in the arms of his wife. Their infant son, Tavin, was fussing and his wife held him close, bouncing him and patting his back as she walked.

'He's a braw lad,' Lachlan said. Never could he have imagined that he could love anyone as much as Frances, but the boy filled him with such pride and joy. Often, he sat by the fire with the infant curled up against his chest, and he could not have been happier.

The clan was prosperous, and they had bought several herds of sheep with the debt repaid by the earl. Slowly, they were rebuilding their lives, and Lachlan was content with his wife and child. Though he didn't doubt that London society would continue to gossip about them, it was no concern of his. He had everything he could ever want, right here.

By the time they returned to the house, Tavin was asleep in Frances's arms. She gave him over to Elspeth. The elderly maid beamed with happiness as she took the infant to bring him back to his cradle.

Frances took him by the hand. 'Come with me, husband.'

The wicked look in her eyes made him wonder what mischief she was up to. 'What is it, wife?'

'I think you're in need of lessons. I am your governess, am I not?'

'You are.' He walked with her to the end of the hallway and clarified, 'Am I needing lessons in etiquette or dancing?' He followed her up the stairs where she led him to their bedchamber.

'Oh, dancing, most certainly.' She closed the door behind him and turned the key. 'But first, you need to be trained on how to unfasten a lady's gown.' She turned around and smiled, waiting for him to help her.

Her words aroused him immediately, and he reached for the buttons. One by one, he undid them, kissing her skin as he bared each delectable inch. An idea occurred to him, and he led her back towards a chair. He sat upon it and continued unfastening her corset and chemise, drawing her to sit upon his lap. Her gown hung open, granting him access to her breasts. He reached to cup one, stroking the nipple as he did.

'Yes,' she whispered. 'Just like that.'

He continued caressing her, then did the same with her other breast until both nipples were erect and taut. Her reaction stimulated his own erection, and he grew rock hard against her plump backside. God, he loved this woman.

Frances inhaled sharply as he reached beneath her skirts and petticoats. When he drew his hand up her bare thigh, he gritted his teeth to gather the remnants of his control. 'What else do I need to be taught, my governess?'

'I've forgotten.' Her voice hitched as he drew his hand between her legs. She was already wet, and he caressed her, knowing how she liked to be touched.

'I think I need to practise pleasuring you,' he said. 'You'll have to tell me when I get it right.'

'You are a very good pupil,' she answered, moaning when he slid a finger inside her depths. 'But, yes, you do need to practise.'

He circled his thumb upon the centre of her pleasure, and she leaned back against him, arching when he found a sensitive place. 'I think you are in need of lessons, too, my governess.'

'In what?' She could barely speak as he rubbed her, and her breathing was coming in swift pants.

'In riding.' He turned her around to straddle him and lifted her skirts, thrusting deep inside. She convulsed against him, and he took her nipple in his mouth, loving the way she came apart in her first climax. He gripped her waist and helped her rise and fall against him as he joined with her. She took him deep, and he could feel her squeezing him in her depths.

'I do like riding,' she confessed, holding his head against her breast. He pleasured her with his tongue while she clenched him inside, taking him over and over. Lachlan felt her rising towards another crest, and he quickened his pace, pounding inside her until she cried out with the force of her release. He joined her a second later, emptying himself within her, and she continued to squeeze him.

His heartbeat was pounding hard, and his wife was collapsed against him, her flesh rosy from their lovemaking.

'You're learning,' she admitted. 'But we might still need more lessons until we get it right.'

He laughed against her skin. 'I do love you, Frances MacKinloch. And if you're wanting to give me lessons for the rest of my days, I will be a happy man.'

'It will be my pleasure to do so,' she answered, leading him to their bed.

And mine, he thought, as he took his wife into his arms and loved her most thoroughly.

* * * * *

COMING SOON!

We really hope you enjoyed reading this book. If you're looking for more romance, be sure to head to the shops when new books are available on

Thursday 31st October

To see which titles are coming soon, please visit

millsandboon.co.uk/nextmonth

MILLS & BOON

Coming next month

MISS LOTTIE'S CHRISTMAS PROTECTOR
Sophia James

'Are you married, sir?'

'I am not.' Jasper tried to keep the relief from his words.

'But would you want to be? Married, I mean? One day?'

She was observing him as if she were a scientist and he was an undiscovered species. One which might be the answer to an age-old question. One from whom she could obtain useful information about the state of Holy Matrimony.

'It would depend on the woman.' He couldn't remember in his life a more unusual conversation. Was she in the market for a groom or was it for someone else she asked?

'But you are not averse to the idea of it?' She blurted this out. 'If she was the right one?'

Lord, was she proposing to him? Was this some wild joke that would be exposed in the next moment or two? Had the Fairclough family fallen down on their luck and she saw his fortune as some sort of a solution? Thoughts spun quickly, one on top of another and suddenly he'd had enough. 'Where the hell is your brother, Miss Fairclough?'

She looked at him blankly. 'Pardon?'

'Silas. Why is he not here with you and seeing to your needs?'

'You know my brother?'

Her eyes were not quite focused on him, he thought then, and wondered momentarily if she could be using some drug to alter perception. But surely not. The Faircloughs were known near and far for their godly works and charitable ways. It was his own appalling past that was colouring such thoughts.

'I do know him. I employed him once in my engineering firm.'

'Oh, my goodness.' She fumbled then for the bag on the floor in front of her, a decent-sized reticule full of belongings. Finally, she extracted some spectacles. He saw they'd been broken, one arm tied on firmly with a piece of string. When she had them in place her eyes widened in shock.

'It is you.'

'I am afraid so.'

'Hell.'

That sounded neither godly nor saintly and everything he believed of Miss Charlotte Fairclough was again turned upside down.

Continue reading
MISS LOTTIE'S CHRISTMAS PROTECTOR
Sophia James

Available next month
www.millsandboon.co.uk

LET'S TALK

Romance

For exclusive extracts, competitions
and special offers, find us online:

f facebook.com/millsandboon

🐦 @MillsandBoon

📷 @MillsandBoonUK

Get in touch on 01413 063232

For all the latest titles coming soon, visit
millsandboon.co.uk/nextmonth

MILLS & BOON

THE HEART OF ROMANCE

A ROMANCE FOR EVERY KIND OF READER

MODERN

Prepare to be swept off your feet by sophisticated, sexy and seductive heroes, in some of the world's most glamourous and romantic locations, where power and passion collide.
8 stories per month.

HISTORICAL

Escape with historical heroes from time gone by. Whether your passion is for wicked Regency Rakes, muscled Vikings or rugged Highlanders, awaken the romance of the past.
6 stories per month.

MEDICAL

Set your pulse racing with dedicated, delectable doctors in the high-pressure world of medicine, where emotions run high and passion, comfort and love are the best medicine.
6 stories per month.

True Love

Celebrate true love with tender stories of heartfelt romance, from the rush of falling in love to the joy a new baby can bring, and a focus on the emotional heart of a relationship.
8 stories per month.

Desire

Indulge in secrets and scandal, intense drama and plenty of sizzling hot action with powerful and passionate heroes who have it all: wealth, status, good looks…everything but the right woman.
6 stories per month.

HEROES

Experience all the excitement of a gripping thriller, with an intense romance at its heart. Resourceful, true-to-life women and strong, fearless men face danger and desire - a killer combination!
8 stories per month.

DARE

Sensual love stories featuring smart, sassy heroines you'd want as a best friend, and compelling intense heroes who are worthy of them.
4 stories per month.

To see which titles are coming soon, please visit

millsandboon.co.uk/nextmonth